A Body in Westminster Abbey

A Victorian Murder Mystery

Published in 2024 by FeedARead.com Publishing

A CIP catalogue record for this title is available from the British Library.

Author's note

Three major characters in this story, Mary Anning, William Buckland, and Henry Mayhew, were significant nineteenth century figures. Those marked * in the Dramatis Personae were also real people

Other characters, together with events in the life and death of Thomas Marshall, and some of the events in the lives of the Anning, Buckland, Mayhew, are the imagination of the author. A few historical events have time-shifted for the benefit of the narrative. Of particular note is that Dean Buckland was rarely in the Abbey after 1849 – his neck and mental problems meant he stayed at Islip until moving to the Clapham asylum in 1852, where he died (and concluded his role as Dean) in 1856.

Major sources of information to give context to this story include

Jan Bondeson	*Victorian Murders*
Douglas Browne	*The rise of Scotland yard*
William Buckland	*The Bridgewater Treatise on ' Geology and Mineralogy considered with reference to Natural Theology'*
David Cannadine	*Westminster Abbey a church in history*
Kevin Chesney	*The Victorian underworld*
Richard Curle	*Mary Anning 1799-1847*
J.S.D.	*The Banker's Clerk*
John Field	*Kingdom, Power and Glory* (an historical guide to Westminster Abbey)
Judith Flowers	*The invention of murder*
Judith Flowers	*The Victorian House*
Judith Flowers	*The Victorian City*
Richard Girling	*The Man who ate the Zoo* (biography of Frank Buckland)
Ruth Goodman	*How to be a Victorian*
Elizabeth Oke – Buckland (Daughter of William Buckland)	*The Life and Correspondence of William Buckland*
Edward Marston	*The Railway Detective* (description of the Devil's Acre)
Liza Picard	*Victorian London*
Peter Quennell	*Mayhew's London* (his editing of the 1861 edition of *London Labour and the London Poor*)
The Times	*Newspaper archive*
E P Thompson & Eileen Yeo	*The unknown Mayhew* (including articles from the *Morning Chronicle*)

Dedicated to

Anne for her example,
and Simon & Colin
for their encouragment

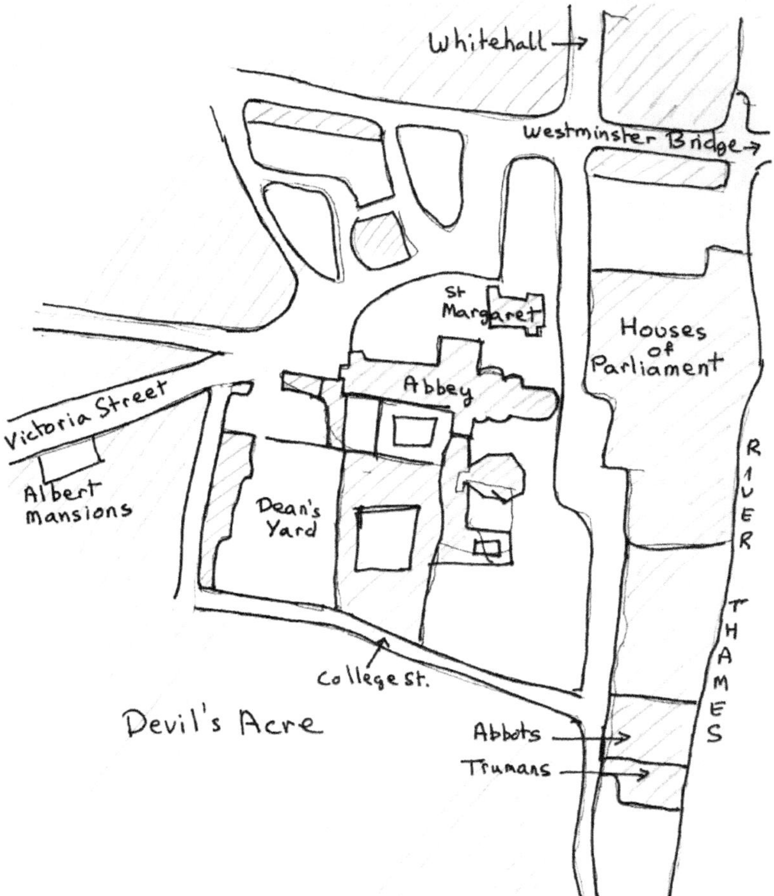

Westminster in 1851

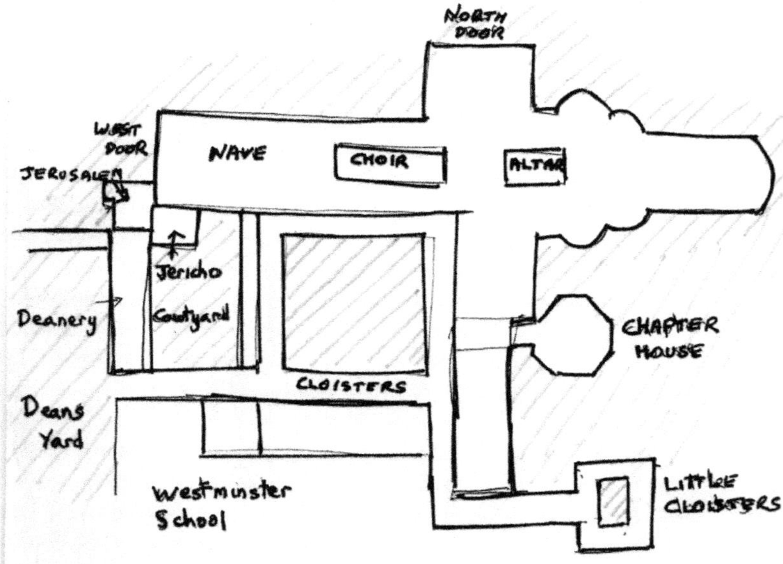

Westminster Abbey

Dramatis Personae

Those marked * were real characters

1. Anning,* Joseph – bank Clerk
2. Anning,* Mary – Palaeontologist
3. Arbuthnot, Ambleside – deputy clerk
4. Bartlett, Ebenezer – judge
5. Bedford, Catherine nee Vincent – wife of Charles
6. Bedford, Charles– new clerk
7. Bourne, Gerald– journalist
8. Boyce, William RA – father of Mary Marshall
9. Briggs, Frederick– Colonel, choir master
10. Brooks, Arthur – Canon, friend of Marshall
11. Brooks, Christine – late wife of Arthur
12. Brown, PC – from Millbank
13. Buckland,* Frank – son of William
14. Buckland,* Mary nee Morland – wife of William
15. Buckland,* William – Dean
16. Bulford, Archibald – senior manager at Bank
17. Burge, Colin - Coroner
18. Burrows,* Esme – housekeeper to the Dean
19. Bush,* John – Superintendent of Clapham asylum
20. Butler, Clive – security guard
21. Chapman, Morris – Abbey server and union member.
22. Charlie – a journalist
23. Clarence, Chipper – senior Carpenter
24. Clark, John - Beadle
25. Clegg, George– police constable
26. Cooper, Walter– leader of tailors
27. Durdin,* John – bank Clerk
28. Evans, Gareth - Beadle
29. Ernest – Coffee seller at Covent Garden
30. Fitzgerald, Reuben– manager of bank
31. George – a journalist
32. Gifford, Christopher – prosecution lawyer
33. Gillespie, Garfield – head of Westminster School
34. Grace – maid of all work for Marshalls

35. Greatorex,* Thomas – former Organist
36. Greene, Arnold 'Ginger'– Brigadier, security officer at Abbey
37. Grey,* Lord – Home Secretary
38. Hall,* Samuel– cataloguist
39. Hamilton,* William – attacked Victoria
40. Holyoake,* Gerald – atheist leader
41. Humphries, Clement – lawyer for Greene
42. Jenny – maid to Buckland
43. Jerrold,* Douglas – publisher of *Morning Chronicle*, father of Jane Mayhew
44. Johnson, Willie – a boy 'runner'
45. Jones, Albert - Detective chief Superintendent
46. Law,* Charles – a Member of Parliament
47. Len – brother of costerboy
48. Marchant – Canon Brooks' maid
49. Marshall, Clara -daughter of Thomas/Mary
50. Marshall, Constance– daughter of Thomas/Mary
51. Marshal, Emily –mother of Thomas
52. Marshall, George –father of Thomas
53. Marshall, Gerald –brother of Thomas
54. Marshall, John –brother of Thomas
55. Marshall, Mary nee Boyce – wife of Thomas
56. Marshall, Thomas– chorister, victim
57. Martin, Mr – Union secretary
58. Mayhew,* Amy – daughter of Henry/Jane
59. Mayhew,* Athol – son of Henry/Jane
60. Mayhew,* Henry – author of London Poor
61. Mayhew,* Jane nee Jerrold – wife of Henry
62. Mayhew,* Joshua – father of Henry
63. Mayne,* Richard – commissioner of police
64. McDougal, Scotty Ian - Carpenter
65. Melbourne,* Lord – Prime Minister
66. Milligan – Doctor, associate coroner
67. Mitchell – Canon at the Abbey
68. Morgan, Charles – publisher
69. Nelson, Chris – woodworker

70. Nelson, Jamie – woodworker
71. Newsome, Charlie – nightwatchman at Abbots
72. Oxford,* Edward – attacked Victoria
73. Pate,* Robert – attacked Victoria
74. Peel,* Robert – Prime Minister
75. Prentice – a doctor at St Thomas's
76. Roberts, Francis – Detective Sergeant
77. Simpson,* John – artist
78. Smythe, Bertie – Woodworker
79. Stanley - at Gravells
80. Temple, Abigail – secretary at Abbots
81. Turle,* James - organist and choir master
82. Vernon,* Robert – artist
83. Vincent,* George– retiring Clerk
84. Watson, John – police Sergeant
85. Wilberforce,* Samuel– previous Dean
86. Williams,* Geoffrey– former organist
87. Wight, Charles – father of Helen
88. Wight, Helen – nurse at St Thomas's
89. Wight, Mrs – mother of Helen

CHAPTERS

Foreword

A Body in Westminster Abbey

London in the 1850s presents the Great Exhibition, the building of the new Houses of Parliament and the creation of the modern Victoria Street. Yet it is also hosts a world of sweated labour and social inequality.

Westminster Abbey experiences its own changes and tensions at that time under the eccentric Dean, William Buckland.

When the body of a middle-aged chorister is found in the Abbey, the new Detective branch, at Scotland Yard, is at loggerheads with the Metropolitan Police.

Why would anyone want to kill Thomas Marshall?

Why, when someone has admitted the murder, and been convicted at the Old Bailey, does the case remained unsolved?

In which of the various aspects of his life has Thomas given anyone a desire to get rid of him?

You will discover both the splendour and the seedy nature of Victorian London, explore the various aspects of Thomas's life and encounter a world of intrigue and tension.

Eventually you'll discover why some people wanted rid of Thomas Marshall. .

Part 1
The Lives of Thomas Marshall

Chapter 1

The family life
October 1805 – February 1850

George and Emily Marshall had not anticipated a third son; indeed, they had not anticipated a third child. George, a graduate of Emmanuel College Cambridge, had married an "older woman", his music tutor, at the age of 24; she was three years his senior. The births of John and Gerald in the first three years of their marriage were a real blessing. Although Emily would have loved a daughter, she and George rejoiced in a family of two healthy sons. The birth of Thomas, 13 years later, as Emily reached 40, was a surprise to them, and a shock to others. On October 21st 1805, the day of the Battle of Trafalgar, as everyone would tell him whenever he gave the date (to which he would always feign surprise), in the bedroom of 27 Grosvenor Square, her parents' home, Emily brought Thomas into the world.

The older children's significant embarrassment at the evidence that their parents were still having sex was not overcome by the arrival of a brother. The attention that they had been receiving from their parents – going for walks, listening to their piano playing, watching their sporting activities – was significantly reduced as their new sibling became their parents' focus of attention. His arrival created a gradual distancing between Mr & Mrs Marshall and their first two sons. The boys would never see Thomas as an asset.

The children grew up in Islington. George owned a publishing business there, mainly books on theology, and Emily, not only a musician but a competent mathematician, assisted with the accounts when time allowed. The main demands on her time were her children, and teaching both singing and piano to the offspring of their social acquaintances.

Thomas's older brothers were always destined for the publishing house, always interested in the books being produced, and from a young age packaging parcels for delivery. A Saturday morning would often be spent with a new volume on Philosophy or early Christian History and quantities of wrapping paper across the large kitchen table. It concluded with precise weightings and an assessment of the funds needed to post them. The highlight of the day was assembling the parcels in preparation for delivery to the mail coach. Painted mauve below and black on top with bright red wheels and undercarriage, with the royal coat of arms on the doors and the liveried driver with his armed guard, it was the most splendid memory of Thomas's early life.

Thomas was an inconvenience once George Marshall had decided that they couldn't really afford to have a nurse beyond his third birthday – and the responsibility for "looking after him for a short while" whilst mother and father went out was not recognised as a privilege or a joy.

He inherited his mother's penchant for mathematics; enjoying sums and puzzles. He was the bane of his brothers' lives from the age of seven or eight when his precocious understanding of mathematics meant that he demanded that his brothers tell him "right away" what fourteen nines were or what prime number is bigger than ninety but less than hundred.

Thomas's parents, or more accurately his paternal grandparents (who had created Marshall & Son long before they had children), decided that he should go to Westminster School. When he started boarding there at the age of eight, he was already learning the piano and had become a competent singer; a scholarship for the Abbey choir greatly reduced his fees. The bulk of the education offered at Westminster was based around Latin and Greek, the languages and ancient texts, with some additional input from members of the Abbey Chapter on the Bible and theology.

In 1821, shortly before Thomas reached sixteen, he was due to leave Westminster. He was summoned by the Head Master, Edmund Goodenough, to his office just days before the end of the summer term.

A summons to the Head's room was normally a signal for a telling off – wise boys would augment their posterior protection on such an occasion. Thomas was not aware of any specific infringement of school rules that might have merited such a command – but nevertheless took the appropriate precautions.

The protocol was that any boy called to attend upon the Head would make sure he was in full uniform and present himself, at the top of the 'Broad Stairs', at the office of the Head Master's secretary (Lancelot Evans, who doubled up as the school bursar and chief finance officer) where some attention would be paid to his presentation before Mr Evans knocked on the solid, decorated, oak door and announced the visitor.

'Marshall of Lower Shell Head Master'.

'Come in'.

Edmund Goodenough, the son of a former Bishop of Carlisle, and himself a future Prebendary of the Abbey and subsequently Dean of Wells, looked up from his carver chair behind a paper-strewn mahogany desk. Thomas was encouraged to step further forward, but not offered a seat.

'Marshall, you're leaving in a few weeks', intoned Mr Goodenough.

Thomas was not sure where this was the result of a recent revelation, or an instruction. 'I am sir', seemed an adequate response.

'I'd like you to stay on'.

'My father is keen that I should find some gainful employment sir. I don't think he feels that I am university material – and so believes that it would be an unnecessary expense, sir'.

'I don't mean as a pupil Marshall, but as an assistant to the staff. You have done so well in Mathematics that you seem to be ahead of some of the teachers, and certainly ahead of many of the most senior boys. The universities are now expecting a better knowledge of that subject'.

The introduction of a Mathematics course into Westminster school when he was eleven gave him great joy – and for each of the next five years he picked up the newly created Norton Prize for Mathematics for his year.

'I would need to speak to my father, sir'.

'Quite right, and that is why I have asked him to come to see me', then he added with something approaching a smile (not a phenomenon normally witnessed on Mr Goodenough's face), 'he knows something of the reason. I didn't want him to think, as no doubt you might have been thinking, that you were in any sort of trouble. He will be with us tomorrow morning at eight. You will be excused morning worship. Meet him at the Beadle's gate and bring him here for eight'.

There was a certain tension in Thomas's response of 'Yes,sir'. He was nervous about his father coming into school, not a regular occurrence, but also a frisson of excitement – he had been anxious about what his father might expect of him, or have prepared for him, upon leaving school.

Next morning George Marshall was as punctual as he always expected his clients and colleagues to be. His tall hat did not disguise the fact that his not-yet-sixteen-year-old son was already his superior in height.

'I'll take you to the Head's room father.'

'Before we do that Thomas, I'd like to say that I am very pleased with this request from the school'. That was the nearest George ever got to saying that he was proud of his son.

The school wished Thomas to become a tutor to some of the younger boys, in return for which a place in the household of one of the resident single masters would be made available. With no anticipated vacancy in the family business, and no desire to welcome Thomas back home to stay, George readily acquiesced to the request for Thomas to be at the school for a further 3 years, on terms that found him "provided for" but with little remuneration beyond that,

One of Thomas's first pupils was Henry Mayhew, an unruly nine-year-old, but one who shared Thomas's love of numbers – and who displayed an uncommon elegance in his writing style. Mayhew did not, however, appreciate the school's focus on classical literature and language.

During the school holidays Thomas would come back to his parents' home. His brothers were now working all of their time in the publishing business and the family conversation over the dinner table was often about Thomas's future. The possibility of staying permanently on the school staff was considered – Goodemough specifically requested that Thomas be allowed to continue his tutoring role beyond the three years agreed, at rather better terms. Thomas – having boarded at the school for nearly a decade – wanted to explore other options.

Returning permanently, however, to his parents' home was not something Thomas had been looking forward to, or that his parents particularly wanted.

Soon after the end of Thomas's final academic year at Westminster it was a more confident young man who was introduced by his parents to Mr Boyce at dinner one evening. George Marshall had met William Boyce RA, a director of the Westminster Bank, at a social occasion when Mr Boyce was wishing to consider sponsoring a "History" of the bank. That venture did not proceed, but a friendship began. George wanted to introduce his new friend to his mathematically gifted son.

The meal was prepared, under Emily's supervision, and served by Daphne, the maid. Only four were sat at table – and when the roulade had been eaten, with much appreciation, Emily withdrew.

‘Thomas’, began his father, ‘mister Boyce has a proposition he would like to make. I hope you will listen carefully’.

They moved from the table into a drawing room and sat at three comfortable chairs around the fire; not that the fire was lit in July.

The arrangement of chairs meant that Thomas and Mr Boyce were facing each other.

‘Well Thomas, it’s good to meet you. Your father has told me about you’.

Thomas wondered quite how much his father knew about him – and what he might have said.

‘He tells me that you are good at Mathematics, that you are reliable and, what’s maybe most significant at the moment, that you are looking for work.’

‘That’s generous of him – and it is true that I have just finished my appointment at Westminster School and need to establish myself in some career’.

‘Well I believe I may have something for you’, volunteered William Boyce, ‘and your father says that he is willing to help you secure the post that I am offering’.

Thomas leaned further forward in his chair, as did Mr Boyce. They were not trying to exclude George – but their actions spoke of both seriousness and a level of confidentiality.

‘I am very interested’, said Thomas.

‘I would like to offer you an apprenticeship as a Banker’s Clerk’.

Mr Boyce explained that a Banker’s Clerk was a highly sought after position. Only those of impeccable character were recruited into its ranks; but there was also the need to provide a “bond”’ of £1000, the equivalent of ten years’ salary, against mistakes, thus taking responsibility for any financial errors short of fraud.

‘And’, Mr Boyce explained, looking towards George, ‘your father is willing to pay that bond’.

While such a guarantee offered the bank some financial protection from staff embezzlement, it also acted as an indicator of the personal reputation of the candidate, since financial stability was equated with good character. It was with some surprise and genuine appreciation that Thomas declared, 'thank you father, that is very generous of you. It does sound like the sort of post that would be suitable for me', and turning to William Boyce, who was now smiling, 'where would it be and when can I start?'

'I would like you to come to my home on Saturday afternoon so that we can go into the details', and he handed Thomas his card.

'I usually go to one of the Banks on a Saturday morning, but will be home well before three – we could meet then'.

'I would be pleased to do so Mr Boyce'. It was Thomas and William who stood to shake hands as the latter prepared to leave. George's face betrayed both his relief that his son was moving towards gainful employment, and his concern that this could be an expensive folly. He realised how little he knew about his son.

The following Saturday Thomas made his way out of London to the Boyce residence in Hampstead. A new-built Nash-designed detached house facing the Heath. That afternoon two important things happened. William and Thomas agreed terms and times of employment, initially at the London Wall branch of the Westminster Bank, and when that transaction was completed, William invited Thomas to join him, his wife and daughter for some supper.

Mary, William and Anne's only child, had brought in the supper and remaining for conversation around the table, discovered a shared interest with Thomas in aspects of Art and Mathematics. Their conversations and their relationship developed over succeeding meetings, and they married in Hampstead parish church during the spring of 1828.

Chapter 2

Married life
1840 – 1850

The Career of a Banker's Clerk was relatively cosseted. Thomas generally enjoyed a higher salary, longer holidays, and more favourable working conditions than his clerical counterparts in other professions – though he never quite provided Mary with the life she aspired to. Thomas was making his way in one of the City branches of the Westminster Bank. The advice of his father-in-law was that he needed to move away from that institution for a period, get a wider experience, and maybe, "in a few years' time" the board might look favourably on any application when a directorship became available.

The Commercial Bank of London had been founded in 1840, with branches in Henrietta Street and at London Bridge. It was George Marshall again, this time through a chance meeting with Reuben Fitzgerald, the bank's chief cashier, at the Oxford/Cambridge game at Lords, that opened the way for Thomas to be one of the first Banker's Clerks in the new venture. A slightly younger man, John Durdin also took a post at the Henrietta Street branch within a month of Thomas's arrival. They would become firm friends. A few years later they would be joined by Joseph Anning, coming up from Dorset to "try his luck" in London.

In early November 1840, at a brisk pace, Thomas set off with a new silk hat and a Malacca cane walking stick, the gift of his father-in-law, to his new job from the home in Charles Street that he and Mary shared, into which their first child, a daughter Constance, had just been welcomed. From the moment Thomas walked through the rather humble single door on the left-hand side of the bank's facade, adjacent to a terraced domestic property, he felt at home. He loved the stateliness of the building's interior, the imposing pillars, the desks ranged in various recesses - creating small rooms for private discussion. He found the ever-busy flow of feet in and out of the main entrance area exhilarating. Here men met, deals were struck and business opportunities created. Those aspects formed the exciting business of the day. Much of his time, however, would be the mundane receipt of and paying out of funds, and the recording of all transactions in registers. Nevertheless, he thrived on the cut and thrust of business life, happy to be a cog in the restless machine that was the commercial world of London.

The Commercial Bank was just yards from Covent Garden Market. The cries of the costermongers, the jostling crowds surging through the market, ebbing and flowing from The Strand; the busy carts and the excited cries, the very heart-beat of the city, thrilled him. He walked to work each day from his house, down to The Mall, along to Trafalgar Square (where many colourful stalls selling clothes and food were already established for the day), past St Martin's church and then a cut across towards Henrietta Street, to the doors of the bank. Each day brought new opportunities, serving in a bank that he was proud to be associated with.

Although Thomas and Mary had established their first home on Charles Street, she always expressed a desire to go "up in the world", hoping, vainly it would prove, to inhabit a property similar to Thomas's grandparents' former home in Grosvenor Square. Even the small terraced town-house off Pall Mall was probably slightly extravagant; but it pleased Mary and her parents, and anything that pleased Mary made Thomas happy. A second daughter, Clara, would be born there eighteen months into his new job.

It was not that Mary was not proud of her home. She, recognising it was essentially her responsibility, had furnished it with colourful carpets and rugs and cheerful linen curtains. There was comfortable furniture, from Willows and Company. She had created a space for her creative skills, embroidery and painting, and the nursery had been developed into a room where the children played. Mary was, however, never fully satisfied that the house matched her position. After a few years at the Bank, and with new responsibilities as well as growing children, the Thomas felt that a change of home would be an advantage, his father-in-law thought it would be necessary, and Mary believed it would be "the only option". Thomas told Durdin and Anning when he had been informed of these two observations, and, as happened in his family, Mary and her father took the initiative and began looking.

- - - - - - - - -

In 1836 Parliament had set up the Select Committee on Metropolitan Improvements to consider London's problems; and their answer, to solve both traffic congestion and the 'Rookeries' (squalid slums), would be to build new roads through the poorest districts. The priority areas chosen were St. Giles (where New Oxford Street and other roads were created), Spitalfields and Whitechapel (Commercial Street), and the Devil's Acre adjacent to Westminster Abbey. At the last of these the new thoroughfare, parliament decided, to mark the Coronation of 28th June 1838, would receive the accolade of being named after the young Queen - Victoria Street. The properties along the new road were advertised as being for the "newly rich" – a category that Mary wanted to identify with; and if a move would please Mary, then Thomas would be happy. This led to their acquisition of a newly constructed "three-floor with basement", terraced property on Albert Mansions, Victoria Street at the earliest opportunity. The purchase was made in February 1850.

Sadly, when the new roads were created, they did not prove an answer to the problem of over-crowding and poverty. There was no provision made for new housing for those evicted from the demolished houses. Church Street, near to Albert Mansions, had housed six hundred and fifty people a decade earlier, but by 1848, during the final construction process of Victoria Street, it was over a thousand. There were still crowded streets of dirty, straggling houses, with now and then an unexpected court composed of buildings as ill-proportioned and deformed as the half-naked children that played on its macadamed roads. There were up to 30 people living in a property on three floors with no more than 8 rooms. It was an area as menacing by day as by night. Within its twisted streets, narrow lanes and dark alleyways danger lurked at every turn. As one writer described it, "bawling adults and screaming children joined in a mass choir whose repertory consisted solely of a sustained and discordant din that assaulted the eardrums. Scavenging dogs and fighting tomcats added their own descant. Smoke-blackened tenements were built around small shadowed courtyards, thick with assorted refuse and animal excrement".

The thousand people of Church Street (within 50 yards of the Marshalls' new home) were mainly Irish. They had no running water, no drains and 49 privies between them. Despite being unskilled many were long term employees, in places like Trumans Brewery and Abbots woodyard on Millbank, others were casual labour. They had social clubs, pubs and even a savings club, there were almost no records of arrests for prostitution connected to the residents, the children were baptised and their parents married, in the Catholic church.

The people had simply moved a few yards to create even more densely-packed slums. This was a situation that distressed Thomas, but Mary chose not to look around the back streets of their locality, preferring to look beyond the Abbey and Whitehall and to develop her relationship with the National Gallery which had opened north of Trafalgar Square in 1838. She also regretted not having a son who could attend Westminster School – now on their doorstep.

Chapter 3

The office life
July 1840 – August 1851

Thomas Marshall proved invaluable to the Commercial Bank of London. He brought several years' experience and became a mentor to some of the new recruits. When Joseph Anning arrived from the West Country it was Marshall who was allocated the role of being his mentor. Although Anning had been working in banks for some time the structure, and the busyness, of the London banks were something of a revelation. In Lyme Regis he had been able to give more time to clients, to enquire of their family (many of whom he would have known). Banks in London had an urgency, and the expectation that customers would be processed as rapidly as politely possible. Joseph was a good pupil and quickly learnt the "tricks of the trade".

The Commercial Bank of London was among several hundred new Bank "brands" in London established in the first half of the nineteenth century. However, the Commercial Bank was also one of a particularly new breed. Rather than being a *private* bank, essentially based on the personal wealth of no more than six partners, it was a *joint-stock* bank deriving its funds from the subscriptions of shareholders and controlled by a board of directors. The creation of such institutions was a reaction against the number of banks that had folded following the bankruptcy of their proprietors. It was a popular new venture, seen as having greater security. It could also be more selective in its staff, with no obligations to employ family members and friends. Thomas's appointment had been on the basis not only of excellent references and that surety of one thousand pounds, but also a competitive interview process that identified a good fit for the new brand. Employees were proud of their positions. The two branches of the Bank, although outside the City of London, were convenient for many of the growing businesses in central London. .

Thomas was fortunate in the generosity of colleagues, and the mutual support of Anning and Durdin, with whom close friendships were developing. Durdin had a family of his own in Camden and Anning lived by himself south of the river.

Anyone walking onto the ground floor of the Henrietta Street branch of the Commercial Bank of London would identify several "stalls" along the walls to both his left and his right. Each stall was the responsibility of a particular Banker's Clerk. The practice at the Commercial Bank was that every Clerk served a specific group of customers, usually, though not exclusively, based on the initial letter of their surname. Some of their daily work involved a small number of moderately wealthy individuals, but the bulk of the bank's work was based around local businesses. Several of these were single enterprises, a book shop on the Charing Cross Road or an importer of Dutch flowers trading from an address on the Strand; others were branches, or the head-quarters, of businesses that operated elsewhere in the country; a chain of shoe shops, or a coffin-maker with branches throughout north London.

Office hours were nominally nine to five, but those would always be extended by at least one, and often over two hours, as books and accounts were reconciled at the end of each day. On Saturdays, when the offices closed at noon, that reconciliation process involved weekly balances and frequently proved quite protracted. Twice a year, on a day at the start of May and again in November, the Bank would close for additional routines introduced for tax purposes. Those could prove the longest days of the year if there was a discrepancy of even a few pence.

Thomas was both adept at calculations and personable to his clients. Most came by appointment, but others had regular weekly times. Some appeared irregularly and without notice.

Marshall had been allocated K to N in the alphabetical division.

One day in the early summer of 1849 Thomas had already created a loan for Kettle's new pharmacy branch, on the security of his home off Regent's Park (having provided the deeds to prove ownership), and produced some of the Bank's own Notes to the value of one hundred pounds for Lord Johnson, who was going on an extensive tour of property in the North and did not want the burden of quantities of cash, when a new client was brought to him.

Henry Mayhew had introduced himself to the clerk at the door who, looking around a pillar and across the room, noted that Thomas was available. He escorted the portly gentleman in his late thirties, attired in Autumnal colouring and a deer-stalker hat, unconventional for banking appointments, unconventional for summer, across to Thomas.

'A Mr Mayhew, Mr Marshall,' said the Clerk with a brief but perceptible bow to Thomas. There was a clear hierarchy in the bank.

A "Thank you" was offered by Mayhew to the figure intent on immediately re-assuming his place by the door.

'Good morning, sir, how can the Commercial Bank help you?'

Mayhew leaned forward and looked over his glasses. 'Did he say Marshall? It is Thomas Marshall, isn't it?'

Feeling self-conscious and at a disadvantage Marshall responded, 'you have the better of me sir, for I am indeed Mr Thomas Marshall.'

'Remember me? Harry Mayhew, at Westminster. You taught me for a while.'

'Of course, sir, how are you? I remember you well.' The, "and not always with great pleasure", was carefully not expressed.

'It is good to see you again. I hope you will be pleased to hear that I have made more of myself than you might have expected.'

Ever the professional, Thomas resumed. 'That is good to hear sir; and how can we help you today?'

'I am planning a new enterprise, writing for the *Morning Chronicle*. I'm going to be based nearby but my normal bank is in North London. There will be times when I need cash at short notice, to pay reporters and others. I would like to transfer some of my funds to your bank to help with that. A current account with some facility to overdraw, is that possible?'

'We can certainly arrange a current account, sir, when you are able to transfer the funds. The overdraft facility, I'm sure, would be in order, provided we have sufficient sureties – a good balance in your other bank may prove sufficient. I'll just get the appropriate forms.'

Thomas knew in which of the many drawers in the racks behind him the necessary documents could be located. This was not an uncommon request. As he turned away to collect them Marshall smiled, recalling some of his schoolboy encounters with Mayhew. He remembered that on his withdrawal from Westminster, or was it expulsion, Thomas was never sure, Henry's father had sent the 15-year-old off to sea. He was evidently more prosperous now than Thomas might have anticipated nearly two decades earlier.

The documents were selected and Thomas turned to put the papers onto the desk between them and drew Mayhew's attention to various sections.

'Here they are Mr Mayhew. I will require your name and address, your signature here and here. The account will be activated when your bill of transfer is deposited, and the overdraft facility enabled when we have a certified copy of your account and a good character from your present bank. We will contact them immediately. Can you include their name here?' He remained upright behind the desk. The bulk of it sloped in his direction, but there was a sufficiently large flat area for forms to be place. He indicated with the index finger protruding from his clenched fist where Mayhew's signature should be entered.

To cover the time taken for the signing process to be concluded Thomas returned to the Westminster conversation.

'Last time I saw you Mr Mayhew, you were getting ready to go to sea.'

'That didn't last long. I preferred *terra firma*. I've spent much of my time since then writing. Some plays, a novel or two, quite a lot for *Punch*, and recently for the *Morning Chronicle*, where this important and vital new series is going.' There was a certain swagger in his boasting. He had achieved something, but felt that his most substantial contribution was just beginning.

The signatures concluded, and so did the conversation. Mayhew recognised a busy man when he saw one. He had already seen Marshall acknowledge the presence of a besuited man on a bench across the room, and so he chose to depart. He had enjoyed the encounter and the co-incidence, but little knew how his relationship with his late tutor would develop. The meeting did not prove significant enough for Thomas to tell his wife about it that evening.

Mayhew made an appointment with the clerk at the entrance door to return to the bank on the following Tuesday.

When that day arrived Thomas Marshall, having received a letter from his bank, was not looking forward to a further meeting Mayhew. Only three years earlier, the correspondence said, Mr Mayhew had been declared a bankrupt. The bank had a firm policy against allowing any credit to such people.

Marshall was busying himself at his office-stall, anxious about his proposed ten-thirty encounter. *Bills of Exchange*, cheques and cash were received, and *Notes* and credit issued, but all the while he was getting more nervous. He knew it was the bank's rules, not his decision, but he felt that, although it was approaching 20 years since they had last met, he was dealing with a man he knew personally. Most weeks someone left their appointment with Marshall disappointed, but here he realised he would feel disappointment as well.

Mayhew arrived promptly. Marshall had five minutes earlier rejected a request from a Mr Kyle to see him urgently because of this ten-thirty appointment, so he was relieved when Mayhew came around the large pillar that obscured Marshall's view of the main door.

'Good morning again Mr Marshall, remember I had to call you that – even though you were no more than five years older than me. My bank tells me that they have transferred a thousand pounds to my new account here and have written to you about the overdraft facility. So, I think my signature will set it all up.'

'Good morning, Mr Mayhew. I do hope you are well. Have you had a good walk here?' stalling tactics were evident, but Marshall knew it was important to get to the point. He had rehearsed his next words.

'We have indeed had the transfer, and your account is now ready to use. However, I am sorry to say that the letter from your bank tells us that just three years ago the High Court declared you bankrupt. I am very sorry but the bank's policy is that we are not able to extend that credit facility to you.'

'I thought that might be the case. I'll need to be careful then won't I Marshall?' Thomas had not expected such a jocular response, and was mightily relieved.

'Thank you for your understanding, Mr Mayhew. We are very pleased to be opening your current account today; and hope to see you again soon.' Once more Mayhew's expected departure was being clearly signalled; and Marshall was able to indicate to Mr Kyle that they could now transact his business.

Other matters were conducted across the next few hours. The working day concluded by making entries into the ledgers.

The bank ledgers were big, weighing around forty pounds. The one Marshall used contained records across all the years since the bank opened. Bankers Clerks were responsible for writing them up with clarity and accuracy using a quill. Thomas had made a note about the transaction with Mayhew, but entering the new account into the ledger was reserved until after the working day – avoiding distractions. Clerks worked at high, sloping desks, either standing or perched on tall stools. Thomas rested his forearm on the desk as he wrote, instead of keeping it in mid-air, where his muscles would soon grow painfully tired. Good, reliable records were fundamental to any bank's success, but creating them was no easy task. Over time Mayhew's speed of writing had increased at a prodigious rate, much to the amazement and approval of his colleagues. It was an occupation he found rewarding, and a place of work where he felt appreciated by colleagues and clients alike.

Chapter 4

The church life
1845 – 1848

Singing in the choir had been one of the joys of Thomas Marshall's school days – and his extra few years as a tutor at Westminster School had given his voice an opportunity to transfer from the trebles to the tenors. He had continued singing in the Abbey choir throughout his time as a bank employee. Through the choir he had made several friends both amongst the choristers and with the Abbey staff. Now, at the age of 40, he was among the more experienced and mature members. The regime was a service each Sunday morning and many Sunday evenings. Choir rehearsals took place on Thursday evenings. Additional services happened occasionally, especially in the days leading up to Christmas and during Holy Week. The choir was his only activity outside of his home and the bank.

The necessity for accuracy in the bank, where a missing five shillings could delay departure from work by an hour, was transferred by Thomas to his singing. The privilege of contributing within a well-trained and highly competent choir meant that he very rarely experienced the frustration of hearing notes a jarring semi-tone out from his fellow choristers. The judgement of choirmasters had always been that his singing was confident and competent. Thomas didn't have the flair or sparkle that identified him as a potential soloist; but he had a solid understanding and delivery that meant that he was reliable. The major change in his appearance when he progressed to tenor was, being no longer a pupil of the school, he could sport a beard and moustache. That was an affectation that was discontinued after his marriage – though he was never forward in identifying whether the decision was his or the new Mrs Marshall's.

The early years of the new Dean at the Abbey in the mid-1840s in the were a difficult time for Marshall, he did not feel so comfortable as he had done. William Buckland, who had taken on the role in 1845, was focussed on "change", whereas Thomas favoured the predictability and stability of the traditional patterns, words and music that he had been familiar with for well over 30 years. He was reluctant to be outspoken on the issues, he possessed a natural deference to authority; but it was soon discovered amongst other like-minded members of the senior choir that it was Thomas who could most eloquently summarise and verbalise their concerns. It was they who elected him to the Music Committee.

The Dean of Westminster Abbey wanted worship that encouraged and challenged worshippers. In creating what he believed was the appropriate environment for it to take place he had faced much opposition. His early years in the Deanery had sometimes been controversial. Although there were not many objections to his decision to replace the choir seats in the Quire. They were redesigned not for added comfort but to create three banks of seating to enable all choristers to be together and, by increasing the depth of the desk, to reduce the number of books and papers dropped on the floor. However, it was the removal of the side screens around the crossing of the cruciform church, which now permitted seating in the transepts and enabled the practical number of worshippers to double, that upset many traditionalists. For Thomas the removal of the 100-year-old screens had been a sacrilegious act.

Buckland had re-introduced daily evening worship; and on the first evening over 2000 people had queued outside to join evensong. He felt it had been the right thing to do. Thomas was not sure why people would want to come to worship without the choir; and whether they were the sort of people that the Abbey ought to be catering for. The minutes of the Music Committee meetings, meticulously Chronicled by Thomas Vincent the long-established Clerk, revealed that some of the Dean's colleagues had not been persuaded, either before or after, of the value of his 'improvements'.

There had been tensions in the Abbey for some time. Every Dean, of course, desires to leave their mark, wishing to be remembered. Each one would be driven by different motives. The changes that Dean Buckland introduced were designed to give greater safety (levelling the cloisters, piping the sewerage), but mainly to enhance worship by introducing new services and providing a more open worship space. The former, safety, matters were not a significant cause of animosity – the latter, liturgical ones, were. The chief opposing voice within the Chapter, the legal executives of the Abbey made up of the Dean and his Canons, was that of Canon Arthur Brooks.

As sub-Dean during the short tenure of Dean Wilberforce, Canon Brooks had been anticipating preferment to the post of Dean when Wilberforce's appointment as Bishop of Oxford was announced. He knew that the curious position of the Abbey, being a Royal Peculiar rather than a Parish Church or a Cathedral, meant that the appointment would be in the hands of the Prime Minister, representing the Queen, rather than the Bishop of London. Anticipating that Wilberforce's period in office might be brief, Brooks had assiduously sought to find favour with Prime Minister Peel - supporting both his Factory Act and the repeal of the Corn Laws. He made speeches in public places, even from the pulpit in the Abbey, that ill-disguised his contempt for the perceived machinations of Lord Melbourne in parliament. Being overlooked for a man of perceived eccentric views and habits, gave the usually taciturn Brooks the stimulus to make Buckland's vision hard to achieve.

In the 1840s the old order tangled with the new; but out of the confusion came an entirely new spirit in the abbey; highly serious, dedicated to compelling and challenging preaching, and to reaching out socially, intellectually, and theologically. Buckland, who always believed that his arguments were persuasive and would eventually be accepted, thought his vision was being achieved. But the demarcation lines of Old and New remained.

By 1848 the interior of the Abbey quire had been restored for worship. The stalls and sittings had been entirely reconstructed, and, despite numerous objections, the Dean had had removed the heavy oak screens in the north and south transepts, thus adding fifteen hundred sittings to the accommodation. He took great pleasure in drawing attention to the woodwork of the stalls, many of the bosses and finials of which were carved from nature by Messrs. Ruddle, of Peterborough, showing that the modern carvers could compete in skill with their ancient brethren in the craft. The cost of these restorations amounted to over seven thousand pounds, a scandalous amount of money some thought. The "marigold" window in the south transept ("Poets" Corner) was filled with stained glass by Dean Buckland, as the "rose" window of the north transept had been by Dean Atterbury a hundred and twenty years earlier. Such actions and expenditures would always be divisive.

On Easter Day, April 25th, 1848, the Abbey was re-opened, with members of the congregation sitting for the first time in the transepts.

The re-opening did not bring the debate to a close. Although there was an acceptance that the old structures would not be reinstated, there was still a loud clamouring in certain quarters for the old worship to be restored. Brooks and Marshall were to the forefront of the Campaign, to give the military title they used that was probably overstating its significance but reflected their strategic approach.

Chapter 5

Marshall and Canon Brooks
Summer 1850

Thomas Marshall's preference had always been to continue to use the Latin Chants that he had been familiar with as a child, and had sung in the Abbey since the time he started as a junior chorister thirty-eight years earlier. He recognised the improvements brought about as Dean Buckland had re-arranged the choir school, adding new facilities – including better lighting and an internal toilet – but he did not appreciate the adding of new music. Some of his colleagues would occasionally attend the Friday night evangelistic services at the Methodist Church at Hinde Street; their desire to include hymns for congregations from the likes of Charles Wesley and Isaac Watts would have stretched even Dean Buckland's generosity. Thomas Marshall believed that those attending worship should participate through their silent attention rather than anything vocal, and he strongly disapproved of the proximity of some of the younger attendees; even suggesting that, as he believed the early church practice had been, males and females should be seated in separate groups.

Colonel Briggs, the choir leader, did not put up with any nonsense. He had access to the Westminster School boys each day; but many of the men, like Marshall, were working. There was an expectation that the men would be there not only for worship but for the regular Thursday practice sessions. Thomas was one of Briggs' great frustrations; capable, he could pick up the tune and the words, but inconsistent, he would often miss sessions without much explanation. This had been particularly true during 1850, but his attendance since Spring 1851 had improved. It would be overstating it to say that the Colonel now felt sorry that he had often shown his frustration towards Thomas. Sorrow was an emotion foreign to him.

It was not as though Marshall had not voiced his concerns about change, both in the formal committee meetings and in private conversations, but he tempered any public comments so as not to reveal his true concerns. This was in order to enable his clandestine briefing of Canon Arthur Brooks to take place after each of the Music Committee meetings. Thomas particularly felt that the sanctity of the Abbey was being attacked when the wooden transept walls had been removed. His anxiety was confirmed when people, let in at the West Door ahead of the service, would rush down the side aisles and scrabble to get chairs near the front of the North - South facing seating, so that they could get a glimpse of the choir. At least when the people were in the Nave the choir were not disturbed by the movement of chairs or the idle chit-chat that permeated the worship.

Thomas did appreciate that Dean Buckland had encouraged a greater sense of solemnity in the conduct of worship. The clergy now knew what they were doing. No longer rummaging through papers on their desks to determine what should be said next. The Dean had instilled in the Canons a deep belief that this encounter with God was something worth preparing for.

Marshall and Brooks both liked the Dean at a personal level, they were both saddened to see his physical deterioration since his carriage accident in Germany in late 1847, but they stood by their position that something needed to be done to bring back traditional worship. They continued to seek ways to frustrate his changes. The Dean was aware not only of their concerns, but he was also very conscious of their influence as senior members of the Chapter and the Choir.

Chapter 6

Gerald Marshall
1840-1850

Marshall and Son Publishing, more frequently simply called Marshalls, was successfully fulfilling the early Victorian desire for inspiring Christian literature. In 1840 George saw an opportunity to consolidate his business by amalgamating with another publishing house called Morgan and Scott, which particularly specialised in theological tomes – reprinting the commentaries of Matthew Henry and providing the sermons of Charles Spurgeon in regular editions, often only weeks after they were first delivered to the Sunday evening crowds at the Vauxhall Gardens. Such an amalgamation would enable both publishing houses to broaden their potential readership. John Marshall, Thomas's elder brother, was a devote Baptist and attended, as did Charles Morgan, scion of that publishing family, the New Park Street Chapel in Southwark where the young Spurgeon was attracting a very great congregation. Marshall, Morgan and Scott would serve the Christian reading community for decades to come.

The merger, with the funds it released, gave Gerald Marshall, the middle son, an opportunity to withdraw from the family business. He had not been supportive of the move within Marshalls towards a strongly evangelical bias in their publications. He looked for new business opportunities elsewhere.

Gerald had been greatly influenced by the writings of Percy Shelley. They had been students together at Oxford when Shelley was expelled in 1811 having published "The Necessity of Atheism". Nineteen-year-old Gerald had even threatened to withdraw from the university himself - but his father's threat to exclude him from the family business over-ruled his youthful atheistic enthusiasm. He had stayed in touch with Shelley, corresponding regularly and occasionally meeting. Gerald was fully supportive of Shelley's arguments, presented a year after his rustication, in "A Refutation of Deism." He agreed that there was no possibility of a middle course between accepting revealed religion and disbelieving in the existence of a deity; and he found that Shelley's new way of stating the necessity of atheism rational, and attractive.

Although he had joined Marshalls on leaving Oxford, Gerald found the positive Christian emphasis in the titles published by his father and brother a continuing challenge. He had sought permission to create an imprint within the publishing house to produce booklets and tracts supportive of his views, particularly to reprint the *Essays* of Francis Bacon; but his desires had been over-ridden.

Gerald became part of a clandestine group, the Anti-persecution Union. A group founded in 1842 by George Holyoake after he had been charged with Blasphemy for the contents of an answer to a question addressed to him following a public lecture. The union's title disguised its purpose Which was to support, encourage and distribute publications that challenged conventional Christian belief.

Gerald took the opportunity of the sale of Marshalls to Morgan and Scott to consult with colleagues in the Union about a place of employment where he could serve their cause. Since the monarchy was a bastion of the Established Church it was felt that he should seek to obtain a job within the relatively new royal household. Lots of posts were being created as the young Queen, under the strong influence of Lord Melbourne, was clearing out some of the men who had served her grandfather and two uncles across the previous 30 years.

At the age of 48 Gerald brought a reputation for skill in editing and communicating, and had impressed Victoria's new husband, Albert, with his fluency at a debate about the future of publishing. Gerald was always careful not to be drawn into any debate about faith.

Within the royal household Gerald proved himself invaluable. His personal researches at Oxford into the theory and philosophy of Atheism had caused him to develop a fluency in reading German and he found it valuable in his new employment to develop his German speaking ability; he became a valuable asset to, and confidante of, Prince Albert.

Soon after Gerald's arrival there was an attempt on Queen Victoria's life by an 18-year-old boy called Edward Oxford. The Queen and Prince Albert had just passed through the gates of Buckingham Palace in their open-topped carriage to "take the air" in Hyde Park. The 18-year-old adopted what was described as a "theatrical pose" and fired a duelling pistol in the Queen's direction. The carriage stopped and Edward, declaring "I have another here", fired a second. He was wrestled to the ground and detained by the police.

Although there was a police enquiry Gerald was asked to investigate on behalf of the royal couple. Edward Oxford was found insane, detained in the Bedlam asylum, and deported to Australia. Gerald found, but did not report, that he was not acting fully on his own initiative. The decision on the day had been his, but he was also part of small anti-monarchist group, the Republican League. The League attracted fanatics, and its leadership sought to encourage a social environment where the slightly deranged found a home for their extreme republican views.

Two years after the Oxford incident a second Republican League member, John William Bean, fired another starting pistol at the same location. It had been loaded with tobacco rather than a bullet. The court determined that he too was insane and ordered that he serve 18 months hard labour. Gerald was again asked to investigate. Gerald's reports supported the police conviction that Bean was acting alone. But he knew differently, and he took the opportunity to ingratiate himself with some of the Republican League's leadership.

Throughout the 1840s the League grew, without any public disclosure of their activities or membership. Newspapers would occasionally speculate on the existence of such a body; but their enquiries did not uncover the identities of its membership or its activities. The nature of the press speculations tended to cause amusement rather than anxiety amongst the League's leadership, which now included Gerald Marshall.

Regal assassination was always considered to be the ultimate goal, but the League continued to find other ways of fomenting opposition to the monarchy; these helped sustain different groups supportive of their ideals. When Parliament, responding to revolutions across Europe, passed the Treason Felony Act in 1848 under which advocacy of republicanism became potentially punishable by transportation to Australia, thoughts of killing the Queen again came to the fore. Within the chartist movement many were believed to have an affinity with the Republican cause.

Early in 1849 Gerald Marshall was walking in St James's Park, less than half a mile from his brother's home, when he was approached by William Hamilton, asking for pennies. Gerald recognised his Army uniform and engaged him in conversation. The unemployed Irishman expressed a contempt for both the monarchy and the English, for failing to support Ireland during the recent potato famine, and the idea that his life would be more comfortable in jail. Gerald offered Hamilton access to some overnight accommodation – and noted his "pitch" in the park.

Gerald's main contribution to the republican cause was his awareness of the royal diary, and he suggested to the leadership of the League that if they furnished Hamilton with a gun there might be an opportunity for an assassination attempt on June 29th 1849 when the Queen Victoria, with several of her children, would be enjoying a ride along Constitution Hill towards Buckingham Palace. Gerald was asked to make the arrangements and issued with a nondescript pistol by one of the League's officials. The day before the intended ride he indicated to Hamilton the most advantageous shooting location along the route to be followed by the royal couple. The next afternoon Hamilton fired a pistol in the direction of the Queen's carriage. It missed. He was arrested and he fulfilled his desire for a prison bed – albeit in an asylum.

Within the periphery of the League's associates was Robert Pate, an ex-British Army officer, known around Hyde Park for his slightly lunatic like behaviour. He became identified within the Republican League as a likely candidate for pursuing an attempt Victoria's life. Gerald was able to inform the group that on June 27th 1850 Queen Victoria and three of her children would be visiting Cambridge House. His attempt, though maybe not the most dangerous, was certainly the most frightening, and Queen Victoria was left with a scar and a bruise for some time; and Pate was sent to the then penal colony of Tasmania.

Whilst his philosophy still looked towards the overthrow of the monarchy, Gerald was continuing to prove himself an asset to that institution. He also remained estranged from his family. He could accept neither the High Anglicanism of Thomas nor the Evangelical Baptist views of John. He despised them both.

The Republican League sought to install its members within places of influence. There were discreet connections with several Members of Parliament. Gerald Marshall being in the Royal Household was a distinct asset.

It was Gerald who introduced Clive Medley into the organisation. Medley had served in the Army but, like so many others, was a victim of the reductions in staffing levels; or more particulalrly the willingness to release any who were either injured or "something of a nuisance". Clive Medley was a man of bearing, well-spoken but susceptible to the influence of alcohol. One evening, at a Soho pub, he was speaking indiscreetly of his contempt for both the Army and the

Monarch. Gerald, drinking at the bar, noted the conversation and approached Medley, and assessed that Medley could be a valuable recruit to the cause.

Gerald helped, nominally through an Army charity, but actually through the Republican League, to set Clive up in a cramped dwelling just beyond the Horseferry, south of the river. Over several months he helped prepare Medley to enter into service. Specifically, Gerald had his eye on an appointment within the household of the Dean of Westminster Abbey. Gerald was familiar enough with the sort of qualifications anticipated from a successful applicant, and also acquainted with people who could produce appropriate documentation. He was able to open the way for Medley's successful application to become the man-servant to the Dean.

Chapter 7
Thomas's other life – among the poor 1848-1850

1848 had been a year of substantial social unrest, including the Chartist meeting held at Kennington Common on 10th April, where Thomas Marshall (although his sympathies were with the movement) was one of twenty-five thousand volunteers from every walk and condition of life who were sworn in as special constables. There were fears that rebellions across Europe might cross the Channel.

1849 would prove a year with a significant cholera outbreak, thirteen thousand Londoners dying in a period of three months. In the wake of these Henry Mayhew had perceived a growing social conscience in the nation and had proposed to Douglas Jerrold, editor of the *Morning Chronicle*, the highest circulation newspaper in London, a series of articles examining the life of workers in the city. Jerrold, who was also Mayhew's father-in-law, wanted to increase his paper's circulation nationally so modified Mayhew's suggestion and introduced three series to run concurrently in his paper. Mayhew would be the "Special Correspondent for the Metropolis" and prepare two articles each week; there would also be biweekly contributions on the Provinces and Rural areas. The scheme was open ended, and began on October 19th 1849. Mayhew had scoped a series to run for two years – and needed many, and competent, colleagues to join him in the task.

Not only had Thomas Marshall been Henry Mayhew's Mathematics tutor at Westminster School, they were also near neighbours off Pall Mall. Their renewed acquaintance, once more at the bank in early summer 1849, had come about when Mayhew, having returned from Paris (where he had gone to escape his debts), and having made an advantageous marriage to Jerrold's daughter, was making his name as a journalist.

Henry's stern father, Joshua Mayhew, was a barrister and Henry was one of his seventeen children. In 1827, aged 15, Mayhew had been caught swotting from his Greek primer in Chapel and given five hundred lines of Virgil to write out. His preference for Mathematics, under Marshall's tutelage, was a distraction from what the school perceived as its true purpose – preparing students for Oxford. Mayhew's failure to complete his punishment meant the senior master told him that he would be obliged to flog him. Mayhew gathered up his books and walked out of the school. After an uncomfortable year at sea Mayhew turned to journalism.

A constant theme in Mayhew's life was trouble with money. While he knew what he was worth as a writer and frequently achieved substantial earnings, often he was in debt. He spent at least three spells in debtors' prisons. Sometimes, but not always, he was bailed out by family or friends. His long-suffering wife Jane and their children, Amy and Athol, had perforce to share these hardships.

Marshall and Mayhew both had the habit, on a Thursday evening, of calling in to the Red Lion on Parliament Street and walking home together. For Mayhew the public house was a source of material, through conversation or overheard remarks, for journalistic articles (members of parliament could be indiscreet after sampling, as David Copperfield was purported to have done at the same location, some "Genuine Stunning"). For Marshall the visit was a recovery from the mid-week choral practice overseen by James Turle, the organist, and Colonel Briggs.

Drinks at the Red Lion were decanted into pewter tankards from casks on the bar. Those who favoured spirits would monitor the bar maid to make sure that the quantity poured from the bottle reached the line on the metal container, little larger than a thimble, before it was poured into a glass – a Standard drink was three such thimbles. Candles on the edge of the bars offered little light – the room was for conversation rather than reading. The wooden floor boards weren't covered; beer spillage was common-place and someone scrubbed them most days. A large open inglenook fire provided some seating in the summer and much valued heat in the winter months.

Their walks back to Pall Mall at closing time were sometimes punctuated by Mayhew's desire to converse with a costermonger, still peddling his wares, or a crossing-sweeper, who was vainly seeking to clear all the detritus accumulated during the day on the patch that he had patrolled for decades. These people, he explained to Marshall, were the exploited backbone of the city – and he was intent on telling their story. Most busy corners, he said, had their regular street sweeper, known by sight and by name. Residents would also ask them to do small tasks and reward them with cast off clothes or food. Morning sweepers cleared the paths for clerks – their job was over by ten. They were often approved by, or even registered with, the local police. Mayhew commented that a recent parliamentary report had written about the area where they were walking. 'Around three cart loads of dirt, animal manure, swept up daily between Oxford St and Piccadilly Circus; that is, my friend, the equivalent of 20,000 tons a year in less than half a mile. These people deserve more. If I can help them I will.'

That evening Marshall, sharing Mayhew's concerns, innocently enquired. 'Can I help?'

There was very little hesitation ahead of the response.

'Yes you can. I need people to do some of my interviews. It's becoming a bit overwhelming, since I've been obliged to get articles out twice a week.'

Although his initial comment may have been impetuous Marshall was genuinely interested in helping his neighbour and fellow Old Westminster, and was happy to accede to Mayhew's request that the following Thursday, rather than venturing to the Red Lion, they might meet at Mayhew's home to discuss the matter further.

Thomas Marshall's day-job did not allow a lot of flexibility in terms of his availability to carry out interviews on Mayhew's behalf. He needed to talk to Mary ahead of his coming conversation with Mayhew, and took the opportunity as they made their usual Sunday afternoon walk through St James Park. Taking the footpath from Great Queen Street they managed to secure a seat on one of the new metal benches looking across the lake where the pelicans, resident for some 400 years, always caused them amusement. The children were encouraged to take a walk around the lake.

'Mary, Mayhew has asked if I can help with some of his research.' At this stage Mary had not been acquainted with what this research was, let alone what any participation by her husband would involve.

'He wants me to interview some people – and to write up some of his notes.' Mary knew that her husband, being a Banker's Clerk, had an immaculate hand. He had often reported being complimented on the clarity of his writing style. It was the other aspect of the job description that concerned her.

'Who would you be interviewing Thomas?' The temptation was to respond, "just a few people", but the honesty of character that made him a trusted worker at the Bank could not be compromised in this tête-à-tête.

'People who work on the streets, the poor of London. Mayhew has a special concern for them – and so have I. I see many of them as I cross to the city. He wants to make sure that their stories are heard, and he hopes that they can be better understood.'

Mary was hesitant, she looked into Thomas's eyes. Although she had less experience of walking through London streets than he did, she was not ignorant of the poverty and helplessness of many of the people that she saw; she was aware of their own privileged position but less aware of others' needs.

'I suppose that if you feel that you can do something to help Mr Mayhew then you should.' His hand reached to hers, folded on her lap, and gave it a squeeze. The most appropriate thing he could find to say was "I love you"; she knew that he would do nothing that would harm that love. Unconventionally they walked hand-in-hand slowly back with their girls to Charles Street, their love and respect for each other enhanced by that brief conversation.

It was with both apprehension and excitement that Thomas rushed from the Abbey to Mayhew's home on the following Thursday evening. Greeted at the door by Mayhew, he was invited into a small study to the left of the front door, lined with books and desks piled with papers. Mayhew handed him a recent copy of the *Morning Chronicle* from July 1849.

'Do have a look at this, Marshall, while I finish my meal.'

Thomas's apologies were rebuffed with an 'I'll only be five minutes.' He took the tendered chair opposite the desk, which was still in receipt of the evening sun. Marshall sat down to read the article at the top of the folded page and learnt about the "habits and amusements of Costermongers". It was evident that Mayhew had not only been observant but had gained the confidence of the purveyors of goods from Covent Garden and the riverside markets. Thomas read of their card games, shove-halfpenny boards and skittle allies; but then there were the reported conversations, the stories shared. A far more intimate knowledge than Thomas had ever been aware of. He was now able to picture the character and business of the costermongers who travelled out from Covent Garden and around the city.

'That's the sort of thing I write, Thomas,' said Mayhew entering at a pace through the study door. Marshall reacted to the suddenness of the arrival with a brief 'what?' and a rapid 'sorry.'

'I'm glad you find it absorbing. I want to let Londoners know about the other Londoners.'

'What do you have in mind for me, Henry?'

'I don't apologise to you for making this request, but I might need to apologise to Mary.' Thomas turned his head quizzically.

'You might need to bathe more often.' Thomas was confident that Mayhew knew nothing of his bathing habits. 'It's dirty work.'

Thomas was invited to stand to look at the map on the desk and see that Mayhew was indicating a point half a mile upstream of Westminster Bridge. Mayhew said: 'I want you to talk to the Woodworkers. Here, and here.' His finger moved across to an area north of the City.

'The work at the Westminster wharf seems to be well regulated, but there's stuff taking place in Spitalfields that concerns me, and I expect will concern you.'

'What sort of stuff?' was the only appropriate reply.

'Mainly to do with exploiting the poor, but maybe also some illegal work.'

'What does it involve for me?'

The way Thomas asked his question already implied that he was signed up to the enterprise.

'You need to spend time with those working there. Not just asking questions – but listening to their stories. You'll need to assess their honesty – though my experience is that once they trust you, they tell you everything. Whether it's legal or not,' here Mayhew smiled, then added, more seriously, 'and not aware whether it could get them into trouble or not. We must be careful how we report it.'

'I'm not the only one concerned about the London poor. Have you read any of Dickens' books, Thomas? I've known him for over a decade, we both worked on the *Chronicle*, we've even acted in plays together. He has brought some of the issues to the public's attention but, as I've said to him, it is facts we need. He and I both have friends in Parliament – but it's hard to influence the vested interests of many of the members, they make their money through exploitation. You'll remember how hard it was for Wilberforce, what was it 15, 16 years ago, when he was arguing for the end of the slave trade?'

Thomas did not need convincing – he was keen to get involved. 'I don't have much time to spare though – it would have to be on Saturday afternoons, or maybe on a Sunday, though I'd need to check with Mary.'

Mayhew suggested that even evenings might be possible, but he did advise not going before work – his colleagues would not appreciate it!

'Do you know the river's edge?'

'Not well,' Thomas confessed.

'Have you got the time for a brief expedition? They might let us in to the Red Lion a bit later, they're not as fussy as I suspect Mary, and I know Jane, is.'

'Happy to do so. Am I over-dressed?'

'We won't go into the water – just look about a bit.' Their walk took them past the Charing Cross and down Whitehall, their destination was immediately beyond the new Parliamentary Estate; an area of high security as scaffolding and stonework for the new tower needed protecting by the night watchman and his hound, whose presence did not encourage any loitering.

As they passed the Brewery Mayhew gave his opinion that it might be worth speaking to some of the people there to get a feel for that business, but that his priority for Marshall would be a few yards further on.

Between the brewery and some parliamentary residencies were several wharfs. There was some activity, but a limited amount of contact between the two well-dressed gentlemen and those about their own business. Mayhew made no attempt to interact with the labourers that evening; but he did point out to Marshall the sorts of activities taking place. The low tide meant that there were some mudlarks and river finders going about their trade, scavenging below the high-water mark. There was also evidence of the storage of imported wood adjacent to a wharf, and some indication within a couple of the buildings that timber was being cut and shaped.

'This is Abbots, one the largest timber yards on the North Bank. They do good work.'

'I know of them,' said Marshall. 'They've been doing work for the Abbey over the past couple of years.'

'That's right. Here you'll learn how a place can be run. I'm trying to look at the best as well as the worst. Do we have time for a drink Thomas?'

Marshall was not disappointed that Mayhew now directed them back past parliament across the still busy road to Westminster Bridge and then taking a turning right, towards the Red Lion. Their conversation was not over. Mayhew's approach took on a deep measure of seriousness as they sat on upright chairs in a corner. Ignoring the frivolity around the bar, they spent an hour over their first glass of Truman's. Mayhew spoke hardly above a whisper as he let Marshall know of his plans.

'Your work is going to greatly help me, but it's not going to be easy. There are many people who are not happy about what I've been doing.' He went on to explain that there were a number of vested interests who profited from the exploitation of the poor – so there would always be a need for caution. Mayhew believed he was well enough known to be protected by his notoriety, but that some who had helped him had been "persuaded" in different ways to step back. He wanted Marshall's re-assurance that if he ever felt in danger or if he was approached by agents of other parties, that he would withdraw from the enterprise. Marshall gave him that pledge.

Mayhew, feeling that the business of the evening had been transacted, declared 'By the way, your Dean has inspired me, Thomas.'

'In what way is that?'

‘I’m writing a book about the Great Exhibition. Frankly I need to make some money and I can dash off one of these quite quickly.’

‘I’m not even sure the Dean has been to the Exhibition,’ responded Marshall.

‘I’m calling it “Mr & Mrs Sandboys and Family, who came up to London to enjoy themselves and see the Great Exhibition” and it’s going to be about all the different food that can be eaten in London at the present.’

‘In what way does the Dean inspire you, Henry?’

‘You’ll know his reputation for eating every sort of animal. Mice on toast is one of his breakfast favourites they say, as is porpoise. Though I understand that some things he only ate once: mole fricassee and bluebottles were not appetising. Well, there is this man Soyer who has created a restaurant in London during the Exhibition with food from everywhere, including, I believe the pigtailed Chinese eating their favourite stewed dog. I’m mocking him when in my book I talk about the option of the stewed missionary of the Marquesas and the roast bishop of New Zealand. Though I understand that when he visited the Archbishop of York’s family home at Nuneham Courtney, that your Dean even ate the heart of King Louis the fourteenth of France.’

‘That can’t be true.’ Was Thomas’s incredulous response, driven by his visualisation of Buckland putting knife and fork to a pulsating heart.

‘It had been embalmed for scores of years I understand,’ replied Mayhew with a chuckle. ‘There are many who swear it is true. You’ve obviously not been invited to share in any of those delicacies.’

‘I’ll stick to beef and mutton I think,’ said Marshall, taking a last sip from his Truman’s.

‘Another drink Thomas?’ Mayhew had now emptied his glass, and Thomas quaffed the last of his. Mayhew’s ruddy cheeks and his portly stance as he stood to move to the bar betrayed a greater familiarity with beer than Thomas, whose weekly indulgence was a Saturday visit to the Lamb and Flag with his colleagues after work.

'No, I must be away.'

'Just let me introduce you to some people.'

The final few minutes of their time at the Red Lion were relaxed and jovial as Mayhew recognised, and introduced Marshall to, Charles Law, the Whig Member of Parliament.

'Charlie has long encouraged me in my work – but tonight we'll rejoice with him that he has got his bill on Marriage revisions through parliament.' Several fellow drinkers were evidently friends of Mayhew, acknowledging him with a nod or a handshake; some others deliberately averted their gaze.

In the walk back, across Whitehall along Downing Street (the home of the Prime Minster, but also the location of a seedy pub, a small prison and a barber's shop), and across Horse Guards parade, towards their homes, Mayhew further outlined his plans.

It had been some time since Marshall was last so excited about a new project. Here was an opportunity to get involved in a very practical way to help the poor of London – none of whom crossed his path in his day-to-day work. When they separated, Thomas proceeded with his head held high and a smile on his face. This was a worthwhile venture.

Marshall knew that the Dean was aware of the needs, and a supporter of work amongst the poor, but Mayhew had asked Thomas to be careful about who he told about their plans. Marshall remembered, as he covered the two hundred yards between their houses, that he had recently been present in the choir when the Dean preached on the poor, and recalled some of his words,

> *The greater number of the poor who perish are the victims of the avarice and neglect of small landlords and owners of filthy, ill-ventilated habitations in which the poorest and most ill-fed and helpless are compelled to dwell. Fatal diseases are continually engendered from*

lack of adequate supplies of water, withholden by the negligence of the owners, or by the jealousy of interference by public officers or public Boards of Health ... It will be the fault of man, and of the selfishness, or the folly, or avarice of the owners of the poor houses, or of the jealousy or pride of officers and interested individuals, and it will be the fault of Parliament also, if we do not instantly begin to remedy these crying evils.

Chapter 8
Marshall meets the Woodworkers
April 1850

Thomas Marshall paid his first visit alone to the Thames-side wharfs on a warm mid-April afternoon in 1850, a Saturday half-day that coincided with Mary taking their children to Regent's Park; their first visit to the Zoo since it had opened in 1848.

As he closed his ledger at one o'clock it was, as always, with both a sense of relief that the figures had matched those on the daily calendars for the week, and also a sense of pride that, once again, he had spent a week serving businessmen and businesses in the great city. He looked across at Durdin and Anning who were also at the point of departure and smiling. They already knew that today Marshall would be excusing himself from "a glass of porter" (which was more frequently two or three). Without being specific he had mentioned an important meeting. They had chosen to suspect he was looking to move, and their visit to the Lamb & Flag (known locally as "The Bucket of Blood", because it "hosted" bare-knuckle fights in the alley outside) would be dominated by speculation about "where?".

His recently renewed acquaintance with Mayhew, and their conversations, meant that Marshall was becoming a lot more observant. He now noticed people hawking matches and rags, cleaning windows and doorsteps, brushing the street and accosting pedestrians. His normal pace of walking, and his very familiar route to work, had meant that he had failed to see how many people were engaged in street work.

Anyone observing Marshall on his walk home and examining his face would wonder whether he was on his way to the dentist or a party, his visage portrayed both his excitement and his anxiety. Mayhew had talked him through his questions, even provided an introduction to Chipper

Clarence, a Superintendent at the wood-working premises. Marshall assumed 'Chipper' to be a nickname, but also hoped it would describe his attitude.

The question of dress had occupied Marshall's mind for some time. Not his working uniform, not his Sunday best, but he wanted to look respectable. He could not pretend to identify with those he met; so had decided upon a cap rather than a hat, some solid shoes, and a jacket over an old shirt. He needed a note-book, he wanted to get the exact words that people spoke; though Mayhew had said that he often edited them to sound a bit more fluent. Indeed Marshall's initial reading of the *Morning Chronicle* articles had given him a false impression of the levels of erudition and vocabulary of many of the interviewees.

One of Mayhew's colleagues had spent some time analysing the 1841 census returns; discovering the number of Sawyers, Carpenters, Cabinet Makers and other trades working in the metropolis. Marshall's task was to be one of small team interviewing workers from each of the categories; and he had also been charged with preparing the first draft of the articles to be published in the *Morning Chronicle*. Mayhew's plan was that there should be ten pieces in all about Woodworkers, which would be published over a period of five weeks.

Marshall felt proud to be afforded the opportunity to be involved in what he perceived as the vital need to understand his city of London. He was particularly aware that many people, including Mary, Durdin and Anning, would prefer to remain ignorant.

These interviews would occupy many of Marshall's Saturday and Sunday afternoons, and several of his evenings, across the next few weeks. He would also be compiling the draft articles that included the interviews conducted by others. His personal conversations would involve the category of woodworkers called Cabinet-workers. Others would be talking with Sawyers, Carpenters, Joiners, boat-builders and coopers. As he set out on the afternoon of April 13th 1850 he knew, according to Mayhew's scheme, that he would need to have the first article ready for publication on July 4th – just ten weeks away.

Marshall was excited and nervous; his pace did not falter until the end of Wood Street as he stepped into the road to cross Millbank. He was distracted from his intention to walk down to the water's edge by noting people coming in and out of the Brewery immediately opposite. The business that he and Mayhew had noticed some weeks earlier.

Thomas had hurried past Truman's Brewery many times. The unpleasant acrid smell had frequently caught his nostrils. Now the three-storey brick building attracted his attention. In the courtyard a couple of large dray horses were being attended to by their grooms, nearby two others were attached to carts onto which men were loading barrels. Another horse was about to leave, pulling a sleigh bearing two further barrels. The jockeys, for want of a better word, were in the livery of the Brewery. There was evidently a foreman controlling operations. Behind, within the confines of the building, machinery, he assumed, would no doubt be pressing and pulping, or whatever beer production involved. Marshall had not previously associated the Truman name, given to the porter he often drank at the Red Lion, with this place of production and employment just half a mile away from the public house.

Marshall's presence was noted, and a cry came across the yard from the foreman

'Oy! What you starin at?'

'Good afternoon, sir. Just passing by,' Marshall said. He realised that even pausing to look at the lives of workers would attract attention. He went on his way. Mayhew's conversations and wisdom meant that Thomas had already achieved the mindset of wondering about the pay and conditions of the workers in the brewery business; but that would be for someone else's articles.

Abbots Yard, the woodworking premises, was situated between the Brewery and Abingdon buildings, off Millbank – the road that ran from Westminster Bridge to the Horse Ferry river crossing half a mile south. The Abbots firm had gained a good, if controversial, reputation when it supplied the benches for the recently completed houses of Parliament, furnished under the guidance of Augustus Pugin. The work and the controversy had, sadly, earned Pugin a place in Bedlam – a location which would certainly be visible, looking south across the river, from the new parliamentary tower when it was completed.

Much of the woodwork involved in the new choir stalls and screens in the Abbey, as well as some of the furnishings in the houses of Chapter members, was prepared in the yard of Abbot and Sons (a name that, it transpired, was created to enhance its potential for working with the Abbey). Much of the work had been completed under the supervision of Canon Brooks, but Marshall had chosen not to confide in his friend Arthur his commission to visit the yard.

As Marshall approached the river, along a path adjacent to the Brewery, he was assailed by its perfume. The sickly hop smells were amalgamated with the Stygian effluence of the Thames. Nowhere in London was free from the stench of drainage. Although, technically, reserved for rain-water the gullies along the edges of roads carried not only the night-soil content of homes, no longer collected, but the detritus of their food preparation and food waste. Yet nothing compared to the odour adjacent to the Thames – sometimes described as the largest open sewer in the world. It absorbed the waste of every drain and channel and stream. The consequence of its tidal nature was that much of the debris of day-to-day life was deposited on the foreshore for periods of time. It was amongst this that the mudlarks, and devotees of allied trades, made their living. The banks also swarmed with bright red worms, called by the Mudlarks "blood-worms." A nose gay would be unlikely to assuage the odorous experience, so Marshall simply accepted the situation, and rejoiced that it was not so evident at the new home he and his family had moved into, not half a mile away, a couple of months earlier; built without the "benefit" of a cesspool cellar.

Marshall was greeted by Chipper. He would prove an exception amongst the cabinet makers that Marshall met over the next few weeks; who were mainly a quite taciturn community. They were skilled and focussed but did not display the wit that "Chipper" possessed. The layout of the site included a wharf onto the river, a yard where wood was stored below tarpaulin sheets under an open-sided barn, several enclosed buildings with woodworkers employed in constructing furniture of all sorts, and a larger barn which evidently contained completed work ready for distribution. Abbots appeared to Marshall to be an orderly and busy establishment. He was pleased that his commission was starting there.

Mr Clarence took him inside one of the workshops. There was a curiously contrasting smell of body odour and the fragrance of the oils used to enhance the colour and presentation of the wood. Men in nominally white smocks leant over an assortment of tools. Each man had his own bench, around the size of a modest square dining-table. Tapers and candles burnt, and were moved around the table to illuminate areas of activity as necessary. Along the edge of the workshop were larger tables, inhabited by groups of three or four, who man-handled larger sections of timber which Marshall assumed would be for beams or other aspects of house construction. He imagined that his new choir stall had been constructed, and its elegant detail created, at one of those desks.

Mayhew's briefing material had informed him that the profession he was considering had four categories General Cabinet-makers, Fancy Cabinet-makers, Chair makers and Bed makers – the last of these was the least skilled, but it was also where many furniture makers learnt their trade and began their labour. The census of 1841 had identified over 8500 cabinet-makers in London, this was marginally fewer than in 1831 – despite a population increase of a third. Marshall enquired of Chipper why he thought this might be. It seemed that the whole of the wood-working industry had been severally impacted by the introduction of Steam Mills which reduced both the time and energy needed to cut wood – and Chipper speculated that it had had an even greater impact in the years since that census because the number of steam mills in London had increased, he thought, fourfold since 1841.

The bulk of the people at Abbots, said Chipper, were General Cabinet-makers who, although usually kept for manufacturing larger articles of furniture such as tables, wardrobes and sideboards must, Chipper insisted, 'be able to make everything, from the smallest comb-tray to the largest bookcase. If he can't do whatever he's put out, he must go.' The final phrase was declared as if it were the firm's motto. It was already evident to Thomas that even amongst professionals and skilled workers, including those working at Abbots, security of employment was fragile.

The Fancy cabinet-makers, and at Abbots they were together on the first floor of the building, made smaller items such as ladies work-boxes, portable desks, gun cases and cribbage boards. Many of Abbots Fancy men worked piece-rates from home and what they produced was either brought in or collected. Marshall was particulalrly admiring of the lacquer work on the first floor, and decided he needed to acquire a small mahogany table for Mary for their new home.

Marshall's observation was that most of the men there were enjoying their work. There was a happy atmosphere, people smiled and greeted one another as they walked past each other's tables. There was a clear focus on the task in hand. Those he spoke to also had a level of pride both in their skills and in what they produced; they wanted to show Marshall their work. The craftsmen enjoyed the company of their fellow-workers and felt that they were well remunerated for their labours.

Some of the staff expressed concerns that their tools, which they had had to provide themselves, sometimes went missing. Most of the woodworkers at Abbots were Society men, working six 10-hour days and earning a set wage each week (and sometimes a small bonus). There was some resentment from the few non-Society men, who worked on a piece rate, that their pay-rate had not been increased for nearly 20 years. The Society men had greater security, and were also paid ten shillings a week, by the Society, when they were not employed; that was through the weekly contribution they each made. You could also join the Society as a piece-worker, but without some of the benefits of, the relatively novel, "contract of employment".

Chipper did explain to Marshall that Abbots was an exception; one of the very few sites where almost all the men were Society members. Marshall was aware of that because the person who had prepared his briefing on the census had also obtained information from the trade societies that across the whole of the profession only one in eight were Society men, amongst Cabinet makers it was one in five. At Abbots it was two in three.

Chipper introduced Marshall to "Scotty" (a name acquired from his Highland origins rather than at the baptismal font). Although Marshall had prepared some questions, he soon found that in general it was better to give his interviewees a licence to express their own thoughts. Chipper, evidently a foreman, was relaxed about his workers having a brief conversation with Marshall – even stepping aside to allow a measure of confidentiality for his colleagues. He was proud of his establishment. He knew that Marshall was helping to compile an article for a newspaper, but he also knew he sang in the choir at the Abbey and believed he could be trusted.

Scotty though, as a piece worker, was speaking in his own time. 'I earn different each week, sometimes over forty shilling – always at least thirty. I'm a Society man, so that helps when I can't work at all – but it doesn't help if I'm laid off for a day or two. I earn enough to keep a wife and child. I wouldn't hear of my wife working for a slop tailor. I'd rather live on bread and water than see that. Slop is slavery.' The so-called slop trade were manufacturers of cheap clothing; many of their 'tailors,' often working at home on piece rates, were, Thomas would read in Mayhew's articles, being exploited. Marshall was, however, pleased to learn of the experiences of piece-workers who belonged to the Society.

A few further conversations took place, mostly very positive about the work and pay and conditions, and Marshall was given a brief tour by Chipper which concluded at his office.

Although conscious that the interviewees were selected by Chipper, Marshall believed them to be a genuine cross section of Abbots employees. Mr Clarence invited him to come back, and, cheekily, asked him to tell Canon Brooks, who had commissioned much of the work in the Abbey, that they were always looking for new work.

Marshall asked how much people were paid at Abbots.

'It depends on whether they are piece-rate, which is true of many of the Fancy workers, or by the hour, as our General workers normally are. Though sometimes they need to work longer to finish a job, and we must negotiate that. Occasionally that will be in their own time because they haven't finished some work that ought to have been completed in work-time. Most will be paid a minimum of thirty-two shillings a week.'

'I suspect,' pondered Marshall aloud, 'that you pay better than many others.'

'I believe we do.'

Chipper undertook to provide Marshall with a breakdown of the pay scales used across the site, from apprentices through to time-served craftsmen.

'I can't lay my hands on them now, but I'll put them together. I'd appreciate it if they weren't published as being from here.'

'I'll keep them confidential.'

'Shall I send them up to the Abbey?'

'I think they would be more secure if they came straight to me'. With which comment Thomas took out some paper from his pocket borrowed a pen from Chipper's table and wrote down his address.

'Send it here, I'll refund your postage.'

That first venture out had been a pleasant surprise. Marshall thought how often he had walked along Millbank not glancing down the alley beside the Brewery, and committed himself to be more observant in future. Once home he wrote up his notes in his immaculate hand. Sharing a very pleasant meal with his wife and daughters, he heard all about their time at the Zoo, and resisted any temptation to give away any details that might have betrayed the location of his afternoon activities.

A week later, this time after joining Durdin and Anning for their end-of-week drinking expedition, Marshall ventured to the East End. He went to Mayhew's office on the Strand to change his clothes, and give a very brief report on his previous week's activities, he also picked up, and glanced through, some of the copy produced by fellow interviewers.

'Don't think much of their writing' was Mayhew's comment, on the style rather than the content. 'None are going to match your copper-plate, and some have an element of Hieroglyphs about them. You'll get through.'

Mayhew had said that he did not want any details of any of the reports until he saw Marshall's first draft. 'There aren't enough hours in the day to go through everything – that's why

I use people like you,' he concluded with a smile, which also expressed his appreciation of his new colleague.

Marshall's attire for this expedition to the East End was not as elegant as that which he had worn the previous week. Even the tie was dispensed with. The Strand was as busy as any area of London, not only a place for Hansoms but also on the route of Thomas Tiling's new omnibus. The omnibuses had twelve internal seats and two beside the coachman. The box seats were favoured by regulars who reserved them with a tip, they were not available to Thomas. Tiling's had the novelty of seating on top of the bus, accessed by a set of iron rungs at the back which led to a knifeboard, where passengers sat back-to-back looking outwards. No women were allowed on top. Thomas, looking at the physical state of the other passengers, felt obliged to climb the steps. The inside of the 'bus was so narrow that the knees of the passengers near the door effectually prevented their fellow travellers from entering and departing, but, fortunately, Thomas's journey was relatively short. The driver wore a white top hat, a blue white-spotted cravat, a clean white shirt and collar, a coat of dark green cloth and well-polished shoes. As Marshall climbed down, completing his journey along Ludgate Hill to Saint Paul's, he paid the cab the four pence he calculated covered the mile he had travelled.

Outside St Paul's he noticed people begging on the steps of the Cathedral; people he had not really observed before. "Others must write about them", he thought as he walked North. Very few of the London streets actually had names displayed. The directions that Mayhew gave Thomas included references to five public houses on his route. Only two hundred yards from the busy thoroughfare was an area with the same levels of deprivation as in the Devil's Acre at Westminster. He walked through, evading eye-contact, not responding to any calls, and avoiding the busy pavements when he could, until he came to Spitalfields.

The reception at “Gravells” on Church Street was of a very different nature to that at Millbank. Although Mayhew had furnished Marshall with an introduction to a man named Stanley (he never ascertained whether that was a Christian name or surname) he initially seemed elusive and, when tracked down, quite dismissive.

‘I don’t know what you wants ere. The men won’t want to speak – they’re all piece-men.’

Gravells was not a work yard but a small enclave of properties. Built, Marshall surmised, at least half a century earlier and not well maintained. It transpired that most were rented. In the East-end the Cabinet-makers did not have a Society, there was no sick or benevolent fund. Marshall would write, “the chair-maker knows nothing of the table-maker next door, and cannot tell whether others of his calling thrive better or worse than he”. The area around Spitalfields had several large stores competing to sell furniture cheaply. Local workers had previously been employed collectively but, said one of Marshall’s contacts, “many a man didn’t like the master or the foreman and so work on his own was the very thing that pleased him, so such a man would try his hand at making and selling to the warehouse.”

Marshall was uncertain about what to do, but had the temerity to knock on a slated and distorted ill-painted door. He was greeted by a stooped, elderly man with a heavy care-worn appearance.

‘Yeh?’

‘Can I come in sir?’

‘Why?’

‘I’d like to see your work.’

‘Why?’

To draw a line under these inquisitions Marshall was bold enough to say, ‘I’d like to help you.’

But the questions continued, ‘can you make tea caddies?’

‘No’

‘Then how are you going to help me? That’s what we do.’

Although not within his brief, and Mayhew would reprehend him subsequently for doing so, Marshall said, 'I think you should be getting more for your work.'

'So does I. How are you going to help?'

'Can I come in and explain?'

The man, Marshall never inquired for or received his name or age but supposed him to be about forty-five, stepped back and Marshall went up one step straight into an ill-lit large room where three other people, whom Marshall took to be the man's wife and two daughters, with very sallow complexions and dishevelled hair. The girls, of maybe sixteen and eighteen years, sat at small tables, eyes closely fixed upon their work. If they were conscious of Marshall's entrance, they made no effort to acknowledge his presence. The room included an unmade bed and some evidence, on a sideboard, that a meal had been consumed.

The man resumed his seat at his table which, like the other furniture in the room, was rather old and mean. Although visitors were no doubt rare Marshall's presence did not halt the momentum of the labourers. In one corner of the room was an assemblage of completed highly-polished rosewood tea caddies.

'You can look around. We make these for Jack's Warehouse. I puts the wood together, the girls line the boxes and Mavis polishes 'em. What you goin' to do to help?'

'I'm going to write in the paper about how unfair it is that you don't have good conditions to work in, and, I suspect, aren't being paid as well as people elsewhere.' He was careful not to be specific about the location of his previous visit.

The man did not feel this needed a response.

Marshall continued, 'how long have you been working from home?' An enquiry that drew an extended reply.

'I've been working near 30-year as a fancy cabinet-maker, mainly these tea-caddies but a few things beside.' He felt no need to raise his head from his work as he continued.

'I started with Browns, I worked at home – but they trained me and bought everything I made. I could earn two pound a week – more sometimes. I was single, living at home then, but I could save – and was looking to get married one day. I met Mavis.' The older female paused to look up, but did not respond to Marshall's smile with one of her own.

'We got married and we got this place. I heard that it was better to work for yourself. I stopped with Browns, but still sold to them – and a couple others. Then the warehouses started being built – they weren't shops, but started selling to the shops. And they would sell cheaper than before – so didn't pay us so much. Today, with Mavis and the girls, some weeks we don't clear much over a pound, for the whole family. I have to work harder than ever now. I sometimes don't know how to lie down at night to rest best, from tiredness. I also must go around the warehouses to sell my stuff, and they pay less and less.'

He was evidently exhausted; a fitter man might have cried – but he did not have the energy for that.

Marshall noted the skill of the family, preparing such elegant tea caddies. He realised that he had one very similar at home – and had given no thought to the makers when he had acquired it at a bargain price in Covent Garden.

Marshall's "thank you" was very weak as he slowly got up and saw himself out.

Marshall arrived at Mayhew's office, where his son Athol opened the door. Marshall was in tears; enraged and frustrated – and feeling that he had something important to say.

'Can I see your father please?'

'I'm sorry sir, Mr Marshall isn't it? He is at the newspaper offices. A meeting with the editor. Can I help? You look quite distressed. Shall I get mother?'

Thomas didn't really want to burden Jane Mayhew with his concerns.

'No, thank you for the offer. I really wanted to see Mr Mayhew – but it'll have to wait. Thank you.'

In the long and slow walk to his home Marshall paused and cleared his eyes. Arriving home his daughters were long in bed and Mary's ill-concealed anger at his lateness meant a night in the dressing room would be more comfortable than a lecture in the marital bed.

Marshall made visits to a couple of other Cabinet-making locations. The contrasts were not as stark as those between the first two, but they contributed to the Letters (as the submissions to the *Morning Chronicle* were described) that he prepared in draft which, together with his summaries of the submissions of colleagues who visited the Sawyers, Carpenter, Coopers and ship-builders, were presented to Mayhew in good time for publication.

Mayhew would edit them, add some comments of his own and supplement the text with statistics from elsewhere, to prepare the Letters for publication. None of his contributors were named in the papers. Marshall was not looking for any accolade, but to read the Letters that he had compiled in the *Morning Chronicles* between the first of August and twelfth of September 1850 gave him the sensation and satisfaction that he was involved in something of real importance.

Chapter 9
Mrs Marshall and Canon Brooks
April 1850

Whilst Thomas Marshall was exploring a new venture with Henry Mayhew his wife was developing a new enterprise of her own.

The eminent art collector Robert Vernon, who had died in 1849, had given a large gift of 157 paintings and seven sculptures by British artists to the National Gallery in 1847. Mary Marshall, the daughter of a Royal Academician and no mean artist herself, had been co-opted by the National Gallery to assist in the artworks' removal from Vernon's house on Pall Mall, which was up for sale, ahead of displaying them in Marlborough House. She had been asked, with Canon Arthur Brooks, to work with Samuel Hall to oversee the publication of the catalogue, under the grandiose title, *Catalogue of the Vernon collection of paintings by British artists; at an exhibition set for June 1850. with a group in marble and six busts, presented to the nation by Robert Vernon, Esq. also, of other English pictures removed from the National gallery in Trafalgar Square, written by S.C. Hall.*

The initial consultation of the small group had taken place at the Pall Mall house. Vernon had occupied the prestigious Nash town mansion, with coach house, for a decade and its elegant portico had welcomed many eminent artists from across Europe. The nearest thing that London had to a Salon.

On April 14th the first meeting in any formal way, took place between Mrs Marshall and Canon Brooks in the context of that committee request.

Although they had discovered a common love of art it had not been a focus of conversation at any time. Being together on the Vernon Committee gave them a common understanding of some of the controversies and issues in the art world.

The most contentious painting in Vernon's collection was John Simpson's Head of a Man. The artist had died in 1847, which, together with Vernon's own death, meant that the reason for its purchase was unknown. The subject had also appeared in Simpson's The Captive Slave, showing the same sitter, but in half-length format, manacled to a bench. The oil-painting had been exhibited in London in 1827.

When the committee had looked at the pictures Mary recognised the person portrayed in Head of a Man. It was the American actor, Ira Aldridge. Canon Brooks was not a devotee of the theatre so had not seen Aldridge's Othello at Her Majesty's theatre in the Haymarket a few years earlier. There had been some debate about whether to exhibit the picture; whether it was appropriate for a wealthy actor's portrayal of a young enslaved man to be displayed. The committee decided that Mary Marshall and Arthur Brooks, on either side of the argument, should settle the matter. They were clearly told that this should be done most discreetly – and that neither should discuss it with others. There were to be two day-time meetings at the Canon's Abbey home to discuss the matter.

Canon Brooks, an Oxford classics graduate, of a latter pedigree than the Dean. Mrs Marshall was pleased to have a sense of using her academic training to both admire and analyse this painting. She walked the hundred yards to the entrance into Dean's Yard and was given directions by the uniformed Beadle into and through the complex cloister network of the Abbey. Beyond the south range of the main cloisters she turned right and then left along short corridors to emerge onto the Little Cloister, some twenty yards square. She had been directed to make her way towards a door opposite. Through this she came upon the site of the former St Catherne's chapel – now an open area with the truncated remnants of some of the historical pillars of the chapel. The entrance door to the canonry was along a corridor to Mrs Marshall's left. Looking up as she approached it Mary could see the scaffolding on the tower being constructed for parliament and, to its right, and closer in her line of vision, the Jewel Tower. Canon Brooks lived on the edge of the Abbey's estate.

Mary was welcomed in and, the Canon having taken her coat, she looked around. Within the Canon's house she noticed some wonderful works of art. A few were copies of famous originals, and some the work of Canon Brooks himself. The lack of orderliness was, no doubt, she felt, due to the recent loss of "a feminine touch".

At their first meeting in the Canonry the two art lovers recognised the sublime craftsmanship of Simpson. They felt a real privilege in having access to the original of the work. It was resting horizontally on the dining table; Brooks did not have the courage to try to hang it. In terms of the quality of the workmanship it would have merited a place in any collection.

Brooks expressed the opinion that it represented a shameful part of English history. He had been horrified back in 1827, as an impressionable young man, making his first visit to an exhibition in London to see people admiring Simpson's The Captive Slave, what he now termed a "bestial presentation" of inhumanity. Mary, however, saw it as a courageous depiction of a beautiful young man – and commended Simpson's willingness to confront prejudice against such portrayals. They were not sure there was a ready compromise between their views.

After maybe twenty minutes of discussion Mary was about to leave and wondered when, or whether, they should meet again when Arthur enquired, 'won't you stay for some tea? Marchant, my maid, has laid something out in the kitchen.'

Mary, aware that it would be some time before her daughters needed to be collected, and that her husband would not be home until much later, was happy to accept Arthur's request.

They moved through to the kitchen where, on a small table, Marchant had laid out some plates, cups, and a teapot with a flask of boiling water. There were serviettes, and a delicate floral arrangement. Mary immediately concluded that Arthur had not allowed his maid to apply such charming gifts throughout the house.

'She tries to look after me. Makes my meals, does my washing. But she does not do things like Christine did. But I must be grateful.'

Mary gently asked, 'how long is it since Christine died?'

'Six months ago. A number of people in the Abbey contracted Cholera; including the Dean and two of his daughters. Most, nearly all, recovered; but Christine was already weak from earlier chest infections. The doctors did what they could. She died here,' his upturned hands indicated and his words confirmed, 'in this house.'

'I'm so sorry. I hadn't realised.'

'Cholera is such a beastly thing. Thousands are dying in the streets outside. The Dean has done some great work in the Abbey, and in the School, sorting out drainage, putting in toilets, getting people to use soap; but too late for Christine.' Mary looked at his hand on the table and his bowed head, she resisted touching either.

The meeting concluded with Canon Brooks looking into Mary Marshall's eyes and saying, 'thank you so much for visiting my home, I don't think we've resolved this though. Maybe we both need to think about it. Can you come back again, I'm free Thursday morning?'

'I think we should, the committee want a final decision next week.'

'Can you come across after Matins; say nine o'clock?'

'I'd be pleased to. I'll think about what you've said,' she then added, rather playfully, 'if you think about what I've said.'

It was good to leave each other's company that morning with smiles on their faces. The smile remained on Mary's face as she walked through Little Cloister, past the homes of other Canons and turned left at the Pyx Chamber to go along the larger cloister, hallowed by the procession and singing of monks through the centuries, into the sunlight of Dean's Yard.

Three days later, her arguments honed, Mary Marshall returned. She brought Canon Brooks a gift of some small cakes, selected from those she had made with her daughters the evening before. At the entrance to Cheneygates, the imposing archway leading into the Deanery courtyard, she acknowledged the Dean's wife, dressed for visiting.

Arthur Brooks had evidently been waiting behind his door, for Mary's knock was immediately responded to.

'Good morning,' they said simultaneously – and laughed. 'Come in.'

Brooks took the proffered coat and hung it on the hatstand and led Mrs Marshall through to the Dining Room. The picture, unmoved from its location few days before, betrayed the fact that Arthur's meals were now normally eaten at the kitchen table.

'I've been thinking about what you said,' began Brooks.

'That's only what you promised,' said Mary with a gentle grin.

'I think you are right. We do need to allow the picture to be shown. I've been invited to speak at the opening of the Vernon Gallery and would want to say something about this portrait and the issues it raises.'

'I think that's a marvellous idea; my thoughts as well. I didn't know you were going to be speaking at the launch. I believe that something could go on the label. Fairly brief; acknowledging that the man portrayed displays, despite his maltreatment, many qualities that we look for in people.'

'Well let's write it. We probably don't need to have the picture with us. Come through here,' and Mary was led into the drawing room. Some upholstered chairs and a small table in front of a settee. As directed, Mary went to an easy chair, declaring 'I could fall asleep in one of these.'

Brooks sat on the settee with the table before him upon which was a sheet of paper and an ink well. Twenty minutes were spent refining the text, securing the correct punctuation, making sure the appropriate points were made, and ensuring, in their minds at least, it was neither too short nor too long.

'I've already asked the National Gallery to collect the painting tomorrow. I can now let them know that we think it should hang in the Vernon Gallery, that we believe it ought to include these words on its label, and that I'll say something about the work when the Gallery is opened next month. Thank you very much. You've done a wonderful job.'

'We did it together.' This time she did, without being at all self-conscious, reach out and, momentarily, rest her hand upon his on the table.

'Shall we have some tea?' he suggested.

'Let's just sit for a few minutes.' And, so saying, she sat down - beside him on the settee. Not a situation Brooks had anticipated. The few minutes extended to half an hour as they each shared something of their stories. Sadly, Arthur and Christine had not succeeded in having children, 'they would now have been so precious to me as a permanent reminder of her,' reflected the Canon.

Mary shared her pride in what Thomas had achieved at the bank, and her wish that maybe he could find more time to be with her and their daughters. They discovered that they both liked the new group of painters called the Pre-Raphaelite Brotherhood, with a common admiration for Holman Hunt seeking to express his faith in his paintings, a distaste for the personality of Dante Rossetti (though a love of his colours), but primarily acknowledged a shared penchant for John Millais and a real appreciation of his recent Christ at the House of his Parents, which they had both seen. Neither had been amused by Charles Dickens' suggestion that the painting "portrayed The Virgin as an ugly alcoholic".

‘I miss talking about art with Christine. She loved the National Gallery. We had planned to go to Italy one day if we didn’t have children, what a stupid thing to say’. The last phrase was reflective and not an intentional part of what he was saying to Mary.

‘Thomas doesn’t have much time for Art any more,’ was Mary’s wistful contribution.

‘I wish you’d met Christine. You have so much in common. You’re both artistic, witty, have taste, are good at conversations, and,’ he added, unintentionally but simply as an expression of his observations, ‘and good looking.’

Predictably that drew conversation to an end. Arthur apologised; but was not going to withdraw the remark.

‘I don’t think I’ll have the tea. Thank you for this morning. I’m glad we’ve sorted out the painting. I’ll see you at the exhibition-opening next month if not before,’ something in her said “I hope it is before”, not words she would have issued aloud.

Chapter 10

The Costermongers
October 1850 – May 1851

Early in 1850 Mayhew's *Morning Chronicle* "Letters" began to have a wider influence. His articles on tailors from November 1849 to January 1850 had proved to be the widest read and led Walter Cooper, a London Tailor and former Chartist, to set up, under the auspices of the Christian Socialist movement, the Working Tailors Association. This was an experiment in co-operative production drawing together tailors, needlewomen and others.

In October of 1850, as the serialisation of Thomas Marshall's contributions were coming to an end, Mayhew fell out with the editors of the *Morning Chronicle* because they had excised a section of his article on the "Boot and Shoe" workers, where a Bootmaker complained about the practice of Free Trade. This was a political hot potato, and the *Morning Chronicle* was firmly on the side of Free Trade whereas Mayhew, and many of his interviewees, recognised a need for protectionism. The final straw, however, was an article in the *Chronicle* commending the business of Nicolls, a Regent Street tailor and an advertiser in the newspaper, praising piece-work, which Mayhew's articles had firmly condemned, and supportive of Free Trade.

Henry Mayhew, after having addressed a meeting of fifteen hundred tailors on October 28th, promptly resigned from the paper.

On Friday November 1st Mayhew summoned a small group to his office from amongst his team of reporters, including Thomas Marshall, to lay out his plan for continuing the series. He had found Thomas to be one of his most lucid interviewers and reporters. For some of his correspondents he had to do a complete rewrite – but Thomas understood not only his motivation but also his style. In the future, Mayhew explained to the gathering, he planned to publish weekly articles himself on the poor of London who were not employed by others, Street Traders. He told the group that this would include everyone from the more legitimate Costermongers and cabmen through to pick-pockets and prostitutes.

Mayhew enquired of the group, 'who will join me?'

Of the eight people assembled, two or three firmly kept their eyes down, another couple were equivocal and looking to see where the balance of opinion lay, but Thomas was one of those whose hand rose immediately.

'It is my intention to start producing these articles next month. I have a plan,' and he indicated a quite extensive list on his table.

'I want to start with the costermongers, the boys and girls who sell stuff from the barrows. I want to identify whether those street traders are being exploited. George, Charlie, Thomas,' he identified each person not only by name but the point of a finger, 'can you help with these?' They each assented both verbally and with a nod of their head.

'You'll need to go down to the markets, early in the morning.'

He turned specifically to Thomas, 'I'll send you to Covent Garden so that you won't be too late for work. I'll need your copy within two weeks.'

Mayhew handed out some details to each of the three before offering work, on a longer timetable, to those who had been more reluctant.

Mrs Marshall did not greet with any pleasure the knowledge that her husband was planning to leave for work before six o'clock on a winter's morning, two hours earlier than normal. Marshall was never confident that she accepted the idea that the bank was insisting staff come in early because they were changing their working practices.

'Are they paying you any more for the extra hours?'

‘No Mary, it’s part of the job.’

‘But isn’t it dangerous going out so early?’ The remark was not only out of concern, but also by way of a reprimand.

‘I can look after myself.’

‘But you won’t see the girls in the morning.’

It was the Marshalls’ domestic practice that, sometime after he had consumed his own breakfast of porridge and some slices of fried bacon, “Daddy” would call ‘you’ll be late’ upstairs to the girls. It was not a sign for them to rise, for they would already be washed and dressed, but permission for them to come downstairs for their own pre-school fare and bid farewell to their father. A moment that was precious to all the family.

‘That is something I’ll regret; but it won’t be for long.’

It was the following Tuesday morning, a day still celebrated with Thanksgiving for the deliverance of King Charles in 1605, it was dark but fortunately not damp, when Thomas, following his normal route, set off through what were surprisingly busy streets towards Covent Garden. The new gas lights which had ‘sprung up’ across central London, about 200 yards apart on his route, were being extinguished.

Mary had not got up for Thomas’s departure – so he had no need to leave Victoria Street wearing his business suit; he could drop off the bundle containing his working uniform, that he was carrying, at the Commercial Bank, literally fifty yards from the market.

This time he had no introductions to ease his path into conversation, just a general description of the sort of people that Mayhew wished him to interrogate. He had not realised the hectic level of activity taking place so near his place of work in the hours before his conventional arrival time.

Marshall understood that Saturday was always the busiest day of the week at the market, with over two thousand barrows being filled as well as three thousand women with shallows and head-baskets collecting items to sell at their various pitches across London. Mayhew had advised that people would probably be reluctant to pause when collecting their produce for the weekend. Monday was often a slack day, but Tuesday was a day for replenishing stores – a good day to visit.

Upon his arrival Thomas noticed the Coffee-stall keeper on the edge of the site. He was carrying cans of coffee from yokes on his shoulders, with a little smudge-pot charcoal fire lit underneath, its small flame readily seen from twenty yards away. He paused for a cup of coffee – and an initial conversation. The carrier had a regular trade, it was a novelty to serve a stranger – and a generous stranger at that. Ernest had assumed his pitch at four that morning and was nearing the end of his shift, so not keen to engage in much talk. Business in summer, Thomas learnt from him, started before three o'clock, by four the crowd and bustle and hum of the morning really began, that was his busiest time. Although nominally official market days were Tuesdays, Thursdays and Saturdays, in fact every day witnessed goods for sale on the site.

He was allowed to go on his way back to Holborn.

Having deposited his bundle at the Commercial Bank Thomas looked around. He noticed that vegetable stalls not only filled the market but also lined the adjacent streets, in the season there would also have been multiple flower stands. There were trestles laden with varieties of fruit, both in the area outside the Covent Garden Theatre and on the steps of St Paul's church.

He had met some men already well on their way, travelling from the Garden to their 'pitch'. Some rugged brewer's draymen in their dark jackets had long set up their wares. Many of the workers from the market were fortified not by a breakfast but by a pint of ale for their morning's work.

Men in varied costumes, from the costermonger in his corduroy suit, to the greengrocer in his blue apron, passed with some urgency – keen to get to their preferred spots.

Marshall noticed the various smells; an herbalist's stall, oranges, the aroma of damp onions. He decided that it would not be prudent to seek to engage in conversation the ladies who carried columns of baskets on their heads. He opted instead, on this first visit, for encounters with younger workers with barrows rather than the older men, many of whom had horse drawn carts for their fruit and vegetables.

After an hour Marshall had recorded the details of a few brief conversations. He felt that he was beginning to understand something more about the place and the lives of the workers there.

He stood back as the sun began to rise at around half past seven. In the morning air of the autumn day the whole of the square could be seen from one end to the other. The rich red and gold of the dawn sky flooded the market scene, the sun rays revealing the vivid colours of the fruit and vegetables. There was no shouting, as at other markets, but a gentle, low murmuring hum of conversation, negotiation, and agreement. He noted, for the first time, that the flagstones were stained green from the leaves trampled underfoot.

Thomas recognised the waggoners by their countryman's smocks, with velveteen breeches and leggings, and their leather gaiters tied below their knees. Other market traders from the country had white smocks covered by either a thick blue or green apron; and that apron, he learnt, was also sometimes covered with a piece of sacking for messy jobs such as skinning rabbits.

Fruit and vegetables were in the main square but around the sides subsidiary sellers set up; selling to other traders. Horse chestnut leaves to put under exotic fruit displays, ribbons and papers to make up bouquets, and tissue paper for wrapping. Shopping bags were for sale near the railings – overseen by Irishwomen smoking short pipes and wearing lurid coloured neckerchiefs.

Some didn't have pitches but walked around – selling seedcake for birds, combs or old caps. Porters with porter's knots – tied around their foreheads and a strap hanging down to hold on to baskets on their backs – were helping to transport fruit and vegetables for those traders who were purchasing larger quantities than they could carry to their carts.

Marshall overheard a conversation beside the stall of an apple seller.

'Give you four shilling for this lot here, mister,' said a costerboy.

'Four and six is my price,' answers the salesman.

'Say four that's all they're worth,' the boy continued, rather audaciously; as much to amuse his friends as to strike a bargain.

'Four and six. Look around, you won't find any cheaper. It's a fair price.'

The costerboy proffered the coins and, with his friends, loaded their carts.

Marshall approached him, 'can I talk with you? You're not in any kind of trouble, I just want to understand what happens here.'

Thomas was able to point across the square and declare, 'I work in that Bank over there, but came in early today to learn about what takes place outside where I work.'

He was not sure whether the lad accepted his explanation, but he did respond, 'If you walks with me, I'm off to Holborn, I'll talk on the way.'

He was a tall stout boy, aged, Marshall speculated, around sixteen, with a face utterly vacant. The grin to his mates, and his cheek to the seller had disappeared. He was very serious now, he had work to do. His distinctive attire included a red handkerchief tied as a cravat and a flat cap towards the back of his head.

'That's all right. I need to be back here by nine.' Marshall immediately set about his inquisition.

'How did you start this work?'

'My father was a waggoner and worked the country roads. He died when I was seven and me and my brother and mother eventually had to move to Golding Lane over there.' A hand gesture indicated somewhere away to the North.

'We had been goin' to school, but never went again. Mother used to go out all day washing for people; Len and I just stayed at home playing. We were devilishly poor; anything we had mum had to sell. We moved to the rookery at Saint Giles. Mum was out from six in the morning till after nine at night – and she usually brought us home something to eat, but not always.'

'How old were you and Len then?'

'We must a bin nine and eleven or there bouts.'

'When did you start on the barrows?'

'A man as know'd mother said to her, "your boys got nothing to do, let them come along with me and earn a few ha'pence"; and so, I became a coster. He gave me fourpence a morning and my breakfast. I worked with him about three year until I learnt the markets. Len and I worked together. One day, with another boss, the two of us together would make half-crown by selling greens in the morning, and going round to the public houses in the evening and selling nuts. We got in about ten, and mum had something for us to eat.'

'Do you and Len still live with your mother?'

'Nope. She died a couple year back and Len took up with a girl and went south of the river. I worked for a man as gave me a shilling a week, victuals, washing and lodging, just as if I was one of his family for a while, but we fell out.'

'Where do you live now?'

'Under the arches at London Bridge, the railway station. It's damn cold, if you'll pardon my language.'

'Do you manage to save any money?'

'Where would I put it if I did? I works seven days a week. What I earns keeps me fed, and an occasionally visit to a "penny gaff" for a dance and a drink, but I never saves nothin.'

They were approaching Holborn and the lad, Marshall never asked his name, declared 'there's my pitch. I've got to set up' and set off at a pace that made Marshall realise that he had been slowing the boy down. He glanced across at St Arthur's church tower and realised that his work would start in under half an hour; he would have to write up his notes later in the day.

There were few public clocks around London. Some night watch-keepers were paid to walk the streets in their drab greatcoats and shake their rattles every half an hour. During daylight hours the public houses often had some form of time-piece inside. It was not uncommon to see people emerging from such an establishment, wiping their lips with the back of their cuff and declaring, "quarter to three" as if that were the sole purpose of their visit.

Two further visits in the following week, also, as far as Mary knew, for necessary Bank work, enabled Marshall to prepare copy for Mayhew ahead of the set deadline. The publications of Mayhew's papers, under the title London Labour and London Poor began in December 1850 and Marshall's contribution was included in an edition early in 1851.

Chapter 11
Street Traders gathering
May 1851

Henry Mayhew's encounters with Street Traders received some unfortunate publicity when he was summoned by the local magistrate court charged with assault against a pedlar woman, his defence was that she had come to his door three times selling her flower stands and refused to take no for an answer. He added that he had sometimes had as many as 38 persons in one day at the door. He produced for the court a list which included collectors of rags and bones, and sellers of crockery, sixpence a peck pea, fine young rabbits, writing paper, slippers, and crochet mats; and one who greeted him with the cry "roots all a blowing all a growing".

In early May 1851 Mayhew got wind of a proposed meeting of the newly formed Street Traders' Protection Association and contacted Marshall. The urgency of the communication meant contacting him through a mutual friend at the Abbey. Mayhew was not aware that Marshall's colleagues there were not aware of his support of his campaigns. The message travelled from mouth to mouth and eventually, via Canon Brooks, to Colonel Briggs ahead of an evening choir practice.

Marshall made his way to Mayhew's home. His greeting was not his normal hearty salutation; Marshall was annoyed that people in the Abbey now knew about their association, and word would probably get to his wife, who had been led to believe that their collaboration had ended. Mayhew was very apologetic and felt obliged to accept that Marshall would no longer be undertaking interviews, a decision regretted by, but understood by, both men. Nevertheless, Mayhew felt emboldened to make a final request, hence the urgency of the meeting.

‘Thomas, I’ve heard that the STPA,’ an organisation he knew Marshall was aware of, ‘are planning a mass meeting on the sixteenth in Westminster. I would like you to attend, too many people know me; but I need to know what their concerns are. I, we, have only sought to help them.’

Marshall, although torn, provisionally agreed to attend. He had seen and spoken to many street traders, and shared Mayhew’s concern for them. ‘But I’ll need to let Mary know what I’m doing. No more secrets, but also an undertaking to her that this will be my last involvement.’

The discussion that evening back at Victoria Street was not a pleasant experience for any of the four family members. Thomas was greeted with an accusation from Mary about his continuing association with Mayhew. Marshall did not know how she had become aware that Mayhew had been trying to contact him through the Abbey; she wasn’t prepared to say. Although their daughters were excluded from the room, it was evident to them that “mother and father” were having a serious row. There were angry words, tears and apologies from both parties. Eventually Mary agreed to his final outing, but she would not forget his apparent priorities. She did agree not to mention it to anyone else. Thomas now found that the dressing room now became a much more regular sleeping apartment for him.

Marshall enlisted the help of Durdin and Anning to make sure he completed his work in good time on the Friday evening before going home, changing, and collecting his note book and walking beyond Victoria Street to the STPA’s meeting venue. It was being held where a large site had been cleared for the building of what was provisionally being called Victoria Station. The area had contained a series of quicksands, mudbanks and old peat bogs that drained from the Grosvenor basin behind the Queen’s Palace. It had been considered too boggy for building, but the need for a railway station at Victoria made it economical - its construction would require the first railway line bridge over the Thames. The six-acre site was marked out – but no construction had yet started.

People were coming from various directions. The Street Traders' Protection Association had summoned peddlers and hawkers from throughout the city. Summoned "to discuss a serious matter".

Mr Martin, secretary to the proto-union, stood on a hastily constructed rostrum, and around the field leaders of the STPA were pleading for silence.

The sun was low, as was the temperature, when Martin began to speak. 'As many of you know that scurrilous journalist named Henry Mayhew has been publishing reports in his paper in which we, the Street Traders and pedlars of London, have been grossly insulted. We have been scandalised, and we are outraged. Mayhew has got up his booklets to suit the tastes and views of the richer classes, and has selected us, the working people of London to be the victims of his slanders – the butt and target to be fired at by public scorn and ridicule.'

He cited Mayhew's suggestion that being a nomadic race the Street Traders' habit of constantly roaming around might have affected their mental capacities and their head shapes. He even jested, to much laughter, 'Mr. Mayhew has himself a great propensity for travelling, and might, according to his own reasoning, very soon degenerate into a donkey.'

One contributor, with a devasting turn of phrase described London Labour as the "spurious abortion of an impure brain."

That Marshall was both shocked and deeply upset would have been evident to any around him. He did not join in their cheers; but he could not refrain from exclaiming 'no' on occasions. Some around him observed this disrespect for Mr Martin, and a short distance away he saw the pointing finger of the lad he had spoken to six months earlier at Covent Garden. Although Marshall was not approached, the lad had accumulated some others around him who noted the direction of his pointing.

On Sunday May 18th Thomas bought a copy of the Reynolds Newspaper anticipating an objective account of the event. He hoped they would accept that when taken as a whole London Labour did not portray its subjects as unfavourably as the speakers had claimed. But the report, accompanying comments, and subsequent letters were vitriolic. Street Traders were describing themselves as honest, hardworking and, indeed, a pious set of men – with normal skull features. According to them, they were the ones living up to the "Standards of respectability", in contrast to Henry Mayhew whom they pictured as a wily imposter driven by pecuniary motives.

Subsequent meetings, which Marshall, in fulfilment of his undertaking, did not attend, created a committee not only to challenge Mayhew's writings but, more particulalrly, to create an embryonic trade union, a consequence that Mayhew applauded since he had long held that creating societies or unions was of real benefit to working people. The meetings also brought together a more sinister committee, a group of vigilantes who were determined that such writings should cease – and those responsible should pay a price.

To avoid not only the Street Traders and other groups, but also his creditors, Mayhew realised he needed to escape London. His publications came to an end. Thomas was now at home much more.

Mary Marshall's occasional morning meetings with Canon Brooks continued. They spoke about art, and about literature. They also spoke about their spouses; the late Mrs Brooks in glowing terms, the living Mr Marshall with less glow. Mary did however appreciate the time Thomas spent with Constance and Clara, now ten and eight; she felt a greater sense of being a family.

Chapter 12
The Great Exhibition
June 1851

Marshall, Durdin and Anning regularly ate at the Chop House in Covent Garden. It was usually a brief interlude in their day, but occasionally it would be a lengthier *dejeuner*, and one such occurrence was on Saturday June 14th 1851 to celebrate the sixth birthday of John Durdin's eldest child Margaret – he now had two further daughters and a son. Most Clerks who could afford it opted for the chop house. Food was principally steaks, kidneys and sausages; leg of beef stew was a staple commodity, as were trotters and pease-pudding. Waiters were not salaried – but customers paid a penny each from which the waiters paid the proprietors a sum. The convention of the three friends was to quickly eat a chop each and have no more than half a pint of porter. Today was different, a celebration. They order a variety of dishes, a pint each would do initially, and they sat back in their chairs to talk.

Marshall and Durdin had started at the Henrietta Street branch of the Commercial Bank of England in 1840, arriving together, Anning joined the staff in 1847. All three had been made aware of the potential and secure nature of employment at the new bank – Marshall and Durdin had transferred from other London banks, Anning from a smaller concern in Dorset, wanting to experience the busy excitement of the metropolis.

The half day on Saturday meant a longer opportunity to be together – after their chops it was Durdin who insisted that they had a drink together at the Lamb and Flag in Rose Street before going their separate ways; he seemed reluctant to go back too soon to the household where his wife Jane had been told to rest, but where the maid, Susan, would, he hoped, be coping with the manic behaviour of the three children celebrating with their sister.

The two married men spoke about their children, but Anning became uncomfortable. Aged 56, Anning had never married. As the drink took its toll, he became more maudlin – with the death of his sister, Mary, five years earlier, he was the only one of his mother's ten children still living. Recounting the experience of his early life where, it seemed, each year a sibling had died, was painful for his colleagues. A passing comment, "and Mary was the best of us – and she was cheated", was noted by Marshall but ignored by Durdin, who was now expressing his desire to get home – he realised he needed to see his daughter on her birthday.

One day the following week, as work concluded, Anning suggested that the three of them might visit the Great Exhibition. He proposed it as a reconnaissance to see whether Durdin and Marshall would find it to be a suitable outing for their families. Durdin, it transpired, had already arranged to go later in the season but, after Marshall accepted the proposal with enthusiasm, he too was pleased to agree to be joining his friends. Everyone was talking about it.

The only convenient time for Anning would be on a Sunday, and the coming, Sunday June 22nd, was proposed for the outing. Marshall's Sunday included commitments in the Abbey for Matins and Evensong (Dean Buckland was adamant that the choir would always be present on Sunday Evening, his predecessors had been less insistent). Thomas would be free from midday until five. Anning, who lived South of the river, off York Road, near the South Western Railway terminus at Waterloo, made his way over the Westminster Bridge, now noticeably subsiding at the western end. His normal walk to work was over the Waterloo Bridge or, simply for the experience, the suspension footbridge to the New Hungerford Market. That day's walk was to a rendezvous with Marshall and Durdin at Storey's gate, then along Birdcage Walk, in front of the Queen's Palace, and up Constitution Hill towards Hyde Park.

There was a measure of excitement as they moved on to the Park –the high mid-summer sun's reflections causing them to lift their hands to shade their eyes coming within sight of Paxton's glass palace.

After a couple of hours Durdin needed to leave his friends, Sunday afternoon tea with his children, often attended by family friends, was a sacrosanct engagement.

Once Marshall and Anning had completed the exhilarating experience of the Exhibition there was need for a rest, and they found a bench to sit on a short distance from Kensington Gore. Although Marshall's time-constraints should have demanded a brief conversation the situation meant that prolonged intercourse took place.

There had not been opportunity at the bank for Marshall to express his concern for the life-experience that Anning had spoken of eight days earlier. To have been so constantly surrounded by death throughout his childhood must have been hard to endure, and Marshall wanted to offer sympathy. He also recognised that he had to play down his delight in his wife and daughters since Anning could not be anticipating children of his own.

His opening comment concerned the conclusion of their earlier conversation. 'You mentioned your sister recently?' was spoken with an evident sense of sympathy, but its phrasing as a question was also an encouragement for Anning to expand on what he had previously said.

Anning turned his face towards Marshall. Both men were already anticipating that this would be a difficult conversation; but both had confidence in the discretion of the other.

'I moved to London when Mary died. Have you ever heard of my sister?'

'I don't think so – but I do remember you said that she had been cheated, what was that about? Was it a man?'

Before beginning his response Anning paused and investigated the middle-distance. He was carrying a burden he had not shared. He prefaced his response by declaring that his remarks would not be brief, but that he hoped Marshall would forbear to hear him out. Marshall expressed his willingness with a nod of his head. Initially staring at the ground, with his elbows on his knees and his hands cupping his cheeks, Joseph Anning spoke slowly as he reminisced and reflected on his family story.

'My father was a cabinet maker in Dorset – but, to make a bit more money, he used to use gunpowder to explode some sections of the Blue Lias cliffs to reveal the fossils; and then he would sell them to visitors. I used to go through the results of the explosions both to select, and then clean up the fossils. Mary, three years younger than me, helped as well.'

His words could not fully convey the pleasure he was experiencing in his head, the last living sibling had supplanted the many deceased ones in his present reverie. His childhood home was so near to the sea that the same storms that swept along the cliffs to reveal the fossils would sometimes flood the property. But the memory of water splashing at their doorstep was not a distress but an idealised image of his early years. He was picturing himself aged twelve and Mary aged nine, sitting outside that small house – washing the finds, cleaning them with a light brush and laying them aside.

'We called them snake-stones and devil's fingers, and dad, actually often us, sold them as curios to people on holiday.

'Sadly, my father fell from the cliff when I was about fourteen and, his injuries with his consumptive disease, meant he died the following year. Mary was only eleven. Mother was desperate. We were so impoverished that we lived by the poor relief.' Anning's mental image was now of the cart that had taken them to what was no more than a hovel.

'But we still collected and sold the fossils.'

He was shocked out of his contemplation by a horse trotted very close by along Rotten Row.

Anning turned his face to Marshall's. 'I don't know why I'm telling you all this.'

'No, go on. We've plenty of time.'

Anning continued, resuming his reverie. 'The next year Mary and I found what would later be called an Ichthyosaur.'

'A what?' Marshall's enquiry did not stem Anning's flow.

'A sort of dinosaur – did you know that word was created by your boss, by your Dean, William Buckland?' He carried on without awaiting an answer; though the thought was novel to Marshall.

'We sold it for 23 pounds, it's now in the British Museum, I've never visited to see it,' he added with some regret.

After a brief pause Joseph resumed, 'at home I trained as an upholsterer – it seemed a secure job. I had to be head of the family. Mother and Mary set up a shop. Mary would go out in all weathers. In her thirties she nearly died in a landslide whilst scrambling along the cliffs where she had lost sight of her dog. But Mary kept going - making friends, writing about her finds, corresponding with all sorts of people. As she was a woman, the men would not allow her to join their scientific groups. When they started the Geological Society Buckland would not let her join, even though she knew more than most. But she did get to know William Buckland well.'

This remark drew a, 'what – the Dean?' from Marshall.

'The very same. He often visited Lyme Regis around Christmas, and he and Mary would search for fossils together in the freezing cold, often out in the snow.'

The image of the Dean with a young lady scrambling amongst rocks in the snow became imbedded in Marshall's head.

'It was because of him that we left the chapel where we had worshipped and where we had gone to school. Buckland said being part of the Established Church would help her; she did get very involved. She was a person of deep faith. He was good to her. When she lost a lot of money, a very foolish investment, he secured a pension for her from the civil list. Twenty-five pounds a year gave Mary some financial security. But then he cheated her.'

'What! Were they engaged?' Marshal's voice was quite shrill as he made the enquiry.

'No, no nothing like that,' was a hasty response. Anning then spoke more precisely, wanting to get the details right.

'She was always reading and writing, but couldn't get anyone to publish anything under her name, except a letter in a magazine. They would work together, but her work was ignored. He did mention her once, in an article about Pterodactyls, but he normally took all the credit for her discoveries. Then one time he came down from Oxford to see her, it must have been in the early 1830s. He had been asked to write an important book by the University. At that time he was beginning to find his way in the church, he was Dean of Christ Church in Oxford. Buckland gave her hundreds of sheets of paper and lots of his books and asked her to put them in some sort of order. She spent a whole year doing that – even got me helping her out. My hand-writing was rather better than hers. She spent hundreds of hours sorting it all out, and would sometimes go up to Oxford with our notes. She hardly ever left Dorset otherwise. Well, he eventually published it as one of a series called The Bridgewater Treatises – it was the last one published. It was about the relationship between God and science. How God had designed everything – and geology and fossils proved it. I can't suggest I fully understood it all. He got a thousand pounds for writing it and, and here's the point, he promised Mary half of that when the book sold. Well, it sold thousands of copies – but he never gave her the money. He did give her fifty pounds when it was published – and made her swear not to tell anyone what she had done for the book or about their arrangement. She never saw the rest, but she kept her promise not to say anything until telling me shortly before she died. I think her faith meant that she didn't want to embarrass a senior church minister.'

Lest Marshall did not believe him, Anning added, 'I can prove she wrote much of it; I've still got her notes from which I wrote up my clean-copy. But,' he added with regret, 'I can't prove he promised her the money.'

Anning's head sank once more and, although not normally a physically demonstrative person, Marshall slid towards him on the bench and reached his arm around Anning's shoulders. His own anger contributed to the strength of the pull he gave to Anning. 'That's terrible Jo, so unfair.' Marshall determined to do something about it.

Marshall's contribution to Evensong was somewhat muted that evening. He did enquire of Canon Brooks whether he knew when the Dean, who had been absent for a number of weeks, would be returning from Islip. The Canon believed that he would be there for the Patronal Festival the following Sunday, June 29th.

- - - - - - - - -

Nearly six million people visited the Great Exhibition, Queen Victoria went several times. Initially she ventured there four months before its official opening, and her last visit was also arranged for June 29th 1851, by courtiers who had forgotten the significance of that date to the Abbey. She would normally attend the Patronal Festival. Victoria would be leaving for Osborne House on July 1st and wanted a last look at her husband's pride and joy. On her desk at Buckingham Palace, which she graced each morning after breakfast to sign official documents, there was laid before her the draft, in pencil, of a letter to the Dean. It had been on the desk for several days. She had intended to consider its contents. Gerald Marshall had been chosen to draft it on behalf of the Queen. He prepared it, as he often did, on the Royal Notepaper – so that the layout and appearance of the final document could also be considered. This direct involvement with the Church of England annoyed Gerald intensely. His anger was intensified when, in the absence of the Queen, he was asked by Prince Albert to attend the service to deliver the document to the Dean.

Several documents for signature lay on top of each other that June morning and Victoria, excited about both the Exhibition and the trip to the Isle of Wight, hurriedly applied her signature to each; a Commission in the Guards, a response to the Prime Minister concerning Egypt, the confirmation of an investiture later in the year, and the note to the Dean of Westminster. Once she had left her room these were carefully folded and put into their envelopes to be distributed to the appropriate parties. Gerald would be obliged to attend the service, but he would pass on the letter to Clive Medley, the Dean's man-servant who would be entrusted to give to the Duke of Kent, representing the Queen at the Patronal service.

Westminster Abbey's curious status as a Royal Peculiar, a Church of England place of worship exempt from the jurisdiction of the diocese in which it lies, meant it was subject to the direct jurisdiction of the monarch. A consequence of which was that the Queen was more closely involved with the Abbey than any other church and had various exclusive rights and responsibilities. Annually Victoria sent the Dean a personal note expressing her appreciation of his work. This letter was traditionally written to be handed to the Dean on June 29th, the feast day of St Peter to whom the church was dedicated. It would be presented to the Dean either by the Monarch or by whichever dignitary represented them at a reception that follows the Patronal Festival service in the Abbey. Unconventionally it was still in its draft, pencil, version when placed into the regally embossed envelope.

The Dean and Mrs Buckland were quite infrequent at the Abbey during 1851. A coach accident in Germany at the end of 1847 had created problems for them both. The Dean was in constant pain and was now slightly stooped. However, the patronal festival for St Peter was an occasion that he could not miss, there would be some splendid pageantry, good singing and Canon Brooks would deliver his impressive sermon on St Peter – though the Dean had heard it often enough that he believed he could probably deliver it in the Canon's stead. St Peter's Day being on a Sunday in 1851 meant the service would also attract the whole choir.

At the reception after the service, in the Jerusalem Chamber, the Duke of Kent (having been handed the letter by Medley when he arrived at the Deanery to change ahead of the service) duly presented the Dean with his letter, and, as instructed, spoke warmly of the Queen's appreciation of the Abbey's work and that she offered her regrets for non-attendance. The Duke knew his expected script: Victoria, in truth, had expressed neither – though no doubt they reflected her feelings. The Dean too, had he chosen to read the epistle, would have recognised the text, it would have incorporated a reference to a particular service in the previous 12 months but otherwise had followed a standard wording. The Dean put down the opened letter, unread, together with its envelope with the royal seal on the back, on the table in Jericho, where he also placed his robes. He joined the Duke, and others, including the Canons of the Abbey, in Jerusalem for some light refreshments. The letter remained on the table, with the robes. These things could be entrusted to Esme Burrows, the official housekeeper and, unofficial, robe mistress. She had been described by one observer as "an excellent portress who worked in the Robing Room (also called Jericho) to air and iron all the linen surpluses of the Canons in residence, as it was highly necessary that those elderly dignitaries should be protected from the well-known deadly cold of the Abbey".

Most of the clergy and guests had left before the Dean retired. Canon Brooks (having been commended, in a conventional but unostentatious way, for his sermon by many who attended) was the last to leave, as he too discarded his robes on the table.

Gerald Marshall left at the first opportunity. He chose to follow the Dean's wife as she left, through the back door of Jericho. She was greeted at the Deanery Door by Clive Medley. Marshall and Medley briefly glanced at each other– as fellow members they would be attending, the following week, a meeting of the Republican League.

Chapter 13
Marshall confronts the Dean
June 30th 1851

Thomas Marshall had a deep great respect for the Dean as a man of faith and a man of courage, but he had been very much against the changes to worship and the modifications to the furnishings of the Abbey. He found his eccentricities hard to accept - wondered why, a couple of months earlier, there had been a Foucault's pendulum installed in the nave, demonstrating perpetual motion based on the movement of the earth. A few years earlier, Dean Buckland had permitted the Abbey to be covered in scaffolding so that the ordnance division of engineers could climb up with their telescopes and survey the city to prepare a map ready to locate all the sewers. Marshall had felt some sympathy for the man after his carriage accident – and recognised that this was debilitating for the ministry and personal life of someone widely recognised as one of the nation's foremost scientists and a significant cleric. Like many others he was amused by the anecdotes about Buckland. These seemed trivial, however, when contrasted with his wanton destruction of Church tradition. Yet he had recently learnt, and needed the Dean to be aware that he knew, that he, Buckland, had been a cheat. Not only claiming authorship of a whole document that was partially written by another, but also depriving that writer of five hundred pounds that would have significantly improved her life.

Marshall knew that the Dean, following the Patronal festival the day before, would still be in residence – indeed he had been at evensong only thirty minutes earlier. He had attended the service, in the choir at the Festal Evensong.

Marshall had mentally prepared what he was going to say as he went to the door of the deanery.

Medley answering the door, asked. 'How can I help you sir?'

'I need to see the Dean.'

'He's resting at the moment; he's just come in from evensong in the Abbey.'

'I need to see him now.'

'I don't think that will be possible sir. Do you have an appointment?'

'It is imperative that I see him.'

A voice from the adjacent kitchen enquired, 'who is it, Medley? What do they want?'

'I don't have his name ma'am; he insists on seeing the Dean.'

Coming into sight behind Medley, Mrs Buckland declared, 'it's not convenient; he's very tired.'

Stepping forward, forcing the man-servant to step backwards, Marshall declared, 'Mrs Buckland, I have to see the Dean and I have to see him now.'

'That really isn't convenient. Aren't you from the choir? What is it that you want?'

Marshall had by now side-stepped Medley and was within a few feet of the Dean's wife. Turning towards the door from which she had entered the corridor he asked, not expecting a response, as he moved towards it, 'is he in here?' Marshall was fairly certain that unless he confronted Buckland immediately, he would never have the courage, or possibly opportunity, to do so.

Without knocking Marshall thrust the door open and stepped into Dean Buckland's drawing room.

'I need to talk to you now Dean, about Mary Anning.'

Seeking to lift his head, but hardly succeeding, Buckland pitifully asked 'what on earth is this about?'

'I know that you cheated her out of five hundred pounds.'

Mrs Buckland, stepping into the same space, exclaimed, 'leave at once.'

'I will not. I must have my say.'

Thomas Marshall stepped past Mrs Buckland and moved further into the large and ornate drawing room. The walls sported portraits of previous Deans against a red flock wallpaper. The heavy curtains in a matching velvet were pulled close across the large window in front of which sat the Dean in a well-upholstered armed chair. The extensive settee beside him had cushions and books. Around the room were various caged animals – birds, including a cockatoo, and what looked like rats. Against a far wall a large water tank housed fish (the invention of Anna, the wife of one of his Canons). Before the Dean was a low cushioned stool for his feet. He was slumped, and did not seem to have the power to raise his head.

It was a very resigned voice that reluctantly offered a seat, 'sit down then.'

Mrs Buckland was still adamant that he should leave, but the Dean declared, 'I will hear him out,' and to Marshall directed a further, insistent, 'sit down.'

'You can't treat the Dean like this, he's not well,' implored Mrs Buckland, once more seeking to move into the space between Marshall and her husband.

'I will hear him out,' came as a weak shout from the Dean.

'Then I shall remain,' declared Mrs Buckland, and assumed what Marshall supposed was her usual chair.

'I am sorry Mr Dean that I have had to come like this.'

He carried on despite the outcry of the Dean's wife, 'no one invited you.'

'I had to come because of a conversation I've had with a work colleague at the Bank. You will not know but Joseph Anning, a man you met, sir, several times a few years ago, now works with me at the Commercial Bank of London.'

'I did not know; I have not followed his career. It was many years ago, as you say, that I knew him.'

'You may also not know that his sister Mary Anning died five years back. She was impoverished, dependent on Laudanum and accused on being a drunkard. She had breast cancer.'

'I did know and I did help her. I secured an annual pension for her of twenty-five pounds a year. I contributed to the window in the parish church at Lyme Regis – though have not yet been able to see it.'

'You excluded her from your Geological Society of London, not allowing women to become members, or even to attend meetings as guests. She was treated as an outsider to the scientific community.'

'I supported her work.'

'You took credit for her work, sir. Things that she discovered were named after you.'

'She didn't have the standing. I was an Oxford professor – people listened to me.'

Marshall had made the initial points he wanted to get across; but he had a body blow to deliver.

'And you stole £500 from her.'

'I did no such thing.'

'Do you deny, sir, that for your contribution to the Bridgewater Treatises you received a thousand pounds? And that you had promised half of that to Mary Anning, who had lost two hundred and fifty pounds the year before in a financial scandal?'

The Dean was evidently nervous, he stammered his next response. 'I had intended to, yes. But I had financial needs. The number of students in my classes was decreasing. I was looking for a better job. We had a young family. I gave her fifty pounds; I was sorry I couldn't give her any more money at the time.'

'But your money was never going to be a gift, it was a payment for the work she had done. Her brother explained to me that for several weeks in the year before publication she came to stay with you. Didn't she, Mrs Buckland?' Mary Buckland was quite shocked as Marshall turned and delivered that rebuke directly at her. To find herself the subject of such a direct question was simultaneously confusing, annoying, and embarrassing for Mary Buckland.

'She did occasionally come to Oxford. A long time ago – and I'm sure she didn't stay that long. What do you mean by accusing my husband?'

She stood to make what she clearly hoped would be her final remark. 'I think you should leave now, sir.'

Ignoring the request, Marshall stood up. 'Joseph Anning tells me that Mary wrote most of that treatise – and that you, Mr Dean,' his finger now pointed, though the man could not, or would not, look up, 'edited them, added the theology and introduced the sketches, many of which were hers. Not only did you fail to credit her work, you also failed in your promise to give her the half of the fee that she had worked for and deserved. She told her brother all this as she was dying. A few days ago, visiting the Exhibition in Hyde Park, he had too much to drink, got very maudlin and told me all about it.'

There was a silence as Mrs Buckland resumed her seat, or rather fell back exclaiming, 'you're being heartless, can't you see he's an ill man. You'll kill him.'

'I expect to hear from you soon,' was Marshall's final remark.

The Dean concluded the encounter, 'you can leave me now Mr Marshall, you will receive what I hope will be a satisfactory response through Colonel Briggs.'

These words were spoken as Marshall left the room, slamming the door behind him. It was only at the bottom of the exterior steps that he sat down and, head in hands, exhausted, shook and wept. In the room he had just left, fifteen feet above, there was silence.

As Marshall arose and left the Abbey through the cloister entrance from Dean's yard he acknowledged Brigadier Arnold Greene, who was there undertaking his duty as a night guard at the Abbey.

Within the Deanery the awkward silence was broken when Clive Medley entered and asked if the Dean or Mrs Buckland wanted anything further that evening.

The Dean didn't respond, but Mary Buckland's declared, 'we've got to do something about that man Thomas Marshall.'

Chapter 14
Letter to the Brigadier
August 1851

Arnold Greene's father, George, born in 1766, had fought with Wellington in the Iberian Campaign as an officer of the 16th Queen's Dragoons. He returned from Spain in 1812 to the comfortable family home in Hatfield with stories of the glorious victories at Talavera and Bussaco. However, a glancing rifle shot had felled him at Salamanca and he needed a period of recuperation. Arnold was completing his time at Eton and, although his mother wished the security of a city job for her son, he was overwhelmed with both pride and fascination by his father's reports, and sought a commission in his father's regiment.

'Are you sure Ginger?' was a question addressed to Arnold by both of his parents. Hoping for different answers.

The protocol for accepting the son of a wealthy officer, a son who had an Eton qualification, was rather perfunctory. The sale of commissions was straightforward. It determined the selection and promotion of officers in the infantry and cavalry. Once officers gained their first commissions through a combination of recommendation and purchase, subsequent promotion was usually determined by age and fortune rather than military accomplishments, with officers usually purchasing their successive ranks using a well-established routine. The purchase system, and the widely condoned abuses of it, worked against either the proper training of officers or any consistently applied career structure.

George and Arnold Greene fought together, with John Vandeleur's Cavalry Brigade, at the Battle of Waterloo. Arnold stayed with their commander, Lieutenant-Colonel James Hay, who was so badly wounded that he could not be moved from the field for a week. This act of courage, and the relevant sums of money, meant an early promotion, at nineteen, to become a Lieutenant. Greene recognised his privileged position. Some impecunious officers who had served as subalterns at Waterloo would be left languishing in the same rank for years, whilst richer men rapidly become the commanding officers of regiments. Greene however believed that his promotions had a significant element of appropriateness about them, he had indeed been a valued and valuable officer.

Greene saw service, with the redesignated Queen's Lancers, in India and the first Afghan war of 1839, reaching the rank of Lieutenant Colonel. A promotion to Brigadier came after the Battle of Aliwal in January 1846 when the regiment charged and dispersed a body of Sikhs ten times its size. It was this encounter, and his memories of Waterloo, that provided the bulk of Greene's anecdotes. He did not speak much about his next military engagement, during the first Anglo-Sikh war, when he was injured at the start of the Battle of Dobraon and had to be taken to the military hospital and eventually returned to UK to be retired, with a good pension, at the age of forty-nine. The injury left him with a pronounced limp and little sight in his left eye (over which he would wear a patch if the sun was shining brightly).

He initially lived with his eighty-year-old widowed father in Hatfield, but when Captain Greene died his son moved to an exclusive property that he described as in Chelsea, but others may have suggested was still Westminster. He lived alone, except for a part-time maid and a resident man-servant.

Greene chose to worship at the Abbey rather than his parish church and he made the acquaintance of some of the clergy and others who worked there. It was Canon Brooks who first suggested that he might accept a voluntary role, greeting Evensong guests and visitors, ensuring security for the Abbey at night. He knew how to wear a uniform, and knew how to deal with people. Greene proved a popular member of staff. He was reliable and his military background gave a respect for authority. The hierarchy Greene recognised in the

Abbey put the Dean and chapter a little below God, and God a little below the young Queen.

Most of the staff at the Abbey only knew him as "The Brigadier". It would have been a shock to hear him being addressed by any name or other title. The nomenclature 'Ginger,' used both by his parents and early acquaintances, was a reference to his youthful hair colour – which no longer applied.

There was a small basement room, in a building on the edge of Dean's Yard, where non-clergy Abbey staff kept their uniforms and where they would occasionally take a rest. Greene's impediment meant that he needed to retire to that space more frequently than some. A wooden open box on the edge of an old table was used as a repository for correspondence, a note about a coming funeral in the Abbey, a request for attendance at a meeting, for instance. It was a colleague who drew Greene's attention to a letter.

'One here for you, Brigadier. It says Private, but you're a Brigadier.'

The joke amused neither of them. The letter was handed across the table and Greene observed that it had been posted, simply addressed to Brigadier Greene, Westminster Abbey. The boldly written and underlined Private, in a hand he did not recognise, suggested an importance that merited pocketing the document until he had returned home.

A couple of hours later, having completed his shift and walked the mile to his home, Greene took the letter out of his pocket. He was seated beside the fire, prepared by his man-servant, that had awaited his return from the Abbey. Although it was late when he got home, he chose to have a few minutes to relax by the fireside and consume a generous Brandy before retiring.

The Royal Crest on the outside had not been noted by the colleague who identified the envelope was for Greene. The Brigadier, however, recognised it from previous correspondence about commissions. It was with a sense of both trepidation and excitement that Arnold Greene opened the envelope. It was with a sense of shock that he collapsed back into his chair, read it through once more, screwed it up and threw it on the fire.

The next day, through his letter box at Albert Mansions, Thomas Marshall was also opening a letter that would seal his fate. It was an invitation to a clandestine meeting with Chipper Clarence the following Saturday evening because, Chipper declared, he had discovered something about Mayhew's work that he needed to discuss. The letter contained no request for destruction. It was filed, in the meticulous way of a Banker's Clerk, in its envelope, upon which Thomas wrote "received August 1851" and "read August 1851" and placed in the appropriate bureaux drawer.

Part 2
The Death of Thomas Marshall

Chapter 15

Finding the body
Sunday August 24th 1851

As he raised his glass William Buckland, seated in his plush and particular chair, was wondering whether anyone should have held the same job for 50 years, but nevertheless issued the declaration, 'George Vincent, for half a century of service!'

There was an echoing "George Vincent" from those assembled in the Jerusalem Chamber, including George's son-in-law, Charles Bedford, who had taken over his father-in-law's post. On the wall before him hung a portrait of George's father – a predecessor of William's as Dean of Westminster Abbey.

The Jerusalem Chamber, an ornately decorated room which was technically part of the Deanery but frequently served as a reception room at the Abbey, was where the Authorised Version of the Bible was first conceived at a gathering, commissioned by the new King James, sixth and first, in 1604. It was where Henry the fourth had died nearly two hundred years before that.

The gathering, in the mid-afternoon, ahead of Evensong, was to acknowledge the service of, and to celebrate the retirement of, the Clerk to the Dean and Chapter. George Vincent had taken on the post, at the age of 28, shortly after his own father had become Dean. He had fulfilled the role for four subsequent Deans. Charles Bedford, the husband of George's thirty-year-old daughter Catherine, had been appointed as the new clerk. Dean Buckland was not confident that such nepotism was appropriate – but the other Canons had over-ruled his concerns. Buckland, now a noticeably stooped man in his sixty-eighth year, was paying one of his rare visits to the Abbey – most of his time was now spent at Islip, a parish in Middlesex where being the Rector was part of the 'package' when he became Dean. For those who could recall the Dean's vigorous promotion of, and active involvement with, the work in the Abbey, he had become a distressing sight.

The general bonhomie was shattered by a scream from Mrs Burrows in the adjoining room. Any verbal content was lost in the agonising wail. The occupants of the Jerusalem chamber first became silent, then looked at each other before those adjacent to the exit moved towards the closed door – carefully putting down their glasses.

Their gaze focussed on Mrs Burrows – hands either side of her head screaming "no". Some twenty feet before them, at the end of a short corridor into the Jericho antechamber, the distraught housekeeper looked down upon a crumpled figure at her feet.

Charles Bedford, the new clerk, at the front of the men leaving Jerusalem, paused a few feet short of the body. Voices behind him were shouting various enquiries. Charles had the wisdom to demand, "silence."

Mrs Burrows, disobedient to the call, screamed more coherently, 'there's a body in the Cassock cupboard – it's Mr Marshall from the choir.' Before her the torso of a man was evident – his attached legs still within the Cassock cupboard that Mrs Burrows had evidently opened (one of a series of cupboards along the wall). Blood was congealed around his face and over some of his clothing.

Bedford's next instruction was gentle and focussed, 'step back Mrs Burrows.' A command she sought to fulfil, but toppled as she moved back – Mrs Bedford was soon on hand to pick her up and seat her adjacent to the round table where she would normally have displayed the robes in preparation for any upcoming service.

Bedford went onto his knees on the wooden floor and carefully sought any evidence of life – neither at the wrist or the throat were there any vital signs. The skin on Thomas Marshall's face that was not discoloured by blood had lost all its own colour.

‘He’s dead; we need the police.’

Most of the former occupants of the Jerusalem Chamber had shuffled through and, having glanced at the body, had stepped back to be close to the large main window of the room.

Dean Buckland asked a question of his colleague Canon Brooks, ‘what shall we do?’

He believed it to be a whispered enquiry – but his advanced deafness, and the few feet separating them, meant that all those gathered heard it. The response of his colleague, ‘we’ll need to call off the service’ was not really the answer he was anticipating or looking for.

Mrs Burrows declaration that ‘we can’t leave him here,’ was no more useful. It was the retiring Clerk who recalled that a member of the Metropolitan police force was usually on duty a few yards away outside the imposing West doors of the Abbey.

His son-in-law, Mr Bedford, assumed a further leadership role and instructed the youngest of the Canons to, ‘go and get the police.’ Canon Mitchell, in clerical collar and dark suit, quickly moved into Samaria. a room between Jericho and the Nave, through a narrow door and down two steps onto the floor of the Abbey.

There was very little doubt whose body it was, though the Dean’s next remark was framed as a question, ‘Isn’t that Thomas Marshall?’ His suspicion was confirmed by the clergy amongst those assembled. Thomas, even in the absence of his choral robes, was recognised as a senior volunteer member of the Sunday choir who should have been, even as his lifeless body was being stared at, in the choir room preparing with his colleagues for Evensong. The choir assumed that Thomas Marshall was, as he often had been recently, “doing something else”.

One of the Canons declared. ‘We ought to let Mrs Marshall know. You were a friend of Marshall, Arthur, do you know where she lives?’

‘I do,’ responded Canon Brooks, ‘not so far away. In one of the new places off Victoria Street. I’ll go and let her know. Would that be all right?’

The final remark was addressed to all those assembled; Brooks being not sure who might be authorising the visit. Those around approved either with a slight nod of the head or a brief, quietly spoken, phrase.

Bedford returned in the company of two police officers at that moment. A further short consultation meant that Brooks’ visit was approved.

‘All right by me,’ said the senior officer, ‘we would normally do it. But since you know her.’

Arthur Brooks acknowledged those in the room and departed. Speaking from the step down into Samaria, , he remembered and turned back to speak to the Dean, ‘I’ll not be back for Evensong – but I’m not leading or preaching tonight.’

The Dean nodded, and after Brooks departure asked, in a general way, ‘should we call the service off?’ No one felt to have sufficient authority to address his question.

The advice of the police, delivered by the Sergeant not long after the question had been raised, was that the worship should go ahead – there were already several hundred people in the Sanctuary area outside anticipating that the barrier preventing their entrance into the Abbey would be imminently removed.

The policemen moved towards the body and indicated to others that they should step away.

Sergeant John Watson, however, knew that his involvement was rather premature. ‘The coroner will need to be called,’ he declared – and dispatched his junior colleague, Constable George Clegg, to make his way towards the river and along to Millbank.

Addressing those assembled Watson said, ‘his office won’t be open, but George knows where the coroner lives nearby.’

Clegg's uniform was a cumbersome mix. As 'a servant' of the people, he wore a tailcoat, in non-military blue. But, needing an air of authority, he also wore a top hat, strengthened with an iron ring at the crown. A stiff stock around the neck, to guard against garrotting, completed the uniform. He also carried, attached to a heavy leather belt, handcuffs, a wooden truncheon, and a rattle to summon help.

Having been asked not to mention what had happened, half-a-dozen members of George Vincent's extended family made their way through the courtyard outside the deanery into the Abbey precincts towards the Clerk's accommodation beyond the Cloisters for a supper that was both earlier, for they had intended to attend evensong, and more subdued, than had been anticipated. Dean Buckland suggested that the other Canons return to their homes – impressed with the instruction not to speak of the matter, and to return for Evensong in half an hour. Only the Dean, Mrs Burrows, Sergeant Watson and Charles Bedford, the new Clerk, remained.

'Best not to mention this to anyone until the coroner's done his job,' advised Watson.

Turning, initially to Mrs Burrows to inquisition her, then, recalling his need for compassion, turned to the Dean. 'Did he have a family?'

'Yes, two daughters I believe, Canon Brooks knows the family well.'

'I'm sorry,' not an apology, but an incomplete sentence that was intended to express Watson's condolences to the deceased's widow and children.

Watson, standing with his back to the large window overlooking the courtyard, surveyed the room. Pointing towards the door to his left the Sergeant asked, 'is there a way out through there?'

'No,' replied the Dean and, somewhat enigmatically the police office thought. 'There's no other way out of Jerusalem.'

‘So,’ looking to his right, ’the body came into this room the same way as we did. Can we just step this way?’

Watson led Bedford, the Dean and Mrs Burrows through into the adjacent “Samaria” and looking around and saw two further doors in addition to the one that they have come through from the Nave.

‘Can I ask where those doors lead?’ asked Watson with his back to Jericho, simultaneously pointing to a door in a recess ahead of him, and a larger one to his right.

Charles Bedford responded, ‘there is a water closet through there that the Dean has just had installed. For the use of special guests at the Abbey. Through that door are steps down to the Deanery courtyard.’

The Dean added, ‘although we are at the moment in my house, I cannot go directly into my main living quarters from here without going outside.’

‘So, the body would have had to come through your house if it was brought in through that door?’ Whilst Watson asked the questions and made the observations, the Clerk was taking notes and looking around. It was he who responded. ‘No, that’s not the case. There’s an open entrance from the rear cloister door into the Dean’s courtyard. There are two doors off the courtyard – one into the deanery and other here.’

Bedford pointed at the door before them.

‘Can we look through it please?’

This time it was Mrs Burrows who responded, the Dean having almost collapsed into a hard chair.

‘I can open it for you. Can the Dean please be allowed home for a while, he has had a busy day – and Evensong a bit later, he needs to see his wife and have some rest?’

‘Certainly he can.’ Responded the police officer.

‘I’ll follow you down,’ said the Dean. A few minutes later they realised why he had said that as they observed his slow and obviously painful progress down the steps into the courtyard and, once through the door into the Deanery, they noted, he would need to ascend a further stone staircase. The

Deanery was a large building; Mary Buckland had never counted its rooms, but was able to identify 15 staircases.

Mrs Burrows sought to direct the policemen's attention from the Dean, and pointed out, 'through that arch and turn right and you are on to Dean's Yard.'

It was the observant Clerk Bedford who noted blood stains on the steps when he looked back, after the Dean had made his way to the Deanery door.

'Here Sergeant Watson. Spots of blood. It looks like the body came in through this door.'

'I think that is unlikely,' contributed Mrs Burrows, 'only the Dean and I have keys.'

'But it was open as we left,' chimed in Watson.

'There is a key hanging near the door on the inside,' Mrs Burrows informed the officer. 'I opened it a few minutes ago so that Mr Vincent's party could leave. I didn't lock it again because I knew the Dean had to leave. But it's a private door – it's always locked.'

'That may be so Mrs Burrows; but this blood suggests the body came in through here, unless you have another explanation?' was Sergeant Watson's response, formed as an enquiry.

'Then someone will have opened it from the inside,' replied the housekeeper.

'Allowing the body to be brought in up the steps. Who has access from the church?' asked the Sergeant, turning towards the door from the Nave.

It was Mrs Burrows who again answered the question, 'although the door is usually closed, and it does have a sign saying "private", it can be easily opened with the handle.'

'So, someone seems to have come in that way, collected the key and opened this door so that the body could be brought in.' Watson's musings were interrupted by the return of Constable Clegg accompanied by the coroner.

Chapter 16

The Coroner
Sunday August 24th 1851

Constable Clegg had disturbed the quiet of the coroner's afternoon, but since his wellbeing and that of his family depended on his income, and his income only came from attendance at deaths, Colin Burge was willing to forswear the imminent evening walk with his wife and daughter and attend the Abbey in response to the slightly hysterical, he thought, beseeching of the police officer. Burge collected his notepad, and picked up his official top hat from the hatstand as he left. There was a momentary pause as he considered whether he needed his tails if he was going to the Abbey – but the constable was not brooking any delay.

Mr Burge felt a tinge of excitement. The conventional destination for an evening call-out to look at a body would be a public house, or somewhere even more disreputable; and this sounded like the sort of lucrative call-out that would entail the summoning not only of a jury but, he hoped, of witnesses and experts as well.

Clegg, being approximately half the coroner's age and rather more fleet of foot, set off at a pace, only to feel obliged to pause and turn every 50 yards. He then set off again each time Burge was within a few feet.

Approaching the construction site of the southern tower of the Houses of Parliament the officer abruptly turned left into College Street and then right into Dean's Yard. He entered the Abbey by the cloister door and then a further abrupt left took Clegg to the steps up to the door of Jericho. He climbed them and stooped to get his breath back. He stood up to open the door as the coroner walked through the Dean's courtyard and up the steps at a measured, funereal, pace and entered first into the room.

Clerk Bedford had been urging Sergeant Watson to get on with an investigation. 'Not until the coroner says I can,' had been his brief reply. After excusing Mrs Burrows, offended to be told she should not do any clearing up, there were several minutes' silence as neither Bedford nor Watson were quite sure what to do.

The silence was interrupted by an, 'evening sir,' from the coroner, with a brief nod of the head towards Bedford, not sufficient to dislodge the top hat, and then to the police officer, 'evening John.'

He responded with an, 'evening Colin.'

The preliminary responses to questions of name, approximate age, and whether the Clerk knew him were conducted and entered his note book by Mr Burge.

'Did he die here?'

'Of course, not.' Came the defensive response from Bedford.

'Then where sir?' requested the coroner in an accusative way, anticipating that he would need to reprimand the police for transporting the body from somewhere.

'He was found here – we've no idea where he came from; but the blood on the steps outside suggest he was brought here by someone.'

The coroner was slightly embarrassed that he had not noted the blood, but mentally excused himself because it was a shaded area, and it was getting dark.

'The gash across his skull makes it evident that he has been killed, probably with a blunt instrument. I'm going to have to get my jury together and come back.'

'But you can't leave him here,' expostulated the Clerk.

'Well, where do you suggest he goes Mr Bedford?'

'There's a room through here,' said the Sergeant – indicating the open door that led through to the Jerusalem Chamber. The Clerk was not of a mind to regard the precedent of Henry the fourth as a justification for a dead commoner to lie there, and the suggestion was made that since this wasn't the scene of the death it would be possible to discreetly remove the body to a basement across the other side of the Abbey's entrance corridor, which was both cold and damp – recognised as beneficial for a corpse to retain some dignity.

So, with the Clerk as a watchguard, and with Marshall's body wrapped in what looked distinctly like an altar cloth, the two police officers and the coroner carried the dead chorister down the stairs, across the Dean's courtyard, across the entrance corridor, along a narrow corridor, down some steps and rested him on a table fortuitously placed in the centre of a cellar room normally only used for storage of objects that would not be harmed by the damp.

'I'll be back in the morning with the jury. Will we be able to get in at eight tomorrow?'

'Will you need me?' asked the Clerk.

'No need for you to be here sir, but I may have some questions, depending on what we discover.'

'I'll ask Canon Brooks to be here – he knows, I mean, he knew Marshall.'

'If this door can be locked, so that no one can go in until the Canon lets us in at eight,' were Mr Burge's parting remarks. They were made as he was already making his way up the steps to the cloister entrance, 'and thank you' he added, believing it to be an apt closing remark to the Clerk. The police officers received an added, 'and thanks to you John and George, you'll be hearing from me soon John.'

The police officers work was not yet complete. They decided to have a conversation with the Beadles at the yard gates. As they left the cloister entrance onto Dean's Yard John Watson went straight ahead and then right and George Clegg turned immediately left.

Watson engaged the Beadle in conversation at his box. He had not been aware of anything untoward in the previous few hours since he had come on duty. He had only admitted authorised people – Abbey and School staff and a few of the Westminster children.

George Clegg's encounter was more fruitful. John Clark was not only on duty that evening, but had been in post throughout the day. The side gate into College Street was not frequently used and the larger main gate at that end was often closed overnight outside of the school term. The role of Beadle at the College Street end was something of a sinecure. There was opportunity to find time to relax. Both the pedestrian and the vehicle gates needed oiling – and had noisy latches; so anyone attempting to enter was normally heralded by the sound of the gate being opened.

'Hi John,' was Clegg's greeting to a familiar acquaintance, they had served in the same regiment – but at different times. 'We need to know if anything strange or different has happened here in, say, the past day.'

'What a strange question. Not much Cleggy – though there was something that might seem a bit out of the ordinary. What's this about?'

'I can't say anything at the moment. But what was it that happened?'

Clark began his account of an out-of-the-ordinary event by recalled that earlier that afternoon he had been distracted by a football game that some of the boys, from amongst those whose parents lived abroad and remained in school during the summer, were playing on the grass. He went across to remonstrate with them, and had detained one of them with a secure grip on the wrist. He had apprehended the runt of the litter as he ushered the others back through the gate into Little Dean's Yard. During the school holidays none of the senior staff were on hand. Clark felt it sufficient to report to a senior prefect, who identified the apprehended miscreant, and who should have been keeping an eye the boys. Clark, being a man of faith, also thought that there should be at least some minor punishment, lines or something, for disregarding the Sabbath.

He enjoyed telling Clegg the anecdote; but the police officer was impatient for him to get to the point.

'Is that it John?'

'I'm getting there Cleggy.' There were few who addressed him in that way, but as fellow members of the Middlesex regiment such familiarities were permitted.

'As I came out from Little Dean's Yard and looked up towards College Street, I saw some guys pushing a cart through the gate. Appeared to be empty. They obviously hadn't taken anything – so must have been delivering something. Doesn't often happen on a Sunday. But they were leaving. They didn't notice me, and I didn't call out to them.'

'Thanks John,' said Constable Clegg and, concealing his hope that it might be significant to the case, but not wishing to give anything away, concluded, 'interesting, but probably nothing. Good night.'

There was an obligation, introduced in the 1830s, upon the police that at the end of each day they put together a route-paper, identifying the unresolved crimes that they were dealing with. These were to be distributed each morning to each of the other 17 Divisions, in case officers there should have information, or might conduct enquires, to progress the investigation. Since the creation of the Detective Branch they had been included in the circulation. The reason why John Watson did not give a full account to his divisional head of his investigations that evening is not certain. He might have believed that the Detectives were bound to find out everything they had discovered anyway. It is also possible that there was a measure of hubris that resented having to hand over the most interesting cases to the new department.

Later that evening six hundred worshippers, some needing to be reminded to remove their hats, came up the steps and through the Great West Door – young couples holding hands, older couples (she behind him), some family groups concluding a day out, and individuals. It was never easy to identify which were devote worshippers, which were seeking to have a glimpse of the Abbey without the expenses of hiring a guide, and which were simply following a crowd. Limited seating meant a number would be standing throughout the forty-minute service. Tonight, the choir arrived, processing through the nave and under the recently installed arch with the statue of Isaac Newton to the left. The absence of Thomas Marshall was not noted by the congregation. James Turle was at the organ, Colonel Briggs conducted the choir, and the Dean, never rising from his seat, intoned the Merbecke setting. The mellifluous words filled the Abbey as majestically as at any point in the three hundred years since they had first been compiled into the English Prayer Book.

The exhausted Dean, as the service concluded, processed back down past the choir stalls and through the arch, and, having walked diagonally across the nave, almost tripped up the step into Samaria. He was the only member of clergy permitted that way that evening. He paused briefly in Jericho, where he discarded his robes, and went out through the door towards the Deanery. A glass of sherry was needed, and a good night's sleep hoped for.

Chapter 17

The Dean's life

Sunday August 24th 1851

The Dean was confident that Mrs Burrows would sort out what attire was needed for next day's Matins. Across the deanery courtyard, he slowly climbed the stairs into his private quarters, wondering quite what he would say to Mrs Buckland – and whether he would say anything to Clive Medley or their maid.

William Buckland was used to investigations, and familiar with dead bodies; but his experience had been restricted to animals, and to animals that had been dead for millions of years. It had come as something of a shock when the then Prime Minister, Robert Peel (under whose behest the likes of Watson and Clegg now had achieved professional status and employment) invited him to be Dean of Lincoln Cathedral in 1844. Although he had been ordained upon leaving Oxford his calling, as he saw it, had been to explore and explain God's work in ancient times, rather than minister to his contemporaries. Buckland was based happily in Oxford, as a lecturer and a Canon of Christ Church Cathedral when Peel made him that offer. Although he had turned it down, Peel had been persistent and when Samuel 'Soapy' Wilberforce, after less than a year in post, was appointed Bishop of Oxford, he once more asked his friend about a senior post in his gift, with the Queen's consent, the Deanery of Westminster. William had been uncertain but Mrs Buckland believed a home in Westminster and a quiet country living in Islip would be an ideal way of seeing more of their family; and that the recognition of a scientist showed Peel to be a man of moral courage. Peel said that it was the appointment, amongst all he made in state or church, that gave him most pride.

Buckland's father and grandfather had been clergy. It was in his father's parish of Axminster, Devon that young William first collected Ammonites. It was no surprise that he became ordained after his Oxford undergraduate degree in 1809; ordination gave an entrée into certain professions and was also an asset on a Curriculum Vitae. He needed a job to enable him to explore the world of geology and ancient creatures, and ordination opened doors to many academic roles.

His professional research had led to several controversies – with both clergy and academic colleagues. He published a paper in 1819 entitled The connexion of Geology and Religion explained. Over time he published further works supportive of a Universal Flood – but suggestive of antediluvian animals. In 1824 he provided the first ever full account of a dinosaur.

Buckland married Mary Morland, herself a noted geologist, in 1828. They had a large family – though only five of their nine children survived childhood.

He was not only seen by some as eccentric in his beliefs; he was also widely recognised as eccentric in his behaviour. On visiting a Catholic shrine that was said to weep blood he bent over to lick the liquid and declared it was bat's urine. His geological knowledge stood him in good stead when lost on a coach journey – he sampled the soil and declared "Uxbridge". His eccentricities endeared him to some, and infuriated others.

At the Abbey he was a man of enormous energy; rising soon after seven, he worked on incessantly till two or three o'clock the next morning, allowing himself scarcely any time for meals and still less for recreation. His focus had been on Westminster School and on the environment for worship within the Abbey.

He encountered an Abbey where it had become uncommon to display a reverent regard for public worship, and he set his mind to ensuring that everything in connection with the house of God should be done with decency and order. The Dean kept a strict eye over the way the services were performed, and corrected many abuses. Finding that the Abbey's junior choristers spent their time between the services in sailing their toy boats in puddles made by the sinking of the gravestones in St. Margaret's Churchyard, or, if it were dry weather, in playing marbles on the flat slabs of the altar-tombs, he looked about for a suitable place in the precincts which could be used for a new Choir School. It would become the heart of musical accomplishments unimaginable earlier in the century.

The Dean kept a menagerie of animals at the Deanery, snakes slithered around an enclosed tank in one corner, monkeys clamoured around the furniture. A hyena prowled the area between the Deanery and the Abbey. Other animals such as hedgehogs, tortoise, an ostrich, frogs and a crocodile, became items on the luncheon menu at the Deanery when they had deceased. and an eagle was tethered on a balcony outside the drawing room. The eagle had created so much mayhem at his son's Oxford college that it had been brought to the Abbey. After it proved a distraction on the day of the Chartist March in 1848, perching on a high pinnacle of the Abbey, it was lured down by a sacrificial chicken and subsequent rehoused to the new Zoo at Regent's Park. Jenny the Monkey arrived with that same son Frank in 1849, when he had finished his Oxford course, and it would also end her days at the Zoo.

Buckland had a good relationship with the police – he had provided men to protect the Abbey, and patrol the local streets with truncheons, during the chartist revolt of 1848 and, indeed, Buckland kept his stock of those truncheons stored in the outer drawing-room for use by the Westminster specials.

In May 1848 Buckland and two of his daughters became ill with typhoid, or " Westminster fever", as it was called. As soon as Buckland was restored to health, he lost no time in applying his scientific knowledge to the making of sewers throughout the school and onto the deanery - though digging up the drains (which removed four hundred tons of foul-matter) accidentally introduced typhoid into the school. He also provided the first washing facilities for the scholars: his system of pipe-drainage was the first of its kind ever laid down in London. Buckland also tried to change the diet of the boys. But the boys objected and, summoning the chef, threw the new-fangled treacle-puddings at him. One of the school masters commented. 'anyone with a less commanding scientific reputation than Dr Buckland, even with all his power as Dean, could not have overcome the prejudice which at that time was entertained against his alterations'.

Towards the end of 1849, a couple of years after that carriage accident in Germany which came to be believed as its cause, Buckland experienced a debilitating illness characterised, initially, by apathy and depression, but it had developed into significant physical deterioration. His doctors recommended the quiet and fresh air of Islip, and the sight of the garden and his favourite allotments seemed to cheer him for a time. At the time of Marshall's death his health was continuing to fail and his presence in Westminster was only sporadic – he did not need this new anxiety.

Chapter 18

The coroner's inquest Monday August 25th 1851

Mrs Burrows had not acted with as much discretion on leaving the Abbey as the Dean and police had hoped – a casual remark to the Beadle at the gate onto the Sanctuary as she went out later on Sunday for a walk, 'that was a shock, finding a body,' together with the description that was necessary to respond to the Beadle's enquiry of 'what?,' meant that Gerald Bourne of the *Morning Chronicle* had been alerted and was standing at the cloister entrance next morning as the Coroner, escorted by twelve besuited men, prepared to go about his business.

'Not you' and 'nothing to say' were the two phrases that Colin Burge used to greeted Bourne.

Canon Brooks, who had spent a couple of hours the previous evening consoling Mrs Marshall and her daughters, was at the cellar door.

'It's terrible,' was the Canon's opening remark as he applied the key and turned it, unconventionally, anti-clockwise. He was reluctant to go into the room – but had little option since thirteen other men needed to enter, each giving him a brief acknowledgment as they pushed by. Burge, who came in last, asked whether the Canon would lock the door and come inside with them.

The twelve jury-men had not moved towards the corpse, covered in its altar frontal, but had stepped aside to stand together. They knew that the proceedings would begin with them being sworn in. Being within the precincts of the Abbey gave to some of them a greater sense of the necessity of acknowledging that they both needed to seek truth, and needed divine aid in that pursuit. The swearing-in ceremony was carried out and the jurors' names entered in Burge's register – eight of the twelve gave a signature, an unusually high per centage amongst adult men, and the four others marked a cross adjacent to their names – Burge's signature was added to each to authenticate their presence.

With a less than artistic style in the removal of the covering cloth the jurors were invited to stand along three sides of the table, whilst the coroner enjoined Canon Brooks, as the nearest thing to a witness, to stand beside him.

'We have to decide whether this death was natural, accidental, suicide or inflicted by someone else,' although nominally addressed to the jurors this was essentially information for Brooks. There were a limited number of people that the Parish Officer, who had been contacted by Burge immediately after leaving the Abbey the previous evening, could approach on a Sunday night, and prevail upon to be available early next morning. Most of those present in the room were familiar with the process.

A knock came at the door, Burge authorised Brooks to open the door with the declaration, 'that'll be Doctor Milligan.' The Parish Officer would only be earning his fee if he could deliver all the necessary cast.

Doctor Milligan, after greeting those in the room, moved towards the table. He carried not only his medical bag but some cloths and disinfectant. He had been called early enough not to need the mask that was often employed in these circumstances. The jurors stepped back a little from the table, though it was evident that the Doctor probably only needed access to the head. The removal of the towel that had been wrapped around it revealed a deep impact wound and some judicious cleaning revealed some evidence of a little cranial material that had exuded from it.

'Seems to have been bashed on the head,' was the doctor's succinct appraisal. 'But I'd better look around the body.'

The jurors took a further step back. Rigor mortis had begun to set in and the manipulation of limbs was neither practical nor necessary. The removal of Marshall's trousers and the opening of his jacket and shirt did not give evidence of any further issues that needed to be considered.

'Did anybody see this happen?' asked the doctor, presuming to pre-empt the coroner's conventional enquiries.

It was the coroner, however, who responded, 'he was brought to the Abbey dead, no sign of a weapon, or any idea of when it was done.'

'This man,' the coroner identified Canon Brooks to the doctor with a gesture that needed no more than a brief opening of his hand, 'knew the deceased, and spent last night with the victim's wife.' Fortunately, the sneer from one of the jurors was only heard by those adjacent to him.

'Do you want to add anything?' the coroner, turning to him, asked the cleric.

'I don't think I can. His wife is obviously very distressed.'

'That is not an issue for us,' remarked the coroner. 'Can you say anything about the death?'

Canon Brooks had earlier mentally prepared his succinct description. 'I'm afraid all I know is that when our robe-mistress (he had created a name to describe her) Mrs Burrows opened the cupboard to select the clergy robes, he fell out. He seems to have been pushed into the cupboard in an upright position, the door pushed closed and the small bar dropped to keep it closed. It doesn't have a key. Mrs Burrows twisted the handle, raising the bar, the door fell open and Marshall fell out.'

'I don't think we need a full post-mortem Doctor, the cause seems obvious,' said Burge, looking across to Milligan and anticipating an affirmative response.

'I'm happy to certify that he was killed with a single blow to the head by an unidentified but heavy blunt instrument, and it would seem that the date of death was on or before Sunday August 24th 1851, certainly the body's condition would suggest no earlier than Saturday, at a location as yet unknown, that'll be for the Metropolitan police to establish' and, turning to Burge, 'I don't believe you need me any longer.'

Milligan had glanced around, not expecting his belief to be challenged, and bade the group farewell before moving towards the door that the Canon had opened. It was then closed behind the departing doctor.

Doctor Milligan gave short shrift to the enquiry Gerald Bourne of the *Morning Chronicle* made at the cloister entrance.

'Gentlemen,' began Burge, introducing his formal summing up of the Inquest to those around him in the cellar room, 'we must determine whether this man, Thomas Marshall, died naturally, by accident, by his own hands, or through the agency of another party or parties. I believe it was the last of those. Do you wish to consult amongst yourselves, or hear any further evidence, or are you happy to indicate that you agree with that verdict?'

There was no hesitation as twelve hands were limply raised.

'Mr Canon. I am now able to issue a certificate to the effect that this man was either murdered or the subject of manslaughter. That means that I am able to say that his family can dispose of the body. Although the Doctor has not requested a full post-mortem, he will nonetheless give a report to the new Detective Police – and I would advise that no burial should take place until they give their approval.' It was a script he had learnt by heart – even though he only saw a few murders each year.

Addressing the twelve jurors, the coroner said, 'thank you gentlemen.'

As they left, they each added their name or mark on the coroner's report, upon which Burge had already circled "Murder/Manslaughter".

Canon Brooks locked the door and decided that Mrs Marshall needed to know the verdict before the Dean. He too was able to avoid the blandishments of Gerald Bourne, but did not realise, as he walked towards Victoria Street, that he was being followed and that Mr Bourne would take a note of the number of the door he was knocking on five minutes later.

Chapter 19

Telling the Detectives
Monday August 25th 1851

That morning Colin Burge, the coroner, knew that the remaining aspects of his work on the case would be essentially administrative. The next hour would be given over to completing forms – this was the point at which he believed he was well worth his guinea fee. Because of the verdict that he, and his colleagues, had just delivered he needed to get in touch with Scotland Yard. Fortunately for him the Headquarters of the Detective Police was only half a mile away at the top of Whitehall. For many of his fellow coroners, who until a few years earlier had simply had to report to their local division office, getting the Inquest result securely to the Detectives included using the General Post Office. Although usually secure and reliable it was known that some people had a particular interest in letters going to the Detectives. Few coroners were comfortable in using the recently introduced Post Boxes, one of which was adjacent to the Abbey.

The coroner went back to his home, and office, at Millbank. He prepared a clean copy of his account of the Inquest on the appropriate form for the Detectives, another for the local Parish Officer and a third for his personal records. He also had to provide to the parish the names of the jurors, so that they could be checked against the approved list and then each paid their four shillings fee.

It was ten o'clock before he was ready to take the document to Scotland Yard. He walked along Margaret Street past the towers under construction at either side of the Houses of Parliament; only pausing to wonder why the people who gathered in that house deserved six weeks off in the Summer whilst he had a week off each year.

Burge proceeded passed Parliament Square to Parliament Street and up the elegant Whitehall, hoping that Victoria

Street would one day look as impressive. Finally turning into Whitehall Place, he came to the door of Scotland Yard. Although there was provision for pushing his form through a letter-box his professionalism meant he needed to make sure it was handed to someone at the desk. That task having been completed he stepped out and faced into the bright sun, content that he had fulfilled his task and would need to give no further thought to the death of Thomas Marshall.

Chapter 20

The Music Committee
Monday August 25th 1851

Frederick Briggs, the choirmaster at the Abbey, responded to Marshall's death by wondering where he might find another such competent singer ahead of the celebrations for the Birth of Our Lady, on September the twelfth, and whether he personally would have the time to go through the music with them.

Canon Brooks' response was rather different. He was wondering where his new "ears" would come from; who his new "voice" would be. For some years Thomas Marshall had been his source of information on the thinking of the Dean concerning worship. As a senior chorister Thomas, elected by his fellow adult choristers, had been a member of a select group, with the organist, and nominal choir master, James Turle, the organist's assistant and actual choir master, Briggs, and the Dean. Turle had had a connection with the Abbey since he was a fifteen-year-old in 1817. Initially he had been an assistant to the Abbey organist Geoffrey Williams, and subsequently deputy to William's successor Thomas Greatorex, whom he succeeded in 1831. When a separate school for the choristers was funded in 1848 Turle, choosing to absent himself from the day-to-day discipline of the boys, had enlisted Colonel Briggs as choirmaster, subsequently he had also passed to him the pastoral care of the men.

Within the Music Committee confidential conversations were held, provisional decisions made and, unbeknown to the triumvirate of other members, these were shared almost immediately after by Marshall with Brooks.

Chapter 21

The Detectives
Monday August 25th 1851

For the officers of the Detective Force their consideration of the death of Thomas Marshall was about to begin. Behind the desk at the entrance lobby of Scotland Yard was the 55-year-old Detective Sergeant Francis Roberts. Twenty-four years earlier he had been amongst the first tranche of candidates to join Sir Robert Peel's Metropolitan Police Service, created to replace the Bow Street runners. He had fulfilled his calling with both distinction and frustration. His task had always been primarily to prevent crime rather than catch criminals; but for a decade now his focus had been on investigating rather than preventing. He had looked to join the Detectives from the time he first heard about their creation, and was amongst the first recruits. A murder on his doorstep excited him. Roberts knew he was coming to the end of his career – and had dreamt of the chance to make the front pages. Such an opportunity was now being presented to him by that strange coroner down at Westminster. It would not, however, be Roberts' decision. He could only hope to be the bag-carrier for a senior officer. He resented that; someone probably less experienced than himself would be credited in the papers with solving the crime.

It was the Desk Sergeant's responsibility to take the case details, neatly prepared by the coroner's hand, through to the Detective Superintendents' office on the first floor; but only once he was sure that another colleague could hold the front desk. Front desk was not an enviable position – you were exposed to all the "concerned" people who wanted to tell you about their neighbours, and to all the amateurs who were confident they had the solutions to the intractable cases that made the Penny Dreadful leaflets. An excuse was always appreciated to get away from the obligation to complete the several "nuisance" forms required when your main desire was to be rid of the nuisances. Roberts' called across to the room allocated to Detective Sergeants, the lowest rank amongst the Detectives, 'can someone cover the desk?' A reluctant colleague appeared, hoping that Roberts' visit upstairs would be brief.

On the first floor Chief Superintendent, the senior officer among the Detectives, Albert Jones was smoking his pipe and listening out the window to the people enjoying their journeys along Whitehall. His fellow Superintendent was also in the room at a desk studiously reading, and making notes from, reports about a series of assaults on local magistrates. Francis Roberts made a bee-line for Jones, knowing that he too was approaching an age where one 'big-one' would satisfactorily top off his career.

'Chief, we've just had this murder in from down the road at the Abbey.' An unsolved death was always initially called a murder, a subsequent conviction for manslaughter regularly came with an element of disappointment. Fortunately for the ubiquitous Penny Dreadfuls, being produced by over a hundred publishers, the distinction was unknown, and "murder" was always the word in bold capitals.

'What's that Frank? Something juicy?' enquired Jones, not yet putting down his pipe, or turning his head in the direction of the Sergeant.

'Someone found dead in the Abbey. Head bashed in.'

Not only did this immediately attract Jones's attention but also that of his colleague at his desk across the room, who put his pen down and lifted his head.

Claiming priority, the chief Superintendent declared, 'this one's mine.'

'Ours I hope,' ventured Roberts.

'Ours,' responded Jones with a wry smile, 'two Welshmen can solve it.'

The chief Superintendent rose from his comfortable chair, put on his glasses, and moved to sit at the desk where

Roberts had placed the document. When he had read through the coroner's report a couple of times Jones declared, 'we need to go down to the scene of the crime, or rather the place where the body was found.'

He stood up with his pipe still in his hand, he had not had the opportunity to smoke the pipe for a couple of days and was not going to relinquish it quite yet. 'We must talk to the woman who found the body, whatever she's called?'

'Mrs Burrows,' chimed in Roberts – having picked up the report from the table.

'Yeh, Burrows, and to see the Dean if we can.'

As they set out a further despatch arrived at Scotland Yard. Delivered on behalf of George Clegg, it was a description of the scene, and conversations he had witnessed the previous evening in the Abbey; although his senior colleague, Sergeant Watson, had chosen not to formally circulate information on the state of play in the case, Clegg believed he should, rather clandestinely, keep the Detectives informed. The document was briefly glanced at and pocketed by Jones as he departed; but it was incomplete, it did not cover Clegg's conversations with John Clarke at the Orchard Street entrance to Dean's Yard.

Fifteen minutes after their departure from Scotland Yard Roberts and Jones were at the Abbey. Both men were familiar with the exterior; but neither was quite sure which entrance to use. One of Jones's proudest moments was when, fourteen years earlier, he had stood close to where they were now holding back, elbow locked to elbow with his fellow constables, the jubilant, noisy, and somewhat drunk, crowds at Her Majesty's coronation.

The Chief Superintendent and his Sergeant walked past St Margaret's parish church towards the impressive, multi gothic-arched doorway to be told by a constable on duty that the main entrance was the West Door.

It took Jones a few moments to orientate himself when the constable enquired. 'Are you here about the murder?'

They had intended to be discreet about their purpose but the Constable was able to produce for them not only a rapidly produced "Penny-blood" fronted by an image of a man wielding a large candle-stick at the high altar and the declaration MURDER AT THE ABBEY in capitals an inch high, but also a more sober account, under the by-line of Gerald Bourne, in the *Morning Chronicle*'s "emergency" edition of the visit of a coroner to the Abbey and a declaration that the victim was a "member of staff" at the Abbey and a "resident of Victoria Street." It therefore came as no surprise that when they came to the Great West Door of the Abbey it was firmly closed with a phalanx of the curious gathered outside. Nominally Jones and Roberts were non-uniform, but their bearing and common non-uniform, including a truncheon, betrayed to several, particularly the few journalists amongst those assembled, that they were "Detectives". Fortunately also amongst the small crowd was a member of the Abbey staff who was able to conduct them passed the vigilant Beadle at the gate of Dean's Yard and through to the cloister entrance. They arrived close to the time that the coroner had suggested to Canon Brooks they might make an appearance; and he was waiting to escort them to see the corpse.

'Is this where he died?' was the Chief Superintendent 's first enquiry as the Canon unlocked the basement door.

'We don't know where he died, I'm afraid. His body was found in Jericho,' the Canon responded.

This caused a momentary, but subdued, 'Where?' from both men. Jones had in his head a Sunday School image of Zacchaeus up a tree, Roberts recalled the journey of the Good Samaritan. Neither were quite sure where Jericho was, but confident it was not in Westminster.

Seeing some puzzled looks, Brooks offered, 'it's one of the rooms in the Deanery. I'll show you in a while.'

Roberts' response hinted at anger, 'who gave permission for it to be moved?'

'The Dean didn't want it in his house, and the coroner needed room for the jury. It wasn't here that the murder happened so he thought it was all right. I wasn't here when he was moved, I had gone to see Mrs Marshall, to let her know the bad news.'

'It shouldn't have happened, but it can't be helped now. They don't make our job any easier.' The last remark was made, somewhat sotto voce to DS Jones. As the Chief Superintendent was speaking Brooks was slowly removing the altar cloth from over the body. Marshall's trousers were still around his ankles and his shirt ripped open; but these were ignored by the Officers who looked at the head, and rapidly looked away once they had seen it.

'We can see what happened,' said Jones. They then both had the courage to give more than a cursory glance at the skull.

The Chief Superintendent looked up at Brooks, 'do we have the weapon?'

'No, we believe that the body was brought to the Deanery from elsewhere. There's blood on the steps up to Jericho.'

'The coroner's report said he's about forty, that seems right,' said Roberts.

Canon Brooks was able to confirm. 'His wife tells me he was forty-two – birthday next week, they had planned a walk out with their children.'

'Can you do a description Jones, or maybe we should ask his wife? Did you know the man Canon? Are there any distinguishing marks on him?'

Brooks, not sure which question to answer first, offered 'yes, he was in our choir – and I notice on his leg a small tattoo.'

Marshall's left leg now attracted Roberts's attention for the first time, on the calf discreetly, but deliberate, the words THE POOR inked in a curve.

'Very curious. Do you know what it means Canon?'

'No idea.'

'Have you completed your description Jones?' A nod affirmed that he had.

'Then we need to make our journey down to Jericho,' Roberts offered a slight laugh at his remembrance of a line from the Good Samaritan, but it was not a joke that amused Canon Brooks who directed them out of the room, locked the door and led them across to the Dean's courtyard.

Brooks drew attention to the blood on the steps that led up to the rear door of Jericho. Roberts glanced back and noted that there was no evidence across the courtyard of any further blood.

Inside the door they found Mrs Burrows. It was evident that she had only just completed her self-appointed task of cleaning the wooden floor. As Brooks stepped across the room and opened the door to the cupboards contained the Clergy robes it could be observed that they were all neatly arranged.

'His body was found in here.'

'Who are you, and what have you been doing here?' asked Roberts, pointing an index finger at Mrs Burrows.

'Esme Burrows, I looks after the Dean,' after a pause she added, 'and this place.'

'You had no right to interfere with the crime scene.'

'I thinks this weren't where he died – so no crime here,' said Mrs Burrows, standing as tall as someone of four foot nine inches could with her arms folded across her chest. 'My job's to keep this place clean.'

Seeking to calm the somewhat tense atmosphere Canon Brooks offered. 'It was Mrs Burrows who found the body. She was taking out our robes.'

Jones, supporting the desire to bring calm, inquired, 'could you describe what happened?'

Mrs Burrows then provided a description of the events of the previous day, some of which Canon Brooks was able to confirm with an occasional 'that's right,' but his remembrances were limited to the period before he had left to go to Victoria Street.

‘I think we need to talk to the Dean and to Mrs - what was her name?’ Jones began

‘Marshall.’ Roberts reminded him.

‘And Mrs Marshall. Where can we get hold of you Canon?’

As Canon Brooks was offering, ‘I live at number five in the Little Cloister,’ Mrs Burrows was insisting, ‘I don’t think you should disturb the Dean, he’s not well and this will have upset him.’

‘One at a time please. Five Little Cloister you say,’ in his mind this sounded like a very exposed residence – but, he thought, “I’ll find out later”.

‘Now, Mrs Burrows, I’m afraid we will have to interview the Dean – but maybe later. Can you make sure that he doesn’t leave this place?’

‘But he’s not well.’

‘Nevertheless, we will need to speak to him,’ said Roberts and, without allowing any further response, turned to Canon Brooks. ‘Can someone direct us to where Mrs Marshall lives? Will she be at home?’

‘I believe she is. I’ll take you myself.’

Offering further calming assistance Brooks turned to his left to say, ‘and thank you so much for your help, Mrs Burrows.’

Chapter 22

Visit to Mrs Marshall
Monday August 25th 1851

Leaving the Abbey with any discretion was not going to be achieved easily, for larger crowds were now gathering in the Sanctuary outside the Great West Door. The Beadle at Dean's Gate was effectively excluding everyone from gaining an entrance, and the Great West Door was closed. Rather than facing the fray, Canon Brooks was able to take the Detectives through Dean's Yard and along Orchard Street, not a street that many of those assembled in the Sanctuary would have cared to venture into. It had absorbed many of those displaced by the construction of Victoria Street, but didn't benefit from the presence of street sweepers, since it was not a location where a living could be made from such a pursuit. Orchard Street did not go directly onto Victoria Street, but the Canon knew how to get to the tradesmen's entrance of Albert Mansions where the Marshalls, or rather Mrs Marshall, lived.

'I said to Mary that I would probably be bringing you over. So, she won't be surprised by a knock on her back door.'

Past the ash cans and some of the detritus that remained from the construction of Victoria Street, they came to and climbed up some steps that led to a rear door, and Canon Brooks knocked. One of the Marshall daughters opened it slowly and, recognising the person that her mother had suggested might be calling, greeted the Canon with a quiet 'hello.' She was already sporting a rapidly prepared mourning of black, with white crepe.

'The girls know me,' said the Canon, addressing the Detectives over his shoulder, 'come in.' The invitation was from him rather than the girl, who led them up some stairs to a first-floor drawing room.

The drawing room was evidently newly furnished. A square table, with four matching upright chairs, covered in a lace cloth with a floral arrangement in a glass vase was in the corner. A dark blue flock wallpaper adorned the three internal walls, but that around the window was lighter. Before the deep window, with pale blue satin curtains, Mary Marshall sat on a two-seater settee with three other upholstered chairs available. The room's furnishings were completed by a secretaire against the wall adjacent to the door they had entered through.

Mrs Marshall had also put together her mourning, bombazine covered in crepe – the widow's cap on the hall table ready if she was venturing out, not something she anticipated doing for a while. She did not rise as Canon Brooks introduced the officers.

'Mrs Marshall, this is Detective Chief Superintendent Jones and Detective Sergeant Roberts. They would like to talk to you.'

'We are so sorry to disturb you ma'am, and we offer our condolences in your loss. We need to ask you some questions if that is all right?' Jones' opening greeting was text book script.

'Sit down,' she said, offering seats by a gesture with her hand.

'Do you mind if I stay?' Canon Brooks' question was addressed to the police rather than to Mrs Marshall – but it was she who replied, 'please do, Arthur.'

Her mother having omitted the conventional niceties, Constance, the daughter, still in their company, took it upon herself to inquire if drinks were required, and, when a general 'no thank you' was received, she withdrew, with the hint of a curtsy to the policemen, to go down stairs to where her younger sister and the maid-of-all-work were sitting in the kitchen.

Albert Jones began, 'I'll talk and my colleague will take notes if that's all right,' delivered as a statement rather than a question – and Mary Marshall felt no obligation to respond.

Detective Chief Superintendent Jones had dealt with a few murders during his time, he had an established line of questioning. However, he was more familiar with interviewing the bereaved in the grim setting of multiply-occupied tenement building, the back room of a public house or his office at Scotland Yard; this was a very different environment. He felt rather less in control addressing an attractive lady, probably in her late 30s he guessed, with a senior clergyman sitting at his elbow. Being seated on an upholstered mahogany armchair was also a novelty in such situations.

'When did you last see your husband?'

'He went out late on Saturday. I wasn't happy, I'm sure it was to do with Mayhew – and he said he'd finished all that. I didn't notice he was missing until Sunday morning; he would have slept in the dressing room. I was about to get the girls ready to go down to the Abbey, I knocked on the dressing room door – but no response told me that he had already left to go to the Abbey, he sings, sang, in the choir. We went down to the service, but he wasn't there. I was so angry,' for the first time she paused and chocked back some tears, 'so angry, believing he was doing something for Mayhew again.'

'Would that be Henry Mayhew – the man who writes in the *Morning Chronicle*?' Enquired Roberts, unaware that the *Chronicle* articles had concluded the previous year.

'Yes, that's him,' replied Mrs Marshall. "He'd been helping with Mayhew's research. The work was dirty and dangerous – and I tried to get him to stop".

'Who was he meeting on the Saturday?' continued Jones, making sure, with a glance, that Roberts focussed on his note taking.

'I really don't know; he's been out a lot recently. He's been helping Mayhew – interviewing people for his paper. He doesn't tell me much – but it was usually on a Saturday or Sunday when he's not at work. But he had promised to stop doing it. He saw the effect it was having on me and the girls.'

'What is, sorry, what was Mr Marshall's job?'

'He was a Banker's Clerk.'

'And where did he work?'

'He worked for the Commercial Bank of London, in their Henrietta Street branch, up in Covent Garden. He'd been there eleven years. But again, I don't know much about his work, he used to tell me I wouldn't understand – but he didn't really give me a chance to learn, he didn't tell me much.'

This last remark was delivered slowly and her head dropped as if she might be about to cry. Jones noted a slight movement forward from Brooks; but the Canon did not get up.

'I'm sorry that some of our questions might be upsetting. We'll only be a couple more minutes, if that's possible?'

This time Mrs Marshall did recognise a genuine question, and replied, 'just a few more minutes will be all right. I need to get back to my girls. Grace, our maid, isn't much older than them – it's hard for her as well.'

'Are you aware of any reason why someone might have attacked your husband? I think that Canon Brooks has probably told you in what state he was found.'

'Yes, Canon Brooks very kindly came over yesterday evening. Thomas was found in Jericho with his head bashed in.' This time there were tears, and the Canon did rise to rest his hand on her shoulder.

'Is that enough?' Brooks enquired of Jones, imploring a positive response.

'Just a final question. Do you know how we might contact this Mr Mayhew?'

'He is,' said Canon Brooks, 'or at least he was, based at the *Chronicle*'s offices. I think I could find out his address.'

'And finally, Mrs Marshall – were there particular friends at work who we might talk to?'

'He mainly spoke about John Durdin and Joseph Anning, they were the people he worked with. I don't really know them; they went together to the Great Exhibition recently. Thomas was going to take us soon. They'll wonder where he is this morning.'

Francis Roberts closed his notebook, as if to remind his colleague that he had promised the interview was ending, and went to get up.

Albert Jones followed his example and pushed himself up from his chair. 'Thank you so much Mrs Marshall. Sorry to have taken your time. We do hope we can find out who did this terrible thing to your husband, and to your family. We will probably need to speak to you again. I also need to say that you are now free to arrange for your husband's burial, we don't need to see his body again. Thank you very much.'

Jones, the more empathetic of the officers, stepped across to rest his hand briefly on the opposite shoulder to that where Canon Brooks' hand remained. 'Canon, I hope you can take us back to the Abbey – we need to meet with the Dean.'

'Certainly,' said Brooks, releasing his hand and moving towards the door, which he opened and from where he glanced back at Mary Marshall, she offered no farewell, her head bowed, her cheeks cupped in her hands, with audible sobs tears were gently coursing down her face.

Conversation was limited as they retraced their way to the Abbey – though Jones did request that Brooks obtain the address of Henry Mayhew as soon as possible.

Back at the Abbey Mrs Burrows was at the foot of the steps to Jericho. 'I've been waiting for you. You can see the Dean now – but only for a few moments.'

She stepped across the courtyard to a door opening onto an ascending internal staircase. She gave them instructions, indicating a door at the top of the stairs, 'they are expecting you, knock and go in, and don't mind the animals.'

Chapter 23

Visit to the Dean
Monday August 25th 1851

The opulence of the Dean's room was not the first thing that Jones and Roberts noticed after climbing the steps from the Cheneygate entrance to the Deanery and being greeting by Medley who, having been awaiting their arrival, ushered them through to the parlour. What they first observed were the monkeys. Sensing their nervousness, the Dean indicated to Medley that he should urge the creatures to leave from the room. He ushered them into the adjacent study.

The Dean, dressed in his canonicals and seated before a large window, invited the officers to be seated on the plush chairs.

'A sorry business, a very sorry business' he opined – as much to himself as to the men now seated with their pencils ready to jot down any significant comments in their notebooks.

'Gentlemen, I note that already a cheap newspaper edition that includes lurid, but inaccurate, details of this crime have been published. I do hope that the police have not been the source of this misinformation.'

His reference, they thought, was to the Penny Dreadful article that they had glanced at the cover of earlier outside the North Door of the Abbey; it had evidently been drawn to the attention of the Dean. However the document that Buckland indicated on the table in front of him was another paper with a graphic image of a body being discovered in the choir stalls – with the eminently recognisable Dean looking on.

Jones replied. 'Neither I nor my colleagues have spoken to anyone. Apart from Mrs Marshall you are the first person we have interviewed, Mr Dean.'

Roberts added, with both a measure of indignation and genuine deference, 'nothing, sir, in the press has come from us.'

'We have some details from Constable Clegg – I wonder whether you can confirm them Mr Dean.' The notes taken by Clegg the day before were taken from his pocket and smoothed out by his hands before he read them out. Except for some confusion over room names, the Dean was momentarily amused that one space was called Bethlehem, and the identification of the formal roles of some of the clergy, Brooks would not have been amused to be called a vicar, the description tallied not only with the Dean's recollection of the events but his remembrance of what had been said.

'Is there anything more you can add sir? Have you been made aware of any other details? We want as complete a record as possible.'

Buckland, who had been hoping that the police might have been trying to solve the crime rather than simply collect more information, leaned forward with his chin on his palm and his elbow on his knee, and spoke in an almost confidential whisper. He offered very little, but suggested that he had found both Marshall and Brooks, who were friends that he thought had met at Westminster School, difficult people to get on with – they had not always supported his vision for the Abbey.

'We will speak to the Canon again later, if you don't mind.' Buckland was not sure whether he was being asked permission or whether this was simply a polite comment, nevertheless he responded, 'That'll be quite in order.'

'We have told Mrs Marshall that she can arrange a funeral, and we believe that Mr Marshall's body will be taken from your basement room to the morgue. We have a copy of the coroner's report. The coroner's jury believe it wasn't an accident, and we agree. We are looking for a murderer. But why did whoever found his body bring it to the Abbey? Do you have any thoughts?'

'Maybe they recognised him.'

'If so, why were they so secretive in bringing the body in? They could have let someone know.'

The Dean began to feel uncomfortable. He was asking himself the same question. 'I don't know. I'm not feeling well. Will that be all?' He enquired, hoping for a positive response.

'A few more things if you don't mind. Somebody has killed one of your choristers. What more do you know about him? And who would have access into the room where he was found?'

'As I said Canon Brooks knew him better than me. Although those rooms are technically part of my home there is no direct connection with these quarters,' and swept his arm around to indicate the space in which they sat, 'but the door from my courtyard into Jericho, where they evidently brought the body in, is not normally open, only my family and Mrs Burrows have access through it.'

'That will be all for now Mr Dean, can you tell me where we might find Canon Brooks.'

The Dean responded. 'If you would like to see Mr Brooks, Jenny will show you.' He rang a bell and, after no more than a few seconds had elapsed, the maid who had brought the policemen in appeared. 'Can you escort the officers across to Canon Brook's house please Jenny?' and, turning to the detectives, who had now stood up, 'thank you for your time. I do hope we sort of this nasty business soon.' The Dean did not rise. He had hardly raised his head to make any eye-contact during the exchange.

Chapter 24

Visit to Canon Brooks
Monday August 25th 1851

Jenny took the Detectives along the southern section of the main cloisters. Initially Jones attempted to avoid walking upon what were obviously gravestones, a Canon here, an eminent musician there, and group of monks further along. He soon gave up his ambition and continued, turning right and then left along a further corridor into and around the smaller cloister and into the St Catherine's ruins, where Jenny stopped beside a large oak door with a generous knocker.

'Shall I see if the Canon is in?'

'If you would please.'

A muffled 'coming' preceded the opening of the door. The initial greeting of 'how can I help you, Jenny?' was not pursued as Brooks noted the Detectives.

'Gentlemen, do you wish to see me again?'

'If we may sir?' said Jones, not anticipating anything other than a positive response.

'Certainly. Come in. Thank you, Jenny.'

Rather than ascending the stairs to the drawing room, Canon Brooks escorted the gentlemen to his left. This was evidently his study. Its walls were lined with books – a selection of which were haphazardly distributed not only on his desk but on adjacent chairs and much of the floor. Papers, letters, and sermon notes added to the tabular ensemble.

'Sorry, as you know I've only just got back to work. Didn't get much done yesterday. I'll shift those.' To Brooks shifting meant removing books from a chair and adding them to a pile on the floor.

'How is the Dean? Since Jenny brought you over you must have seen him.'

'He's wanting to get this all resolved; and directed us back to you. We hadn't realised that you were a close friend of Marshall's, we took you simply as our escort to his home.'

'Thomas and I have known each other for many years.'

'The Dean thought you may have known each other at the school.'

'It's true we both attended Westminster – but I had left long before he started. I suppose my friendship with Thomas was, curiously, because we were both against some of the Dean's actions. We both favoured a more traditional form of a worship, and the established layout of the Abbey. The present Dean came in 1845, after the brief tenure of Bishop Wilberforce, or rather Dean Wilberforce at the time – he's now Bishop of Oxford. Thomas joined the choir when Dean Ireland was in post. He changed things, yes, but he allowed people to do what they were meant to do, canons and choristers amongst them. He didn't interfere with the services, with the language, with the times of worship. He made sure that what we did was done better. He was a great Dean – and Thomas and I, though we both only arrived towards the end of his time, liked him, liked his attitude, liked what he did.'

'And did things change with the present Dean?' asked Roberts.

'They did – in all sorts of ways. The language changed; parts of the building were removed. It was a mess. Some of things that both Thomas and I, and my late wife, cherished were thrown out. He and I, with a couple of others, sought to get onto the committee that made decisions, but the Dean was too canny, he had his 'yes' men who would always agree with him. But Thomas became a member because his fellow choristers voted him on, believing he would represent their views.'

'Yet you chose to stay at the Abbey? '

'I did believe at one time that I might be asked to be Dean, that isn't going to happen now. I never stopped campaigning, I suppose I'd call it, on musical and liturgical matters but for the past few years I've been looking after Christine. This has been a good place to be, lots of friends around, good doctors. I couldn't have taken on a new job and moved house whilst Christine was ill. I'm getting a bit old now – anyway now would not the time to move on.'

'Sorry to hear about your wife,' said the sympathetic Roberts, 'you must miss her?'

'She died, cancer of the breast. Some months ago, a year and a half now I suppose,' he added wistfully and paused. 'Forgive me, sorry, now about Thomas. We would meet and talk about the worship and the Dean's actions, usually privately; often here because I was looking after Christine. I didn't see so much of Thomas in recent times. He had moved on to a new cause as it were. He wanted to fight for something else, and so got involved with Henry Mayhew.'

The Chief Superintendent decided to be direct. 'Are you aware of anyone who might have wanted him dead?'

'Frankly, no. Though I know there has been some opposition to the sort of thing that Mayhew is printing; but I don't imagine that many would know that much of it was Thomas's work. He did get involved with the woodworkers, and I hear that some of their leadership are getting angry – they were, let us say, not presented in a glowing light. Thomas's name wasn't there though. They wouldn't want to get rid of him, would they?'

'Our responsibility is not to speculate – but to follow every lead. We will want to talk to Mr Mayhew.'

Brooks concluded his contribution to this part of the enquiry by expressing a hope that the matter could be resolved speedily and declaring that he would keep his ears open and be available at any time the policing agencies wished to contact him. Jones concluded his part by expressing appreciation for Brooks' help.

'I think we can find our way back to the main entrance. Thank you for your time.'

As they walked back to Scotland Yard the consensus was that Brooks' story was interesting, but they were not sure it added much to their knowledge.

Chapter 25

The Police at work

Tuesday August 26th 1851

The journalist Gerald Bourne stood, in top hat and a slightly disreputable suit, near the Headquarters of Metropolitan Police Division B (Westminster) at Vine Street, Millbank.

His was a curious relationship with the Detective department. They had a way of controlling the news agenda. They expected the stories they wanted to be given prominence to make the front page; but they were not very forthcoming in conversation. He would very rarely be seen "hanging around" outside their Scotland Yard offices.

Gerald preferred to have a closer rapport with the Metropolitan police. Although not technically employed by the *Morning Chronicle* or the Evening Standard he regulalrly supplied both with stories and information. It was useful to work with both a morning and an evening paper. He was also privy to the conversations and speculations within the newspapers' offices. This made him useful at times to Sergeant John Watson. They had an " I'll scratch your back, you scratch mine" relationship. Hence Bourne was at Millbank rather than at Whitehall Place.

John Watson was not surprised to see him outside his office that Tuesday afternoon. He invited him in with the question. 'What've you heard, Gerry?'

'Something of interest to you, if you've got something I can get into the Standard,' negotiated the sleuth-cum-reporter.

'We'll see,' was all that Sergeant Watson offered for the moment – but both knew that their association only lasted because both found their conversations rewarding.

Watson indicating to his colleague, Constable Clegg, that this was a private meeting that he was not to be disturbed. He closed the door of his office and Clegg sat opposite, on a bench normally reserved for those waiting to speak to an officer on the front desk.

Bourne, who had himself written about Mayhew's project, recognised Marshall's name as being associated with the articles in the *Morning Chronicle.* He would never have disclosed such names, but the situation had changed. Bourne's pieces questioned Mayhew's motives, and he had learnt that Abbots yard was the location of one of the *Chronicle* articles. Bourne quickly began his trading of information.

'Your man Marshall had been hanging about Abbots yard,' indicating the direction of the river, not unfamiliar to Watson, 'talking to the Truman brewery men down there and the woodworkers at Abbots. Some of their wood was used to repair the Abbey,' he pointed, un-necessarily again, in the vague direction of the said church, 'come from there. I think Marshall was sent down by his mate Canon Brooks to negotiate, Brooks has overseen getting some of the best wood for the Quire. Some say that he negotiated a bit too much for himself and had fallen out with the Dean.'

This was better than Sergeant Watson could have hoped for. He would need to go away and digest this information – what could he offer Bourne? He needed to give him something.

'You know you've guessed wrong about where the body was found. I can confirm that it wasn't in the choir stalls: it was in the Deanery – in the bit where all the clergy get changed. They call the rooms after places – all very strange, I don't call my bedroom Wapping or my kitchen Chelsea – it was in Jericho, in a cupboard.' The exchange of intelligence seemed mutually acceptable – and hands were shaken, either confirming a sort of bargain or simply as a prelude to parting.

'Come on constable, we've got work to do,' Watson called to Clegg, who always knew not to listen in on conversations his colleague had with the Press. Best to be ignorant of what intelligence was being shared. Clegg joined his senior officer and drew up their plans to visit Abbots Yard.

The stench of the river on a hot August afternoon was bad enough on Vine Street it would be terrible at the river edge, they resolved to visit at a less noxious time. They would go early the following day.

Chapter 26
Visit to Commercial Bank of London
Tuesday August 26th 1851

Thomas Marshall's employers had not been best pleased that one of their Bankers Clerks was, without explanation, absent on Monday morning. Punctuality was a priority and Marshall had not requested time off – yet his desk was vacant all day.

The concerns of his closest friends at the bank, Joseph Anning and John Durdin, were more for his personal well-being than the well-being of the bank. When his absence continued into the Tuesday morning there was greater consternation. Mr Bulford, the senior manager, was declaring that this was a ground for dismissal – and had Marshall not thought about the clients he was meant to be meeting. Anning and Durdin were wondering whether he was ill - and how they could find out. They had been to his previous home but he had now moved to Victoria Street, so how could they find out his address? They soon discovered that that was not information that senior staff were willing to divulge.

These two forms of concern, from management and colleagues, met each other when Anning and Durdin were summoned downstairs to Mr Bulford's office. Although not sure what to anticipate from the meeting, what they were not expecting was an encounter with two of London's Detectives.

Chief Superintendent Jones was seated beside the bank's senior manager Archibald Bulford, Detective Sergeant Roberts stood behind them. Bulford addressed his two employees in a tone they were unfamiliar with. Compassion was not an emotion that was frequently employed in the Bank.

'Durdin, Anning,' said Bulford, looking directly at them, 'Mr Jones has something dreadful to tell you. Please sit down.' Mentally both surmised this was about Marshall, but neither anticipated what was about to unfold.

‘I’m sorry to tell you that Mr Marshall is dead, someone killed him on Sunday.’ said Jones directly and without emotion. ‘His body was found in Westminster Abbey just before the evening service on Sunday. I have spoken to his wife, who is obviously very distressed, and she identified the two of you as his closest friends here at the Bank. We hope you can help with our enquiries.’

Anning’s question, ‘who did it?’ was obviously not anticipating an answer – but did receive one, ‘we intend to find out.’

‘If I may talk with Durdin and Anning alone sir,’ requested Jones of Bulford, who seemed a bit flustered that he should be expected to vacate his own office.

‘Of course,’ responded Bulford, who selected some papers from his desk and moved them into its top drawer, which he deftly locked before leaving the room.

‘We can’t give you all the details. To be honest there is a lot that we don’t know – and that is why we need to speak to you. When did you last see Marshall?’

Durdin volunteered, ‘I’m sure he was here on Saturday morning when we were cashing up for the week. He must have been. But I don’t know when he left. We sometimes used to have a drink afterwards – but not last Saturday.’

‘In fact,’ Anning interjected, ‘he and I did have a brief drink afterwards. We had something to talk about.’ This information came as a shock to Durdin – he could not recall any time when only two of them met.

‘And what was that business Mister Anning?’

‘I’m afraid that I can’t tell you.’

‘Mister Anning, I ask you to tell me what you spoke about. This could be vital information.’

‘I’m afraid I’m not able to, it involves someone else who is not here.’

Evidently frustrated, Jones drummed his fingers on the mahogany table. ‘If this case ever goes to court, I do hope that you will not regret your failure to tell me. If it does go to court, you will be under oath to tell the whole truth.'

'I am aware of that, and I am truly sorry that I cannot say any more.'

Durdin's anger was growing, 'tell the man what he wants to know, Jo. For God's sake, Thomas is dead, we must do all we can to help.'

Calmly Anning responded, 'I will do all I can, there are some things I cannot do. I will speak to you,' he offered looking at Jones, 'at another time, but not here.'

Durdin was almost incandescent. 'So you've got secrets from me.'

'Yes, I have,' came the measured reply.

It was Roberts, busy taking notes, who recognised the necessity of moving the conversation on.

'If you can let us have details of how he can be in touch with you, Mr Anning, that would be appreciated. But we do need to ask – are you aware of anyone who may have had a reason for harming Mr Marshall?'

Durdin, who no doubt thought he was answering for them both, responded 'not at all.' Roberts made a note that Anning had not replied.

'Gentlemen, we do appreciate your time; and we know your distress at the death of your friend and colleague. We may need to talk to you again. Mr Anning if you would please give Sergeant Roberts your address – and yours as well please Mr Durdin. We will take our leave of you, thank you again.'

Anning, who knew Durdin's residence, offered to write both their addresses. He had an immaculate hand for which Roberts expressed his gratitude. 'We've got to write neatly sir – one of the Bankers Clerks was dismissed a few years back for his poor handwriting,' Durdin declared.

During the walk back from Henrietta Street to Whitehall Place, Albert Jones commented to Francis Roberts, 'we'll need to talk to Anning again, and soon.'

Back in the office they found a request from the Dean, apparently delivered by one of the younger clergy at the Abbey, for the police to issue a statement. The desk clerk reported the priest as saying that everybody seemed to have heard about the crime – and there were lots of rumours and incorrect stories, and several garish images and scandalous speculations.

Detective Chief Superintendent Jones felt that now was the time to put something into the press. He sat at his desk, with the notes from Roberts – and realised that he did not really have a lot to say. He nevertheless prepared a few sentences for *The Times* – which appeared the following day without alteration.

Body at Westminster Abbey

On Sunday evening last the body of Thomas Marshall, aged 42, was found in Westminster Abbey. It was apparent that the man, killed by a blow to the head, had died before being brought to the Abbey. Anyone who can offer any assistance is asked to contact Detective Chief Superintendent Jones at Scotland Yard, Whitehall Place, LONDON.

Chapter 27

Meeting with Mayhew
Wednesday August 27th 1851

Albert Jones was anxious because the pursuit of the killer of Thomas Marshall did not seem to be making much progress. Sitting, with his wife, at the kitchen table in the small Camden Town house eating a late supper on the Tuesday evening he was musing about the crime. In the back of his mind, he was confident that he had heard of Henry Mayhew – maybe even read something by him. He mentioned to his wife that he would be meeting the following day with a Mr Mayhew and she reached across to a pile of newspapers, 'he wrote these' and she produced several copies of the *Morning Chronicle* stashed under a table.

'You'll remember how important I thought they were,' she added, (he had not remembered). 'He writes about the life of the poor here in London. I think it's so sad. We see them every day. But no-one seems to help. I've tried to get our vicar interested – but he says he's too busy looking after the sick here in Camden. The Cholera is still so bad.'

Albert had not always paid attention to his wife! He picked a copy from the pile, one that his wife had evidently been reading. It was dated December 11th 1849, "nearly two years old, surely out of date" he thought. He decided however to look through it, probably useful for his meeting the following day.

Forty minutes later he put the paper down, having read and reread the article. Mrs Jones had not often seen him absorbed in the newspaper, he would usually only glance at any stories under the general heading "Crime" that she identified, and then focus on sporting activities, he was always following the Horse racing and was interested in the Cricket now that Middlesex had a team nearby on their new ground at Lords.

Albert observed to his wife, 'I didn't realise that there are over 21,000 tailors working in London – and this Mayhew seems to have talked to lots of them. Very interesting. Were they the people who had a meeting last year?'

'Yes, down at Blackheath I think,' said Mrs Jones looking up from her embroidery; there was enough light in August to carry on such work into the evening.

'I'll ask him about that. But time for a wash and bed now.' This was a bit early for Albert; usually a sign that he was nervous, or maybe anxious, about something. They needed to make some progress.

The Detective Chief Superintendent and his colleague met early at Scotland Yard the next day. Henry Mayhew had kindly agreed to meet with them at their office. He had said that he was quite used to summoning people to his office for conversation.

Albert briefed Francis on what he had learnt from his wife and the article he had read. 'I'm really not sure whether this person is a rabble-rouser or is doing a service highlighting these issues,' he observed.

The clock on the mantle shelf above the fire place in the Detectives' first floor interview room indicated that 8 o'clock was fast approaching as the desk clerk knocked on the door and introduced Mr Mayhew into the room. The Detectives' room was a significantly more informal environment that those attached to the Divisional Police Headquarters where colleagues in the Metropolitan Police held their interviews. There was, potentially, a fire, light from an open window and chairs arranged with only one desk, for the clerk, or in this case Sergeant Roberts, to take notes or collect relevant papers.

The man admitted to the room was dressed comfortably rather than fashionably. He moved forward purposefully, obviously a man in a hurry, and offered a hand to the two men in turn with the same greeting 'Henry Mayhew.' He turned, noted an unoccupied chair, took off his top coat and hat, resting the former on the chair back and putting the latter on a hatstand by the door, sat down, and said 'how can I help you?'

After Albert Jones had formerly introduced himself and his partner he responded to Mr Mayhew, 'we would like to talk to you about Thomas Marshall.'

'I thought that might be the case – I've just seen your item in *The Times*,' he indicated the paper, in the inside pocket of his coat.

'We have been told that Marshall has spent a lot of time with you over the past couple of years.'

'A lot of time working for me,' Mayhew corrected, 'not necessarily a lot of time with me. We would meet to talk about a particular area of a trade, or business or job and I would suggest where he might meet people, and probably give him some contacts. Thomas would do the interviews and write the report which I would edit, sometimes asking for more information about a certain aspect, and we would meet to discuss the copy before I submitted it to the *Morning Chronicle*. Most of our meetings were down at the Red Lion.'

'Yesterday, at home, I read your article from the *Chronicle* about the Tailors – my wife had kept a copy.'

'Quite controversial I believe,' added Jones, looking up from his note taking.

'Yes – though that wasn't one that Thomas was involved with – his main focus was on the woodworkers, that material came out about a year ago.'

'Was that also controversial?' asked Roberts.

'It was. You'll know that Thomas was involved with Westminster Abbey,' both officers nodded agreement, 'somehow people recognised where he was writing about and, as a result of his articles, some of the cabinet makers involved in work elsewhere sought to create or join societies, we tend to call them unions now. They demanded more pay, comparable to that earned by those working at Abbots for the Abbey. Other yard owners were furious at Abbots' generosity in terms of wages and their foolishness in permitting their publication.'

'We've not been made aware of any personal animosity towards him,' said Jones, glancing across to Roberts who shook his head to suggest agreement.

'But more than that, Thomas was involved in the recent meeting of Street Traders.'

'Like the meeting of Tailors at Blackheath?' Roberts thought Jones was showing off.

'Not as big – but just as important. They met a month ago across the river at Vauxhall – Thomas was there, he spoke to some people, it was on a Sunday afternoon.'

'How many people were present?'

'The papers said two hundred, Thomas thought there were maybe three, the Union people put it at five. Who knows?'

'Thank you.'

'I did see Thomas a couple of weeks ago. I had planned a new project for him. You may know I'm no longer working for the *Morning Chronicle* – I'm publishing my own material. I was asking him to do some research into the Mudlarks – the poor nippers who scavenge down by the river. But when we met, he expressed a concern that his name had appeared in the papers, from the Vauxhall meeting, He understood that some people weren't happy. Most importantly his wife wasn't happy.'

'Had he been threatened?' asked Jones.

'No, not that I'm aware of. He didn't say anything.'

'Mr Mayhew, this has been very helpful. Can you let us know if you think of anything else?' Requested Jones.

'I certainly will. Are you thinking that it was to do with our work?'

'I'm really not sure. We need to find out more; but we are grateful for your time and we may well be back in touch with you.' Jones was already standing and Roberts pushing his chair back as this sentence was spoken. Henry also stood to take his leave of them, ‘I do hope you make progress soon, gentlemen. He was a good man. We need to know who killed him. If I can be of any further help please be in touch.’

Mayhew collected his hat and coat and left.

Chapter 28

Meeting with Anning
Wednesday August 27th 1851

Joseph Anning had contacted Scotland Yard to ask if he could come to see them after he had completed work on that Wednesday afternoon – about six thirty he suggested. Although they had not formally responded, Jones and Roberts, knowing Anning's sense of urgency the previous day, were waiting when a slightly flustered Bank Clerk arrived shortly before seven.

The desk officer was also anticipating his arrival and so was able to address the man who came to the office front door, 'Mr Anning?'

Joseph did not affirm his identity but simply said, breathing rapidly from his exertion 'I'm sorry, so sorry. The numbers didn't balance. I'm sorry.'

'That's all right sir. The Detectives are waiting for you upstairs. Can I take your coat?' the offer was well received, the tail coat was taken and hung on the hat-stand, the tendered hat was placed on an adjacent table.

'The door straight in front of you at the top of the stairs, it will be open.'

Although normally Anning may have ascended stairs two at a time his progress that afternoon was more conventional. He had recovered his breath before arriving at the interview room door, where he repeated, verbatim, his earlier apology.

'That's quite all right sir,' said Jones, 'we understand, do take a seat.'

Occupying the chair that Mayhew had done earlier, Anning brushed his hand through his hair, took out a handkerchief to wipe his brow, and used the same device to clean his glasses.

‘Thank you for coming this evening’ (the word ‘evening’ made Anning more aware of his lateness, but did not provoke a further apology).

‘You said that you would like to speak to us privately. What have you got to tell us?’

‘My name is Joseph Anning. You may have heard of my sister Mary.’

Glances across the room suggested that neither of the Detectives were familiar with the name, that was confirmed when Jones said, ‘I don’t think we do.’

‘Mary is, sorry was, a Palaeontologist.’ Similar glances followed this remark.

‘You’ll need to explain that word, if it is relevant,’ said Jones.

‘It is certainly relevant. A Palaeontologist is someone who studies and collects ancient fossils.’ The relevance of the testimony of the sibling of a fossil collector was not immediately obvious to either of the officers; but they did not interrupt.

‘Mr Buckland, sorry Dean Buckland, whom I’m sure you’ve met at the Abbey, is also a Palaeontologist, a fossil collector.’ This may have been interesting, but was it important?

‘I’ll go back to the start if I may,’ said Anning.

‘Please do,’ said Jones, sitting back; both he and Roberts, making himself upright at the desk and ready to write, felt this could be a long story.

‘Mary and I were brought up in Dorset – we were the only two siblings in the family to live beyond ten years of age, our brothers and sister died young. Our father used to make some money selling fossils, the cliffs near Lyme Regis produced a lot of them, particularly if there was a landslide. I am a few years older than Mary was. She died a few years back. She and I would go out looking for fossils after the rains fell, and hope that the cliff faces could be scraped away.

'One day, when I was about ten, and Mary seven I think, I found the head of what seemed like an old fossil. I didn't have much time to work on it – but over the next year she spent hours releasing it and laying it out, it was well over four feet long.'

The Chief Superintendent felt this was probably the right time to interrupt. 'I'm sorry Mr Anning, this might be fascinating family history, but neither Sergeant Roberts nor I are Paleo whatevers, we are not particularly interested in fossils,' turning his head to Roberts the remark was readily agreed. 'How is this relevant to the death of Thomas Marshall?'

Anning continued, 'I'm getting there. Over the years many famous fossil collectors came from all over the world, even the King of Prussia, and Mary became quite famous. One of those who came was William Buckland, now Dean Buckland, though then he was simply Reverend Buckland. They spent a lot of time together – and exchanged a lot of letters. He was a busy man; he was a lecturer at Oxford and something at the Cathedral there. One day he was asked to write something about God and Fossils. A man had died and left lots of money to a group of people to say that the existence of Fossils didn't mean that God didn't exist – or something like that. Well, he was so busy that he did not have the time to write it all – and asked Mary to write some of it for him but, he said, she wasn't to tell anyone – and he would let her have half the money, five hundred pounds he was going to give her.'

Anning concluded by saying, 'he published the book and she didn't even get mentioned, and she never saw the money.'

'Well, that sounds very unfortunate for your sister, but since this was years ago and she is dead I still can't see why its relevant to the death of Thomas Marshall,' said Jones, hovering between frustration, indifference, and annoyance.

'I'm just coming to that. Mary didn't say anything to me about this until just before she died, four years back. I kept it to myself, as you say she's dead, and it was a while ago but it always niggled me. Earlier this year I went with Durdin and Marshall to see the Great Exhibition. Durdin had to go home, and Marshall and I had a drink, well rather too much drink really. I got a bit maudlin and when Marshall said, "I don't really know much about your family", I told him about Mary, and that story. He was incensed, I assumed that that was because he had also been drinking. "I'm going to see the Dean", he shouted out, very embarrassing for us both. I'd got no idea that someone who occasionally sings in the choir, which I only learnt that day, would know the Dean. I can't remember whether I egged him on or told him to forget it, there's lots I don't remember from that night. But last week he told me he had spoken to Mr Buckland, who had said that the idea was ridiculous, but that he would do something. But Thomas believed me rather than the Dean. That's all I know. But I thought you ought to know.'

Jones said 'thank you' and Roberts, who had written at speed, and believed he had the gist of what was said, also declared a similar appreciation. Both were struggling to determine whether what they had just heard would be relevant.

After a few moments consideration Jones concluded the interview. 'Mr Anning we very much appreciate you coming to see us. The Sergeant and I will consider what you have said. I think you were wise to see us by yourself. We will not include your story in anything we say to the press – but you must understand that if it proves useful it will obviously reveal a connection to you.'

'I understand that.'

'I think we,' speaking directly to Roberts, 'may need to have another word with the Dean,' and turning to Anning, 'thank you again for your time.'

Part 3
The killer of Thomas Marshall

Chapter 29

Visit to Abbots Yard
Wednesday August 27th 1851

The police officers, Watson and Clegg, believing that they ought to engage in some further investigations before passing on their discoveries to the Detectives, chose the early morning to make their visit to the Abbots Yard. This was following up on the information they had received from Gerald Bourne.

Six o'clock was already a busy time, but the river smells were not as powerful as the previous afternoon would have been. They needed to discover whether the intelligence Bourne had given them had any basis in fact. Bourne, as a writer, was known to exaggerate for profit. There was always a greater nervousness when people saw the appearance of members of the Detective branch than over the approach of members of the regular constabulary. The Detectives' mission was always recognised as being of specific intent, regular police were maintaining contacts within the communities where they worked.

They chose to introduce themselves to someone who, by the way he urged and directed his colleagues, appeared to have the status of a foreman.

'Sergeant John Watson, Westminster Division of the Metropolitan police,' was the formal introduction – though his appearance betrayed no ambiguity.

Although not obsequious, the man he addressed was respectful as he replied, 'Bertie Smythe, sir, how can I help?'

Constable Clegg, having sucked the pencil nib to make it more effective, was already jotting down notes, 'spelt?' he enquired.

'S M Y T H E sir.'

Stepping a little aside from a group of interested wharfmen into a dark corner Clegg got straight to the point. 'Do you know a man called Marshall, Thomas Marshall?'

‘I don’t believe I do. Did he work here?’

‘He was a chorister at Westminster Abbey and did some writing for Henry Mayhew.’

‘I know of him, I read the articles – and only afterwards learnt that it was about us. I wasn’t involved. I don’t really want to talk about him. My impression is that he let us down. We have been told not to speak about it with other journalists.’

‘Is there anyone here we can talk to?’

‘I think it was Mr Clarence that he dealt with – but he’s not around today’

The police officers looked at each other, and stepped aside for a brief conversation. They concluded that Clarence’s absence was unfortunate, but probably not critical. There would be other opportunities if it proved relevant. They were often in the area. They had confirmed, at least, that there was something in what Bourne had told them. There was no need to mention anything to the Detectives – nothing to report.

Chapter 30

Basement Conversation
Monday September 1st 1851

As a matter of course rumours travelled quickly around the members of staff at the Abbey. An overheard remark, a speculation, an exaggeration – all would add to general levels of unjustified certainty about what had really happened.

There were essentially three groups of people employed in or around the Abbey.

There were the clergy, in 1851 that consisted of the Dean and eight Canons – appointed by the Monarch, through the agency of the Prime Minister. There were also several ordained members of staff at Westminster School who, depending on the company they kept, would usually declare their status as academic instructors, but in some other contexts as working at Westminster Abbey. Appointments to this group were made by the Dean and the Headmaster of the school.

There were liturgical staff, headed by the organist, Turle, the choir master, Briggs, and the Sacristan. Some of these would have access, for laying-up purposes, to the precious silverware of the Abbey such as candlesticks, chalices and patens, but others would focus on the more mundane aspects of stewarding worshippers and, at times, crowd-control. This group included all those involved in the musical traditions of the church; choristers and musicians. Appointments to this group were made by the Dean and Chapter, supported by the said Organist and Sacristan. These appointments were often made on the recommendation of friends and colleagues.

A third, much broader, group covered administration, cleaning and security. Some of these were members of the Dean's personal household; others were nominally appointed by the Clerk, the role George Vincent had played for 50 years, but in practice most gained their employment through the good offices of his deputy Major-General Ambleside Arbuthnot and, unsurprisingly, many were drawn from the ranks of the military. People the Major-General thought could be trusted – and who respected rank. Many of his team were volunteers, and could afford to be because of their Army pensions. Within Arbuthnot's ambit came the security of the Abbey, headed by the Beadles, and including those who acted as night watchmen as well as those who had the responsibility of showing visitors around the Abbey. This last role was quite lucrative, and Arbuthnot would often select people in particular need for such posts.

The three groupings remained quite distinct, and had their own gathering spaces. Historically the clergy would have used the Chapter house, but in 1851 that was a repository for many parliamentary records (which had proved a godsend in 1836 when the fire across the road that destroyed the Houses of Parliament could so easily have eliminated all the historical documents). The Jerusalem Chamber, technically part of the Deanery, was now their meeting place.

The liturgical staff had a new place of gathering thanks to the creation of the choir school by Dean Buckland. Their room was accessed via a recently created door knocked through the south wall of the cloisters.

The administrative team were based in a building, no longer required by the school, on the west side of Dean's Yard. There were offices on the two main floors, and in the basement a place to store uniforms and leave possessions, secure behind a door-keeper who knew everyone entitled to enter. The basement was also their main location for preparing for or relaxing after a shift.

In each of these three gathering spaces conversations were taking place, based more on rumour and speculation than upon any facts, about the "murder in the Abbey" as the newspapers had christened the event of eight days earlier. There was an undeclared, but closely followed, regulation that such discussions were confidential within the groupings. Of course, if an external agency, the Police or the Detectives, made enquiries of an individual they would divulge what they knew; and then tell other members of their group precisely what they had said.

The most animated of those discussions was within the membership of Arbuthnot's group in the basement on Dean's Yard, though he personally chose to take time off in an office within the small cloister which he had shared with clerk Vincent in recent years. The Beadles spoke of the murder victim's association with Abbots Yard long before that was general knowledge. Among those asking the more detailed questions was Brigadier Arnold Greene. He was less taciturn than normal, being quite inquisitive about what people knew and what people thought.

Any intelligence vouchsafed to the police or to the Detectives was reported and discussed within the grouping.

It was early that Monday morning. Greene had just come off his overnight shift when one of the Beadles commented to anyone in hearing range, 'they saw a cart coming into Dean's Yard.' He was not specific about who "they" were.

Greene enquired, 'did they talk to them?'

Someone else asked Greene directly, 'weren't you on duty that night? You normally do Saturday, don't you?'

He had paused before a non-committal, 'I didn't see anything,' and then corrected himself, 'in fact I was off last weekend.'

It might have rested there had not one of the Beadles, Gareth Evans, remembered, 'but I saw you walking along Millbank late on Saturday, t'other side the road, I called "Ginger" but you were obviously in a hurry to get home, you didn't hear me, or at least you didn't respond. I've never seen you walking so fast – I remarked upon it to Charlie when I took over my duties at nine, didn't I Charlie?'

'I think you did.'

'So, I obviously wasn't at work. I'd been out for a walk,' declared Greene, quite defensively.

'And "obviously" eager to get home Ginger.' Military titles were rarely used "off-duty", but nick-names were carried on, a measure of military solidarity - with an almost masonic mystique.

Greene decided that the need to have any further conversation had gone. He picked up his bag, slung it over his shoulders and made his way, very deliberately neither addressing nor observing others, to the steps outside. His injury always meant that these were an issue – but there was, today, a determined intention to tackle them head-on with no suggestion of problem or pain.

'What's got into him?' Evans enquired, but it was not a question that merited, or gained, any response and conversation in the basement moved on to other aspects of the case.

As he made his way through Dean's Yard Greene's pace slowed down. It was not simply a result of the exertions on the steps but the mental turmoil of feeling exposed. What did Evans know? Were people talking about him? But he had only been doing his duty. He was also aware of a painful cut on his right hand. Those step-exertions had exacerbated the discomfort he was feeling, even through the gloves he had taken to wearing in recent days.

When he reached home, he took off his gloves. The cut was looking "vicious". Greene had seen serious infections on the battle fields of Europe, he had even witnessed the amputation of infected limbs in crude medical hospitals in the Waterloo campaign. The cut, self-inflicted when wielding a length of wood with a nail protruding, bore a superficial resemblance, on a small scale, to the sword wounds he had observed when assisting the medical orderlies in Afghanistan. The swelling and the throbbing informed him that medical attention would be a necessary next step.

As a retired senior officer, Greene had access to the out-patient department of St Thomas's hospital in Southwark.

Taking a third Brandy to address the pain, and assist the process towards sleep, he resolved to attend the following day.

Chapter 31

Visit to the Hospital
Tuesday September 2nd 1851

St Thomas's Hospital in Southwark and adjacent to the Thames, was situated in one of the poorest areas of London, which it had already been serving for some 700 years. Its main clientele were the ragged and underprivileged local residents, but Greene was aware of the privileged access afforded to his class, and he took a Hansom to the edge of the nearby Borough Market. He chose to wear some campaign medals to give authenticity to his military claims and sought, despite his limp, to approach the hospital doors with an upright bearing – carrying a cane and sporting a top hat. He made a quite incongruous appearance as he tried to avoid the detritus in the streets and make his way through the crowded Borough Road market.

At the hospital entrance he received what he accepted as an appropriate welcome. He was invited to avoid and by-pass the queues of the malnourished and often, from the sounds they emitted, consumptive locals; to walk past the crippled children and desperate mothers to locate a door marked "Officers" and be greeted as 'sir.' Once inside, however, it was evident that the main function of the door was to enable priority but not necessarily more professional treatment. He was granted a chair but the recording of his name and rank was a perfunctory activity, and no immediate enquiry was made as to the reason for his visit. Within 10 minutes, as a care-worn heavily pregnant girl, carrying a screaming infant, left a consulting room he was admitted. This would be no exclusive encounter. Around the room were an assortment of chairs with a range of occupants. It was evident that the doctor was moving from person to person having a brief conversation, making a rapid observation, and quickly determining an appropriate remedy. Some would have a note for a bottle of something, whilst others would be dismissed with no apparent solution to their ills. Greene overheard one wretched man, with an evidently broken limb, being instructed to go further into the establishment for what would presumably be additional treatment.

The doctor making his way around the circle of chairs was, Greene surmised, approaching the end of his career. He was accompanied by a nurse who not only recorded some notes but was also responsible for moving a three-legged milking-stool from place to place for the doctor as he moved along – she stood holding a board with some lined paper clipped to it and upon which she recorded any necessary details. She also carried some smaller rough-cut papers which would be written on and given to the patients. These either accessed some medicine or provided access to further treatment.

The balding and ruddy-faced Doctor Prentice, who had served as a medical orderly in Afghanistan and supplemented his skills with some additional training upon his return to England, wore what had been a white smock which bore a badge revealing his name. His manner with Greene demonstrated a measure of respect. There was even an enquiry as to his name and where he served, the nurse only recorded the former. Greene received a more deliberate examination of his injury than was afforded to most.

'How did this happen?'

'A nail from some wood.'

'It's gone quite deep. How long ago?'

'Just over a week.'

The unsympathetic response, 'why didn't you come sooner?' was not unexpected – and was recognised as a reprimand rather than a question.

'I think the nurses can handle this. Through there.' A thick digit indicated an opening, which might once have contained a door; the doctor moved on without appreciating the "thank you" that Greene offered, and the Brigadier picked up his cane and hat, received a chitty from the nurse, and moved to join another queue.

In front of him was a mother and baby, with two toddlers in tow, all malnourished, including the mother who looked strained and, surmised Greene, probably younger than the thirty plus she looked. The youngsters were in khaki shorts but without socks or shoes. She was behind a man, his couple of badges confirmed he was an army veteran, with a wooden leg to the knee, supporting that side of his body with a crutch which resembled an inverted kitchen broom.

Ten minutes later, as he came to the front of the queue and through the doorway, he rather unexpectedly heard a greeting, 'Brigadier Greene,' from one of the pair of nurses, each seated behind a broad table festooned with bowls and bottles and the effluent of minor treatments, discarded bandages and swabs.

'Fancy seeing you here. Come over.'

The nurse, Helen Wight, was a regular worshipper at the Abbey who recently had had cause to appreciate the assistance of Arnold Greene when she needing to be escorted home after a fall some months earlier.

'What have you done?'

The contact between them, and his knowledge of her familiarity with the area around the Abbey, meant he offered some precise information. 'I was down at Abbots Yard and cut my hand on a piece of wood.'

Naively she continued the pleasantries of the conversation; she so rarely dealt with people she knew. As she was cleaning the hand, in water from a bowl which, Greene assessed, had probably been used to clean many hands before, she continued, 'and what were you doing there,' and even offering a possible reply, 'another part-time job?'

He sought to stall any further enquiries. 'I might have got that wrong, it may have been somewhere else. I'm not sure. I'm not even sure when it was. What can you do?'

‘I need to take your temperature and measure your heart rate.’

‘I have started feeling quite hot and my breathing is fast – but I was putting that down to the exertion of walking the last few yards through the Market.’

She rested the palm of her hand on his temple. It was damp from perspiration – and revealed a level of heat that Nurse Wight was quite familiar with. ‘You have quite a high temperature Brigadier.’ There was a pause as she dried her hands.

‘I also need to measure your heart rate. I will need to hold your wrist and observe the second hand on this watch as I count.’ To avoid being drawn into any conversation she always counted the heart-beats aloud, albeit not loudly, as the 30 seconds of testing time elapsed.

‘You also have a very raised heart-rate; not just from your walk.’ The evidence of the two readings was that the level of fever was already significant.

She then undertook a closer inspection of Greene’s right hand. She was deeply concerned by what she saw. It was not just the redness of the cut, but its depth and the pus accumulating at its edge.

‘If we had seen it earlier, I might have recommended honey; and that will still be useful over the next few days. But this has gone deep and the infection is spreading. I am going to have to apply some Bromine. We’ve only recently started using this. It is very effective at burning off the infection – but it is very painful. Fortunately, we have a supply of Nitrous Oxide which I will ask you to breathe in, that will help dull the pain initially – but the pain will return, and it will remain painful for a few days afterwards. If we don’t do this, you might be back in a few days to have your hand cut off.’ The final comment was quite dispassionate, neither meant as an expression of concern or to cause anxiety but simply her medical conclusion.

The Brigadier quaked slightly at the prospect of an amputation. The pain of the Bromine application would have been just about tolerable, but he was relieved to hear that he would be partially numbed from its effects by the laughing gas.

'Come through here.'

The nurse's, 'I'll not be long,' was for the benefit of the growing number of patients awaiting her attention or that of her colleague. Within a space barely larger than a wardrobe, and with no windows, but a high-level grill to the outside world, the nurse asked Mr Greene to hold a cloth mask, with a pipe going onto it, tightly around his nose and, when she had left the room, to turn a lever on a canister through ninety degrees for the duration of ten seconds.

Nurse Wight delayed her return for a further 20 seconds. The application of the Bromine solution to the cut took only a short time. Almost uniquely the cloth used for this process had not been used before and would not be used again. The Brigadier, despite the anaesthetic, winced as she sought to cover the whole infected area and allow the liquid to go deep into the wound.

'I see you have brought your gloves. We would advise wearing them with a piece of linen against the wound which you change each day. It will be painful for at least two days, probably longer, that is from the Bromine attacking the infection; but the redness should decrease.'

Superficially it would prove to be as she had suggested; but the latent infection would, over a short period of time, develop, as she speculated in her rapidly scribbled notes, to a full-blown blood-poisoning. A threat to both his sanity and his life.

Chapter 32

Duty at Westminster School
Tuesday September 2nd 1851

Helen Wight returned home, exhausted as usual, from a long shift at St Thomas's to have supper with her parents. Her mother, worn down with the care of seven children, of whom Helen was the oldest, would always try to ensure that when her husband, Charles, and her daughter arrived in from their work, there would be food on the table. Mrs Wight was conscious that the two bread-winners deserved a good meal. The younger children had already had something less substantial, and she would sometimes, as tonight, eat a stew with Charles and Helen. Charles's job was delivering for a furniture company, usually on a horse-drawn vehicle – but now-and-then pushing a hand-cart. To make a few extra pennies he had recently made himself available for the occasional shift supporting the Beadles at the Abbey, this was his response to the kindness shown by the Abbey staff to his daughter following her fall. Charles Wight would be covering for an event at Westminster School later; a celebration of some sort with a meal.

Mrs Wight, who did not often hear much about, though was always interested in, what happened at work from either her husband or daughter, would sometimes try to use the opportunity of eating together to ascertain what it was that had occupied their day.

Her enquiry, 'busy day?' was unspecific as to its intended respondent. She hoped it might be a conversation starter. She ate rather slower than the other two – and the absence of conversation from them meant that they would often be waiting for her to finish.

Charles replied first, 'chairs and tables mainly. We are doing well from those new places off Victoria Street – but they all seem to have steps, not only to get into the house but often up the stairs once you're inside. We supplies mainly the kitchen and study and sometimes dining room, but we get to glimpse at the posh stuff they gets from the Pantechnicon, or special made by Abbots or someone else.'

Confident that this was the extent of her father's contribution, he having resumed consuming his stew with his spoon, Helen added, 'you remember the man who helped me home from the Abbey a few weeks back, one of the security staff I think, he mentioned Abbots. Got a nasty cut across his hand when he was down there, must a been a week ago Saturday. I applied some Bromine – it'll be hurting like heck tonight. Brigadier Greene he was.'

That exchange didn't continue. Eating his meal rapidly, ahead of going out, didn't give Charles the opportunity to contribute too much to the conversation. When his wife and daughter started talking about the fashions they'd observed on the street, he chose not to expend the energy required to participate.

He used an 'I'll be on my way,' to temporarily interrupt their discourse. His remark was briefly acknowledged, but the flow of the ladies' conversation did not permit anything more demonstrative. Charles had no expectation that it would. He left the room to change into dark trousers, shoes rather than boots, and a white shirt. He would collect his jacket from the basement room on Dean's Yard.

The first forty minutes of his duty were hectic, so many people arriving for the meal at the school. Charles' responsibility was to identify whether the carriages that wished to park within Dean's Yard had the appropriate permissions. He had a check-list of those being entertained – and had to direct people to the apposite pre-meal drink gathering. Once that had been accomplished, and all the guests were suitably acquainted with their drinking venue, there would be a hiatus of a couple of hours until he, and others, would be marshalling departures.

A colleague was despatched to obtain a flask of ale from the Albert off Victoria Street and the four Beadles on duty that evening, including the two *irregulars,* decided that for half-an-hour they could leave their duties and catch-up.

One of the regular Beadles, Gareth Evans, was full of the fact that he would be having a further police interview the next day. The police had spoken to him, and now it was the turn of the Detectives.

'Why can't they work together?' Evans' query reflected the thoughts of them all.

He explained that it had come to light that the body had been brought to the Abbey from down by the river, from Abbots Yard. Charles, excluded from much of the discussion, because its topics were familiar to the permanent Beadles but obscure to him, found here an opportunity to be involved.

'My daughter, a nurse across at Thomas's, met someone today who had hurt his hand down at Abbots.'

'It's a dangerous place,' suggested Evans, 'saws and nails and rasps and planes, I'm surprised there aren't more incidents.' With such a remark Charles' intervention was dismissed; and soon afterwards Mr Evans instructed that it was time to get back to their posts.

The final carriage was directed through the gates and off in the direction of Whitehall, the last pedestrian departure had been a few minutes earlier. Charles and Gareth had offered to do the final survey of the site and ensure that the gates were locked, and the handing over of responsibility to the Abbey's night patrol.

Departing from the basement for the final time, having hung up their official jackets, Gareth took the conversation back to Charles's earlier remarks.

'The person who hurt his hand at Abbots. Was it someone you knew?'

'No, but you might. Greene, I think, a military man. He sometimes does a duty here.'

‘I do know him; the Brigadier I think he’s called. Do you know when it happened?’

‘It must a bin Saturday before last, or possibly Sunday, because Helen said it was eight nights ago – she specifically said ‘nights’ which now strikes me as odd. She wondered why he’d waited so long.’

Gareth Evans’ final remarks, as he locked the gate into Dean’s Yard, were ‘I do hope he’ll get better soon. Have a safe walk home Charles.’

Chapter 33

Interview with the police
Wednesday September 3rd 1851

When Chief Superintendent Jones and Sergeant Roberts formally spoke to anyone they tried to ensure that the conversation had a measure of privacy. Their experience was that people were often reluctant to say things that they were not certain about, or were not confident were germane, in front of others. There was always the anxiety about being embarrassed by irrelevant remarks. Jones, through the new Clerk, had had a little-used office in the Little Cloister made available to them during their enquiries. He even held one of only two sets of keys for the room.

Gareth Evans was, as he always was, punctual. His twenty years in the navy had impressed on him the need for discipline and precision. A delay here or a hesitancy there could prove fatal, as it had for some friends in his first engagement as a fifteen-year-old rating against the French at Toulon in November 1813. His first, and only significant, naval battle had formed his attitude to time in both military and civil life.

Evans wrapped his knuckles against the door as Nicholas Hawksmoor's clock on a western Tower of the Abbey struck ten.

'Come in.'

The small room was made even smaller because it had served as a repository for various pieces of furniture discarded by the Canons, who resided in adjacent rooms. Jones had instructed his colleague to create an ensemble of three chairs and a table from the available items. He had decided to use an ornate table, almost entirely because it was both heavy and already in situ at the centre of the room. A judicious push across the floor enabled three chairs to be placed around it – the decision that their guest should have the Windsor Carver was to facilitate the exposure of two other chairs as the carver was lifted over the table.

The window in the room faced South, but the layout of the cloisters and nearby properties did not enable much light to penetrate, and no artificial lighting had been provided.

'Sit down please,' said Jones.

'Thank you for coming,' added Roberts, to ground the meeting in a measure of civility.

'I know you weren't on duty on the day, either the Saturday or Sunday, when Marshall's body seems to have been brought to the Abbey. But you do have a senior position amongst the Beadles. We are talking to a lot of people today; believing that someone will be able to help us.'

Jones and Roberts then heard words that they had hoped for, but not anticipated.

'I think I can help you. I believe I know of someone who may have been involved in Marshall's killing.'

They looked at each other, and then looked across the table at Evans.

'Tell us more,' said Roberts.

Jones felt he needed to add some words of caution before they heard any more. 'I do need to say that we will be taking notes of all that you say. It sounds like it might be important. Please let us know what things you are sure about and what things you believe but may not have evidence for. Although this meeting is confidential, if we use any of the information you give us in a court case then you will be named, and if you say things that are untrue, or if you mislead us, then you will have committed a criminal offence.' Evans often wished that there was a specific form of words for this situation like those used when they arrested someone.

'I accept what you are saying. What I am going to tell you is only what I have heard, but it comes from trustworthy sources. You will need to speak to others to establish my account.'

'We accept that. As long as you are happy for what you say to be associated with you when we speak to others.'

'I am.'

'Then please tell us what you know, or rather, what you believe to be the case.'

Evans proved to be concise. What he said was summarised by Roberts in his report of the meeting:

Mr Gareth Evans, a Beadle of Westminster Abbey, reported being told by Mr Charles Wight, an occasional Beadle, late on the evening of September 2nd, that, earlier that evening, he had been told by his daughter, Miss Helen Wight a nurse at St Thomas's Hospital, Southwark, that at eleven o'clock that morning she had treated a Brigadier Arnold Greene for a serious injury to his hand which she believes was caused by a nail from a block of wood. They had been previously acquainted when Mr Greene assisted her home form the Abbey following a fall. When she asked about the wound, he revealed both the time, 9 or 10 days earlier (that is the Saturday 23rd or Sunday 24th), and the location, Abbots yard. He knew she was aware of the yard because they passed it when he was taking her home. She treated the wound with bromine and discharged him, encouraging him to subsequently use honey. Mr Evans is aware of Mr Greene as a member of the night staff of the Abbey.

Both officers were enthusiastic in their appreciation of what Evans had to say, but they also sought his discretion, asking that he instruct a member of the Abbey Staff to contact Mr Wight's daughter, as soon as possible, imploring her not to speak to others, and to inform her that the Detectives would like to talk with her at her earliest convenience. They were prepared to give him a small sum of money for whoever would go immediately to St Thomas's to impart their advice – and to charge Miss Wight to be available to speak to them at midday when, they believed, she might have some respite from her nursing responsibilities. In the meantime, they would seek to contact the emporium for which Mr Wight worked to speak to him to ensure he spoke no further on the matter. They would also find out from the Clerk of the Abbey, or his staff, the address of Brigadier Greene and seek to arrange for a constable to be located near his house to observe his movements.

All three participants, as they stood to shake hands, believed that this had been a vital moment in the police enquiry, and would be likely to achieve a significant result.

Chapter 34

Nurse Wight interview
Wednesday September 3rd 1851

Jones hastily wrote the note that Evans would pass on through the athletic 19-year-old son of one of the Canons, home from Cambridge for the summer. He was prepared to undertake the delivery swiftly for enough money to buy a meal for himself and his brother later that day. Helen Wight received and read the note, and acquainted the courier with the knowledge that she could be available to talk to the Detectives for fifteen minutes from a quarter past twelve. A further runner had delivered a note to the furniture business that employed Mr Wight, he received a commitment from a staff member to deliver it into Wight's hands upon his return from making a delivery.

The Clerk's secretary, in an office close to the Detectives' "interview room" furnished Detective Superintendent Jones with Arnold Greene's address, and the ten-minute walk to Vine Street, and an urgent request, meant that a police officer was stationed before a quarter past eleven outside the home of Arnold Greene. Police were not a novelty in the area – and it would have been a very discerning observer who knew the purpose of the constable's presence.

The Detectives, recognising that they had time to kill, decided to walk to St Thomas's. They made their way over Westminster Bridge. Along the south bank of the Thames, through to Borough Market and down to St Thomas's adjacent to the new London Bridge. There was a measure of self-congratulation as they walked. They felt a resolution was close.

A few minutes ahead of their scheduled time the Detectives arrived at the hospital. They were anticipating a positive meeting with Nurse Wight. She had informed Doctor Prentice of the requested consultation with the Detectives, and he had arranged space in a gazebo within the hospital's private grounds. It was Doctor Prentice who greeted Roberts and Jones. The gazebo, he explained, was created because it was important that the nurses, during their brief breaks, should be away not only from the stench of their working environment but also away from the risk of the toxic miasma invading their lungs. "The Gazebo" was hexagonal – with two open faces and benches along the other four sections. Doctor Prentice gave them assurance that they would not be disturbed in the fifteen minutes allocated for their meeting.

Things had moved very quickly in the 24 hours since Nurse Wight had treated Arnold Greene. Helen Wight knew this meeting related to that encounter and her first enquiry, stepping into the Gazebo where Jones and Roberts were already seated, was as to the Brigadier's health, a matter upon which Jones was supremely ignorant. He momentarily regretted that that probably suggested that he did not care.

'We have been speaking to Mr Gareth Evans, a senior Beadle, who we understand to be a friend of your father's, he is a Beadle at Westminster Abbey.'

'I don't know him personally – but my father speaks highly of him, they sometimes work together.'

'This morning we met with Mr Evans who informed us of a conversation that he had had with your father concerning the treatment you gave to a Brigadier Greene yesterday morning.'

At this point Nurse Wight became quite defensive. 'I am not at liberty to speak of treatments given to patients.'

'You felt at liberty to speak to your father, miss. I must inform you that we are making enquiries in relation to a murder, we have just spoken to Doctor Prentice who has authorised our questioning of you, and assured us that it is your duty to assist us in our enquiries. Is that understood?' The tone was neither as friendly nor as calm as Jones had hoped. There was a tension. He wanted to respect the nurse's allegiance to her oath regarding patient confidentiality, but longed to know what she had learnt from Mr Greene.

He assured her, 'I believe that our questions today may lead to the arrest of a murderer.'

'A murderer? Where? Here in the hospital?'

'Not here. Maybe you have heard or seen details of a death in Westminster Abbey last week.'

'Yes, I saw something about it in the *Morning Chronicle* – and dad has talked about it.'

'We believe that Mr Greene, Brigadier Greene, may have been involved. Your father has been requested, in a letter from us this morning, not to speak to anyone about this. If what you tell us is consistent with what Mr Evans has said then we would certainly be interested in interviewing Mr Greene and potentially arresting him in connection with the murder of Mr Marshall. I don't say this to frighten you, but to remind you that it is supremely important that you tell us what you know.'

Helen Wight, although shocked, and disbelieving as to the culpability of the Brigadier, was persuaded that it was right for her to shed any inhibitions she had on the matter and to fully co-operate.

'How can I help you?'

'We understand that Mr Greene said that the wound that you were treating was a result of holding a piece of wood with a protruding nail, that he did this at Abbots Yard in Westminster and that the occasion of the doing of this was, by a calculation from what he told you, on the Saturday 23rd or Sunday the 24th of last month?'

'That is what I deduced, and indeed it is what I have recorded in my notes. If I had not met Brigadier Greene recently, when he helped me home and we walked past that yard, I would not have sought such information. We simply treat the injury; but having previously met he spoke more freely about the situation.'

'We believe that Thomas Marshall, the man who was found dead in Westminster Abbey, was in fact struck over the head with some sort of club at Abbots yard during the night of Saturday to Sunday that weekend. The evidence that you have given – and the evidence we will see in Mr Greene's hand when we arrest him, suggests that he committed the murder.' Jones knew that he was taking a risk by using the word 'arrest', but he needed to focus the nurse's thoughts

'Why would he do that?' was the pleading response..

'That, Miss Wight, is what we are trying to find out. Are you able to let me know what his condition is? I'm sure you realise that this is vital for our enquiries.'

'He has a very deep-seated wound. It is unfortunate that he delayed getting treatment for it. It is likely, from the appearance and colour of the wound, that blood poisoning has already taken place. I applied a bromine solution which, hopefully, will attack the poison in the blood. It will certainly cleanse the surface of the wound, but it will be painful for some time. The fear is that the blood poisoning will already be taking hold.'

'What effect will that have? Is it fatal?'

'It can be. The Brigadier was already exhibiting some of the common signs of the infection spreading – he had a very high temperature fever, a very rapid heart rate, and, I believe, was already confused. Blood poisoning can lead to a significant level of pain and loss of sanity. It can be fatal. A week's delay in getting any treatment makes that much more likely than if he had let us know immediately.'

The allocated fifteen minutes was approaching its conclusion. The Detectives obtained some further contact information from the Nurse and an undertaking that she would not speak of this to others, though she sought, and gained, permission to speak privately with her own father. Helen Wight also said that she would be available, if necessary, to speak as a witness in court should the matter come to trial and her testimony need to be examined.

Nurse Wight walked the twenty yards what would have been a lawn if it was properly maintained, washed her hands under an external tap, and returned to her demanding, but often rewarding, work. Jones and Roberts looked at each other with a measure of contentment. This would be the "big one" that would enable them to retire with a glorious achievement.

Chapter 35

An arrest
Wednesday September 3rd 1851

Since his return from St Thomas's, Arnold Greene had not gone out. The initial sense of euphoria on taking the Nitrous Oxide, and the sensation of a dull pain as the nurse applied the treatment, had terminated before his return home had been completed. The pain was now being addressed by quantities of brandy, measured out by his man-servant and duly taken by the disciplined Army Officer every four hours. He had had little to eat and had not gone outside his home in the previous 24 hours. Even if he had risen from his chair and observed a police officer walking past his door at regular intervals, he would not have suspected that he was the cause of the constable's presence.

Rather foot-weary, and with a measure of urgency, Roberts and Jones summoned a Hansom Cab to make the journey from St Thomas's to Greene's home on Vincent Square. The Hansom, created by the architect Joseph Hansom, was an improvement on the two-wheeled, single horse cab – since it had larger wheels and a lower centre of gravity. The driver sat high up at the rear of the vehicle. For the first time passengers could see where they were going and keep inside. They would be paying eight pence a mile, the same cost as both of them travelling on an Omnibus. The cabstand near the river was conspicuous, it had sufficient space for a dozen cabs with their horses, a water pump and a refreshment shed for the cab drivers; however access to a cab in that location also meant stepping through the ever-present smelly mix of dropped animal feed, water and manure. Jones, in uniform, could at least assume that his cab-driver would not be reckless.

As they came onto Vincent Square they observed Police Constable Brown pacing slowly towards them at the far end of the nearly deserted street. During the school term pupils of Westminster used the fenced-off green at the centre of the 13-acre square as their playing field, with sundry pitches and pavilions; over the summer holidays the grass grew. The officers decided to take the cab beyond Greene's house, number 57, and stopped just short of the Police Officer.

Emerging from the Hansom, Jones enquired. 'Has he left the house?'

'No sir. Not since I've been on, and PC Clegg reported that the door hadn't been opened before that.'

'Thanks. We are planning to arrest Mr Greene, and have retained this cab to take him to Millbank Police Station in Vine Street. Can you please now return there to prepare for our arrival. Is there a back entrance to the station?'

'The cab might not be necessary – it's only 100 yards away. Go down,' here he pointed across the square, 'towards where they're going to put the new bridge, the back entrance to the station is in an alley to your left, just after the posting box. I'll make sure they are ready to let you in.'

'Thank you. On your way.' Constable Brown set off at a more respectable pace than the patrol-step they had witnessed earlier.

'We'll keep the cab, Roberts, just in case. Can you let him know?'

The Detective negotiated the wait with the Hansom driver, and ventured some payment as a deposit to retain their patronage.

'I understand he has a man-servant who will probably open the door. If not, we may need to find another way in.' Jones was not sure how that might be achieved as he ascended the six polished steps to the olive-green arched door that sported the double-digit number above a lion-headed door knocker. He lifted the lion's head and deliberately hammered it down. He took a slight step back and looked at the closed curtained windows on either side for any sign of disturbance. His heart rate always increased in these situations – though on this occasion he was not anticipating any resistance. The sound of both key and latch preceded the door opening to a sufficient degree for the head of the man-servant to survey the Detectives and offer the single word greeting 'gentlemen,' an observation that recognised their occupation and simultaneously questioned their purpose.

'May we come in? We are members of the Detective Department of the Police; we wish to see Mr Greene.'

'The Brigadier is not well at present, but do come in and I will attract his attention.'

They were directed to chairs on the left of the hallway. Once seated, the man-servant knocked on and, without awaiting a response, opened a door to their right. He stepped into the room, closing the door behind him. It was a matter of a full two minutes before he opened the door once more and begged them enter. The two minutes had been sufficient to prepare Arnold Greene in an upright chair in front of the wall opposite the door. The wall consisted of book cases replete with multiple leather-bound volumes. Two other chairs, placed a few feet apart, were set in front of them; evidently brought across the room for their benefit. The small table before the curtained windows provided evidence of the consumption of a significant quantity of spirits. A tired carpet in a dark green covered the floor – a tall 'grandfather' clock stood in the far corner. Over the mantel piece was an engraving of the flight into Egypt in a frame of polished brown wood. Other walls carried large portraits of Greene and a person the officer surmised was Green's father – together with some battle scenes. A two light chandelier hung from the ceiling. The two minutes had also been appropriated to furnish Greene with his array of military medals.

The Brigadier offered the same single word enquiry, 'gentlemen?'

'My name is Albert Jones and I am a Chief Superintendent of the Metropolitan Detectives, this is my colleague, Detective Sergeant Roberts, can you confirm that you are Mr Arnold Greene?'

'I am Brigadier Greene sir.'

'I would like to ask, if you are happy, that your man-servant remains present with us'

'Of course he may.'

'Thank you, he may need a chair'

'I'd prefer to stand, sir.' Declared the tall man who moved to stand adjacent to Greene's chair.

The identification preliminaries having concluded, the Detective officers sat down and Francis Roberts took out his notebook.

Superintendent Jones announced, looking directly at Greene, 'my colleague will apprise you of the reason for our visit.'

Sergeant Roberts then read a familiar summary of the events of a few days earlier and concluded, 'we have reason to believe that you were the person who struck Mr Marshall, possibly at Abbots Yard, and killed him.'

This was another point at which Jones's heart rate usually increased. He would be taking over the interrogation and would occasionally need to respond immediately to a belligerent denial, an aggressive defence (both verbal and physical) or to a tearful confession. He felt himself tense up as he awaited Greene's reply. When he heard Greene's next words, he was not sure whether to laugh or, as he did as a responsible Detective, seek elucidation.

'I did it for the Queen,' was Greene's unapologetic and very deliberate response.

Roberts could not resist a smirk at what was an unusual, in his experience unique, and implausible defence.

'You are saying, Mr Greene, that you are admitting that on that night and in that place, you killed Mr Marshall?'

'I am,' was again spoken as confidently as any confession Jones had heard, but it came with a qualification.

'I did it because I was instructed by the Queen to do so.'

Fortunately, the Superintendent was aware of the effects of blood poisoning. Nurse Wight had already reported the high temperature and the increased heart rate, it was no surprise that the additional symptom of confusion was already being manifested. He did momentarily pause to consider whether such a situation would bring into question the confession that had just been made. He believed that in agreeing to the accuracy of Roberts' summary Greene had made a voluntary, formal, and complete confession. Nevertheless. He felt it would be helpful, if not necessary, to hear that confession once more.

'That's as maybe. I need to be clear, and you are speaking here before two police officers and your man-servant, that you personally killed Mr Thomas Marshall.'

'I did, and I thought that I had pushed him into the river, but maybe the tide was going out.'

No mention had been made of the specific location of the body within Abbots Yard, so this confirmation that it had been left at the water's edge was, Jones felt, sufficient for him to issue a formal arrest. If only they could find more evidence that associated the crime specifically with the woodwork yard there.

Jones stood and rested his hand on Greene's shoulder, a mechanism initially introduced to identify which of a group of people was being arrested, but rather superfluous in this instance.

He made a formal, and familiar, declaration. 'Mr Arnold Greene I am arresting you for the murder of Mr Thomas Marshall on or before Sunday August 25th 1851. You have declared before witnesses that you are guilty of this offence, and I am taking you into custody.' He did conclude with an additional, 'you have five minutes to prepare before you are removed to a police cell, from there you will be removed to a prison cell and await a court hearing. You may only bring with you such as you can carry in one case. If there are people you would wish to inform of your arrest, may I advise you to tell your man-servant during those five minutes. Sergeant Roberts and I will stand at the two exits from your house and, after five minutes, will take you, in a Hansom cab, to Millbank, Vine Street, police station.' After a brief pause, he concluded, 'do you understand?'

Greene's response was a clear and distinct, 'I understand.' The officers left the room and stood inside the doors at the front and rear of the property. There was some movement from the man-servant up and down the stairs, and he was evidently making some notes as well. The Detectives chose not to overhear any conversations.

Greene came, with his man-servant, towards Jones at the front door. The officer informed him, 'your case will be examined at the Police Station. Please follow me.'

Jones led down the steps to the Hansom; Greene, leaning on his man's arm, followed and Roberts brought up the rear.

Chapter 36

A Prison cell
Wednesday September 3rd 1851

An examination in the police station cell by a police doctor confirmed Arnold Greene's high temperature and fever, and a rapid heart rate, consistent with the assessment made the previous day by Nurse Wight – but neither examination had sufficient precision to determine whether Greene's condition was improving, deteriorating or stable. The evidence of the hand, which was redder over a larger area than described by the nurse to Jones and Roberts, confirmed the previous diagnosis of blood poisoning, but suggested a deterioration. This reinforced Jones's view, passed on to George Clegg, that anything that Greene said should be treated as the babblings of a mad-man (not Jones' exact words, but Clegg's interpretation).

Greene's suit-case was examined. His clothes were removed – and squashed into the bag, whilst he was dressed in police-issue prisoner clothing.

Later that day Greene was transferred the one hundred yards along the Millbank to the Penitentiary House close by Vauxhall Bridge – its sixteen-acre site and its function as the 'holding prison' for up to four thousand people sentenced to deportation annually made it the largest prison in England. Greene's temporary incarceration was because of its convenience rather than its prescribed function.

Greene was not escorted beyond the entrance gate, and had to struggle unaided into the jail. The reception area was full and Greene was directed to sit on the bench to await his turn. Men sent there before him were still being processed. Greene was then obliged to remove his recently acquired clothes, to be returned to Millbank Police station.

For the first time in the whole enterprise fear was now the dominant feeling that Greene was experiencing. He had been aware of a sensation of privilege and responsibility when first instructed to undertake the killing of Thomas Marshall. Going to Abbots was a reminder of previous military exercises, an element of risk – but the prospect of a sense of commendation for service, of fulfilling a mission, of a successful engagement. He had lived for a few days wondering how his service would be acknowledged, or was it sufficient, as the Ignatian Prayer he had learnt at school said, that he should ask for no other reward except that of knowing that he was doing, in this case, the regal rather than divine will? He had been cautious about reporting his injury – questions might be asked, but he would be discreet. He was flattered to be engaged in conversation with a young nurse, and maybe had said more than he ought. Now something had gone horribly wrong – where was the senior officer who would testify to the nature and authenticity of his commission? He now regretted the delay in seeking medical assistance; and the overheard conversations about blood-poisoning and potential loss of sanity caused him some anxiety – but his biggest fear was that he was now alone. He had always worked with people, both under authority and with authority, but also with comrades-in-arms. He had not experienced fear in the face of an enemy – but now experienced fear, partially because there was no enemy, no one he could test his strength against. He was alone without friend or enemy.

It was the practice at the Penitentiary House to greet each new occupant with a bath, the water of which bore traces of the preceding bathers and was tepid rather than warm. As Greene emerged, naked, he was given a ticket with a number on it, ‘hold on to this’ was the instruction. He then dressed himself in the clothes provided – in what some of the prisoners named the “Millbank suit”. It comprised trousers, jacket, and shirt, all odd colours and rough cloth; together with red-ribbed stockings, ill-fitting boots, and a cotton neckerchief. A similar square of cotton acted as handkerchief. The prison rules were read to him and several other new "guests", a procedure that occupied half an hour. These preliminaries complete, Greene was taken down a corridor, across a yard and from thence up a spiral stair to a cell on the river side of the hexagonal building – not that there was a river view to enjoy. He entered the cell, surrendering the ticket he had been clutching, and saw it placed above the door. He would now be a number and not a name.

The warder immediately reappeared and brought work to be done. Initially a prisoner was set to do "light work", especially one like Arnold Greene whose stay was expected to be brief. A pile of rough material was delivered, together with coarse thread and a blunt needle. On the top of the pile was a finished example of the work. The warder briefly explained what was required and bade him to set about the task until the hour of the next meal, which would be indicated by the tolling of a bell.

Before the meal-bell was rung a further humiliation was inflicted on Greene with the arrival of the barber. Unceremoniously he was shaved and his hair cut short. The meal, a watery soup, concluded the day and, for the moment, Greene was a single prisoner in a cell designed for two, so he could choose which of the hard boards to lie on. Sleep was not easily achieved – and became an impossibility when, an hour after nightfall, a reluctant companion was admitted to his cell. His invective was directed at various people and institutions, and his language not unfamiliar from the army barracks. The prison noises were such that it would have taken a man with nerves of iron to sleep well. Sometimes Greene could hear women, in an adjacent 'wing,' screaming and lamenting, but mostly the sounds were of angry and fearful men. His cell-mate did not seem keen on conversation, and Greene was not going to initiate any; both slept only fitfully.

Greene's residency at the Penitentiary House, Millbank, would be brief. No one visited him during that time, except the single appearance of a doctor whose one achievement was to secure an overcoat that could be worn at night to challenge the shivering. Although the blistering on the hand seemed, visually, to be reducing, the palm continued to a distinct red hue and beneath the blood poisoning was progressing. Medical practitioners in prisons were divided over whether a fever was a mechanism to draw out an illness, or a symptom that should be treated. A compromise was the provision of a bowl of cold water and a cloth which it was advised could be applied four times a day, but not to interrupt his work-schedule of 12 hours a day.

Greene would be at the Penitentiary House, Millbank for a week before being moved to Newgate.

Chapter 37

Police enquiries
Wednesday September 3rd 1851

George Clegg, a traditional police officer, personally could not see why there needed to be a Detective Department. Had he not, joining amongst the first roster after Peel created the service, been solving crimes and apprehending criminals for decades? He knew that the politicians wanted to see crime prevented, as he did, but the people wanted to see crimes solved and offenders behind bars. He knew his patch well – better than any of the Detectives could.

Clegg asked his senior officer, John Watson, whose regard for the Detectives was no greater than his own, whether he might interview the Beadle again. Westminster Abbey Beadles had proved valuable witnesses in the past, from their vantage point looking out onto the Sanctuary, and, now also the terminus of Victoria Street. They were aware, 24 hours a day, of activity. They knew the tradesmen who could legitimately bring their wares for the Abbey residents or the boys' school. There would also be a Beadle at the other end of Dean's Yard, but often only during daylight hours. A team of people paid for by the Abbey and the School and usually ex-military, as John Clark, who he had spoken to the previous week, was.

Being part of his 'beat,' it was not unusual to see Constable Clegg around the Sanctuary, and he would regularly pass the time of day with whoever was on duty at the Beadles' box. Rather than arrange a formal interview he would take the next opportunity when Clark was on duty in the day-time, which would usually be three or four times a week, at one of the gates to Dean's Yard. The Beadles worked a seven-day rota that paid little attention to the Lord's Day.

Constable Clegg's patch included the area to the South of the Abbey between Great Smith Street and the river. Robert

Peel's ambition to have one police officer to every 450 people had not been achieved in this area – Clegg and his two fellow constables covering this section of the Westminster B Division observed the lives of over 2000, a population that had recently significantly increased as those evicted from their accommodation along the route of Victoria Street had moved a few hundred yards at the most. Buildings previously occupied by ten now had 15 people in them.

This patrol area frequently meant walking through the College Street gate and across Dean's yard to emerge onto the Sanctuary. On one of these occasions late in the week after the discovery of Marshall's body Clegg was on his customary perambulation, hoping John Clark might be on duty, when he was hailed.

'Cleggy, can I have a word.'

'Certainly John. Indeed, I was looking out for a chance to talk with you again.'

'You didn't tell me there was a murder. Do we know anything more about what happened on Sunday? I've been thinking about what I saw. It was the cart that gave it away, I thought it was familiar. It was bigger than most of the carts that come through bringing food and the like. It had three sets of wheels rather than two. The only people I know with carts that size are Abbots down at the timber wharf. They had them specially made for bringing in the stuff for the choir backs, you know the side walls of the choir.'

This was the link they needed. Grounds for an exploration of the work yard at Abbots. Things were beginning to slot into place.

'And you don't think anyone else has carts that size?'

'Sure of it.'

'Have the Detectives spoken to you yet?'

'Not seen hide nor hair of them. You is the only person I've spoken to about it.'

'Can you keep it under your hat for a while? I said the Detectives aren't talking to us. I don't want to talk to them either. I can do my own detecting for the moment.'

'Surely Cleggy. I'll keep quiet. But if you do find out anything, can you let me know?'

'Sure John. I know Chipper down at the Yard. I'll go down and see him.'

There was a significant jauntiness in the step of Constable Clegg as he turned to take the short walk down to Abbots Wharf. Not only was he making some progress in the case, but he was getting one over on the Detectives.

Clegg was not an unfamiliar figure to the businesses along the river front. It was he to whom they reported petty pilfering and needless minor vandalism. It was he who they often wanted to "do something about it" when groups of men seemed to be acting suspiciously. Yet he was also a reassuring presence, his bearing carried weight and he was always looking to help; and, since many of the miscreants also inhabited his patch, he would sometimes be able to retrieve what had gone missing through his local network, with a small consideration to whoever gave him information.

Abbots was not a business site that gave him particular concern. They paid their own watchman to keep an eye on the site.

Walking onto the premises he enquired of the first person he saw whether Chipper Clarence was around – and a finger pointed him towards one of the workshops. Clegg walked across, acknowledged by a couple of the staff en route, and entered the open door. Two thirds of the way through his 180-degree survey he noticed Mr Clarence leaning over the bench of a slight man chiselling some fine work onto the leg of a table.

Not wanting to disturb, or distract, the labourer Clegg made his way across and, as the worker looked up, drew Chipper's attention to his presence.

'Mr Clarence, can I speak to you for a moment?'

‘Certainly.’ He left the craftsman with some words of encouragement and invited Constable Clegg to step into the yard outside.

‘How can I help you Cleggy?’

‘You may have heard that a body was found in Westminster Abbey last weekend.’

‘I did, I saw it in the paper. Was it the same Thomas Marshall who I met a year or so ago?’

‘He was certainly Thomas Marshall. Used to be in the choir. I don’t think he was a carpenter though.’

‘He spoke to me last year for his newspaper. He was working for the Mayhew chap, wrote things in the *Morning Chronicle* about London workers. He talked to us about Woodworkers. We featured in one of his articles – not by name of course. I think he quite liked us. But the articles made them, Mayhew and his team, unpopular with others, very unpopular. In fact it has since become tough for us. Although we weren’t named word got out that we were the outfit that he paraded as the best example, and our workers the best paid. People who don’t pay as much as us are upset.’

‘It sounds like the same man.’

‘I haven’t seen him since so I don’t think I can help.’

‘I think you can’ said Clegg, taking out his notebook – and noticing that in his excitement he had not recorded his recent conversation with the Beadle.

Clegg continued, ‘I was speaking a few minutes ago with one of the Beadles at the Abbey. We, the police, believe that Mr Marshall wasn’t killed at the Abbey – but that his body was brought there. This Beadle believes that there was something brought on a cart through the gate into Dean’s Yard that evening. Although it was curious, he didn’t think much about it until he learnt, from me, our suspicion that the body came from somewhere else. He has just said that he thinks that cart may be one of yours, since you are the only local firm that uses six-wheeled carts.’

'We do have them, we don't like them, terrible to turn. We had one specially made for the work we were doing at the Abbey a couple years back. I don't suppose we have used it at all this year. It's stored behind that shed,' Chipper indicated a building towards the wharf, 'takes up too much room to be inside.'

Without further conversation both men walked in the appropriate direction and behind the shed, under a tarpaulin, rested the trolley.

'That's curious,' suggested Chipper pulling back the tarpaulin.

'What are those sheets doing on top of it? What's that blood about?'

'I think the answer is that this cart was used to transport Mr Marshall's body into the Abbey.'

'You saying that Mr Marshall was killed here?'

'I can't reach that conclusion yet on the evidence I have seen so far, but it wouldn't surprise me.'

Clegg was now not only excited but also recognising that his language needed to be precise. He did not want to be quoted in a way that implied he had jumped to conclusions.

'What I can say is that this cart was almost certainly used to transport Marshall's body from somewhere to the Abbey, and that it was brought back here at some point afterwards. The presence of the sheets suggests immediately afterwards. Do you have sheets like that on your premises?'

What were being termed sheets were actually more like bed blankets. Chipper held a corner and felt the fabric.

'I have to say that they are probably the ones we use to wrap around the larger items that we move.'

'So, I think we can say that the cart and the sheets came from your yard. Circumstantial evidence, as we say, points towards, but does not confirm, that a dead body was brought from here to the Abbey and left there.'

'How many people here knew of Marshall's association with the Abbey?'

‘I did. He spoke to a few other people. He may have mentioned it to others. He spent more time with Scotty, Ian McDougal, than anyone else. Can I fetch him over here?’

‘If you would.’

Constable Clegg began to make some notes in his booklet whilst looking around the site. It was not often that he experienced such a sense of excitement. This would be a feather in his hat. Maybe an award, a commendation, promotion. He needed to make sure he held on the story. Tell others not to speak about it. Ensure that word didn’t get to the Detectives, quite yet. They might have their man – but he had the evidence necessary to convict him. He needed to act circumspectly, but quickly.

A few moments after this internal reflection concluded, Chipper returned.

‘Constable Clegg this is Mr Ian MacDougal, one of our senior workers.’ A man, clothed in a white apron and some glass-screened eye protectors in his hand stepped from behind Chipper.

‘Good afternoon, sir. How can I help you?’

Clegg was aware of a nervousness in his enquiry, or maybe it was related to his accent.

‘I believe, Mr McDougal, that a year ago you had a conversation with a Mr Thomas Marshall, a journalist, concerning work in this yard. Is that correct?’

‘I did, though he wasn’t really a journalist – he worked in a bank he told me.’ That information was news to Mr Clarence, and Constable Clegg remembered he had heard it – but wondered whether it was relevant.

‘Is that so? Did he tell you anything else about his life?’

‘I think he mentioned a wife and daughters; I mentioned I had two daughters and he said that he did as well.’

‘Anything further?’

‘The second time we spoke he had to finish because he was off to the Abbey, he had to go to a choir practice. He also talked about having just moved.’

'So you knew he was involved at the Abbey?'

Scotty became conscious that he was maybe saying too much, he needed to be accurate speaking to the police – so therefore only say what was necessary, and nothing more. 'I think so,' was an unconvincing reply, Clegg was certain that he knew so.

'Mr McDougal. We believe that Mr Marshall's body was taken from here to the Abbey on the back of this cart. Do you know anything about that?'

There was a pregnant pause, Scotty lowered his head, the fact that he was composing a response, when an outright denial could have come immediately, betrayed, thought Clegg, an involvement. He repeated his enquiry, but it now took on the tone of an inquisition. 'Mr McDougal. What do you know about that event?' He re-arranged his question to imply that Scotty knew something. The continuing silence only confirmed it.

Before receiving a reply, Clegg was emboldened to say, 'Mr McDougal. I believe you were involved in taken Mr Marshall's body from this location, Abbots Yard, to Westminster Abbey and leaving it there. I also believe you may have been involved in his murder.'

It was this last remark that finally induced a response.

Scotty looked up and spoke directly to Clegg. 'He was already dead.'

It was the turn of the other two to be silenced.

'We should go to my office,' Mr Clarence offered, turning to the others, 'follow me.'

Office was a grand name for the secure space where invoices and plans were kept; in a very orderly way, Clegg observed. It was occupied when they completed their 20-yard walk.

'Miss Temple. I wonder if you could vacate the office for a while, I have an important meeting with these men.'

Pushing papers together, at the smaller of the two desks in the room she asked. 'How long will you be, Mr Clarence?'

‘I really don’t know; but is important that we are not disturbed. Please leave us Abigail, and don’t let anyone in.’

‘I’ll make sure of that sir, I’ll sit outside with these invoices,’ and, putting the documents into a small folder and picking up a pencil, she left, closing the door behind her.

Chipper sat at his desk, Constable Clegg behind the recently vacated desk, and before them Mr McDougal slumped onto the third chair in the room, normally available to those who came to see Chipper.

Clegg remembered that he was meant to administer a form of warning. He had not memorised the appropriate text and so sought it from one of his pockets.

‘I need to say these words. Mr McDougal “I am not charging you with any crime; but I am making a record of what you say and if you are charged with any crime then what you say can be used as evidence”. I advise you to tell the truth.’ He had added the final words; they evidently carried weight.

‘I will tell you the truth sir.’ There was a pause. Scotty was waiting for a further question, when it did not come, he continued.

‘A week ago on Sunday morning I was the first person to come to work. Not so many people work on Sundays. Mr Clarence here doesn’t normally come in on a Sunday. No one’s really in charge, but some of us get on with some work – maybe we’ve got an urgent reason to conclude the task.

‘I arrived early’, Scotty continued, ‘not really sure what time. The nightwatchman was still here. He knows some of us, and is allowed to unlock some doors for us. I walked down towards the river when I arrived. I like to look at the Thames flowing along, it’s a magnificent river. When I got near the water’s edge, I saw a body on the foreshore. It looked like someone had tried to throw it into the river, I’ve got no idea how long it was there. It wasn’t wet – I don’t think it had come from the river. But the tide was coming in. I was by myself, except for Charlie Newsome at the gate. I was expecting others that I knew to come along. I went closer and recognised it was Mr Marshall, the man I talked to last year.'

As he spoke his eyes moved from one to the other of the two men in the office with him.

'Hold on a second please,' requested Constable Clegg, 'I just need to get all this down.' After a few moments he read out his summary which Scotty accepted.

'What happened next?'

'I checked that he was dead. He obviously was. There was a great gash in his skull.'

His pause, and distant stare, suggested he was reliving the situation. He carried on.

'Jamie and Chris Nelson, two brothers, arrived together a few minutes later. They were talking and laughing, but I interrupted them with a sharp "shut up. Look at this". They stepped down to the foreshore and asked, what are we going to do. Jamie even turned and asked, "you didn't do this did you Scotty?"'

'I think I swore at that point – but the gist of what I said was "No. I've just found him here". Jamie asked, "what are we to do?". Chris and I obviously had the same question. I declared "I know him. He's from the Abbey"'.

Scotty went on to explain that they decided that they did not really want to have the responsibility for a body; but that something ought to be done before others came into the yard or the tide came in, they certainly did not wish the body to be taken downstream. They also felt that it would be something that the Abbey could be better at dealing with. Apparently, he spotted the long cart behind the shed and suggested that they get some of the wrapping blankets and put the body on the trolley under the tarpaulin and decide later quite what to do. That was done and Marshall was left there throughout the day.

He continued, after a brief pause whilst Jones brought his notes up to date and then said, 'carry on please. I suspect this isn't easy.'

‘It wasn’t an easy day then either. All three of us were nervous when other people came to work. In fact, we spent much of that day finishing off a job or two together so that we didn’t need to get involved with others. Early afternoon other people were leaving, and quite surprised that we were staying so long. Eventually, by two o’clock, there were just the three of us. Charlie was just coming back on for the Sunday evening and night watch. His first duty is to go around the site making sure that all the buildings are empty of people before he locks them. We saw him going into the main building and said “We’ll be gone whilst you’re in the warehouse”; and we expressed the hope that he would have a quiet night.

‘That afternoon,’ Scotty continued, ‘finished by taking the cart and body to the Abbey. Jamie knew something of the layout of the Abbey, he’d been involved when the work was done. His first task was to go along College Street and Orchard Street and through the Sanctuary and into the Abbey. The West door was often open on a Sunday and people came into and from services. Meanwhile Chris looked to when the Beadle had moved away from the top entrance. Fortunately, he was distracted by some students playing. Then he and I wheeled the cart through Dean’s Yard and through the cloister entrance into the Dean’s courtyard. Jamie had gone into the Abbey and made his way around to the door into the Deanery and through a room, curiously called Samaria, and opened the door into the courtyard using the key that he knew hung there.

‘Chris and I decided that we could not leave the blankets behind so manhandled the body off the cart, up the steps to Samaria and through the door into Jericho and then we put it in the robe cupboard, and closed the latch. We didn’t want anyone to find it for a while – we wanted time to get away; and maybe it would be some hours before it was found. We wheeled the cart back to Dean’s Yard and, seeing no one at the rear gate, proceeded to go through to College Street. Jamie locked the door and went back out through the church and ran around to Abbots ahead of us to see when the watchman went off on a further patrol of the site. We then returned the trolley to its previous location.

'That's the honest truth.' Scotty concluded.

'I believe you,' said Clegg, 'but to confirm it I need to talk to Jamie or Chris before you do. Is either of them in today?'

'I saw Jamie Nelson earlier. Shall I go and get him?' offered Chipper

'If you would. Bring him back here – and I want you on your honour not to say anything about why you are fetching him. When he comes in, I want you, Mr McDougal, to wait outside with the young lady who was here earlier. Is that all right?' Both Scotty and Chipper agreed.

Within a few minutes Chipper had returned with Jamie Nelson, who was able to confirm in some detail the account that Scotty McDougal had given.

Constable Clegg concluded the session by instructing the three people he had spoken to to swear that they would not speak to anyone else on the matter. It was conceded that Jamie should speak in confidence to his brother and enjoin him not to say anything to anyone, and to let him know that he could soon expect to be interviewed by the police.

Clegg left the yard and walked back along Millbank to the divisional office at the junction of Vine Street. Sergeant Watson was, Clegg was told by the front desk, in his office. He walked around the desk, through the doorway behind it and knocked on Watson's door and entered when 'come in' was heard. Clegg stepped into the room and closed the door behind him.

Clegg's pleasure at explaining how he had resolved the matter was quickly dashed when Watson reprimanded him for not bringing the men from Abbots Yard with him. Why had he not recognised, following Clegg's full account, that various serious offences had been committed, including the concealing of a dead body, concealing a crime, and transporting a corpse without consent? Clegg was instructed to bring Abbots men, under arrest if they chose not to comply with a request, to the Divisional Office so that they could be charged with such offences – and then allowed to go back to work whilst other enquiries continued.

Clegg found it dispiriting to walk back to the yard to ask the people who had, he felt, generously explained the situation and to bring them back to the police station. Although Scotty and Jamie came reluctantly but without protest, they were conscious that being escorted from the yard by a police officer, albeit in conversation and not cuffs, was doing nothing to assist the discretion that was being asked of them. They had to agree, with Watson at the office, on an alleged petty misdemeanour to explain the situation when they returned to the yard.

To not complete and distribute to the Metropolitan Divisions and the Detectives the "route paper" itemising updated material on all crimes that had not been resolved at the end of each day was a significant offence. Watson and Clegg committed such an offence that day.

Chapter 38

Further investigations
Thursday September 4th 1851

What was most amazing, Watson felt in conversation with Clegg next morning, had been the failure of the Detectives to secure in their investigations the information that they had received from Abbots Yard the previous day. It confirmed his belief that that new branch of policing was a rather redundant enterprise. There was a deep sense of pride that they had secured a charge in the affair of "The Body at Westminster Abbey" that had eluded the Detectives. They may have detained someone for the murder, but still did not have the full story.

It was, Watson felt, appropriate to do two things – but the timings needed to be right. They did need to tell the Detectives what they had done, but it was also time to contact Gerald Bourne. The former would be with a measure of gloating, and the story in the press would serve to exalt the detecting work of the Police and embarrass the Detectives.

'Wily' Willie Johnson, a ten-year-old lad living around the corner from Vine Street, would run a mile to take a message for thruppence. He would soon be despatched with a message for Bourne, whereas a note later in the day would be sufficient to bring the Detectives into the loop. Within an hour of the dispatch of Wily, Gerald Bourne was at the front desk in Millbank, and Watson felt it was the appropriate time to send Clegg up to Scotland Yard with the parting words, 'don't rush.'

The Detectives had already signed off the case with the arrest of the "Murderer" – and Clegg's additional information was not particularly welcomed. Neither party came out well from the ensuing argument about the failure of the police to provide information and the failure of the Detectives to properly investigate. The Detectives felt obliged to open the case again – although they were confident of a conviction for the crime. There was a need to determine whether the additional evidence of the carpenters, having being charged at Millbank, could assist in determining who might have initiated the murder. What they had heard that day gave greater credibility to Greene's claim that an outside agent had instructed him, and that his actions were not on the grounds of his mental health. Would there be grounds for delaying the imminent trial?

Part 4
The Trial concerning Thomas Marshall

Chapter 39

Newgate prison
Monday September 8th – Friday September 12th 1851

On Monday September 8th at the Old Bailey the Grand Jury was meeting to assess the cases proposed for the session ahead. Their purpose was to determine whether there was sufficient evidence to bring each individual case before a trial jury.

The consideration by the Grand Jury as to whether the case should go forward in the Brigadier's situation proved a formality. His prosecutor declared that since the Brigadier had confessed, and there was no ambiguity as to the identity of the body, there were no grounds for withdrawing or not permitting the application. Although provision was made for the defence to contribute, the Grand Jury believing it to be what the Americans, they understood, were now calling an "open-and-shut case".

The elegantly besuited clerk, present for this meeting, advised that an Old Bailey trial seemed appropriate and no objection was raised by the propertied men of the Grand Jury and the case was approved as a "true bill". This meant that its seriousness merited a formal trial and that there was a likelihood that sufficient evidence was available for any decision made by a jury and judge to be secure.

By the evening of that day, with the prisoners who would face trial identified, the Newgate Calendars of Prisoners were drawn up, listing the prisoners and the charges they faced and the dates for their trials. Greene's name was added to the Calendar, the charge of Murder entered next to it, and date set for trial would be Monday September 15th. The Brigadier's appointed law firm consulted the list next morning and allocated Mr Humphries from their list to defend him.

Clement Humphries had been called to the bar in 1843. He was regarded as a man of integrity with somewhat Radical views, he had some sympathy for the Chartists and, promoting their cause, he had fought for, and lost, a parliamentary seat in Norfolk. He had also represented Marie Manning at the Old Bailey two years earlier. She had been accused of the vicious murder of her lover Patrick O'Connor. Although she, with her husband, had been hanged, Humphries had nevertheless gained, through the trial, a reputation as a powerful defendant in a seemingly lost cause.

Greene was moved to Newgate on Tuesday September 9th. Newgate was just yards from Smithfield and not much further from St Pauls. There in the very core of the city, at the heart of its business, adjacent to its Cathedral, next to where the vendors of soup and fish and damaged fruit were plying their trades, scores of people's lives were brought to an end – many through public executions.

Greene had his first meeting with Humphries the following day, one of only two meetings that were permitted. With the case coming to court the following Monday, both meetings would need to be that week.

Although Greene was accommodated in a shared cell, provision was made for him to meet Humphries alone, save only for the guard continuing his constant walk up and down the corridor. The door was kept open for the protection of the lawyer, though the Brigadier, despite his charge of murder, was not thought a flight risk and there was no expectation of any violence. His physical condition meant he had been supported to the interview cell by the guard with his arm around Greene's shoulders.

Humphries used his conventional opening gambit as they sat in the restricted space of a one-man cell. 'Mister Greene,' he chose not to use the military role except in court, 'did you commit the crime with which you are charged?' He had discovered that such an approach could save a lot of time.

'I did kill him as part of my service to the Queen.' The Brigadier was evidently a very weak man. He had not stood as Humphries entered, and only looked up intermittently, from his position sitting on a rough stool, during the meeting.

'We'll come to that, Mr Greene. But I need to ask a couple of other preliminary questions. Did you do this act deliberately, and was anyone else involved with you?'

'I did it by myself sir, as requested by the Queen.' The lawyer took this to be an affirmative answer to both questions.

Feeling obliged to pursue the matter that Greene had raised, but having received a note about his potential health condition and its symptoms Humphries did not believe it would be a particularly fruitful approach. He nevertheless asked, 'and how was Queen Victoria involved?'

'She wrote me a letter with instructions to go to Abbots Yard on Saturday August 24th 1851. I recognised Mr Marshall, I knew him from the Abbey, and, as requested by Her Majesty, killed him with a blow to the head with a heavy stick I had taken with me.'

'How did Her Majesty give you these directions?'

'In a personal letter.'

'Do you have that letter Mr Greene?'

'No, she instructed me to destroy it.'

'Mr Greene. I find it hard to believe that such a letter existed. I will need to find out from the Queen's personal secretary whether such a letter was sent to you.'

The Brigadier, briefly looking up with something of a smirk said, 'he won't know anything, she told me in the letter that no one else must know. She would be unlikely to tell her aides that she was requesting someone to murder one of her subjects, would she?'

Another line of questioning was obviously required. 'How did you know Mr Marshall?'

'When I retired from the Army I acquired a post at Westminster Abbey. Two nights a week I patrol from late afternoon through to the next morning. There are two of us, we have some breaks, but one of us needs to be alert all the time. I work with Clive Butler. We do Sunday and Monday nights – which means that we see the choir at Evensong, Marshall will, sorry, would, sometimes have a brief conversation.'

Humphries returned to his previous area of enquiry. 'Were you given a reason why Mr Marshall should be killed?'

'I was not sir.'

'Do you have any grounds for believing that it was a reasonable request?'

'I obey orders sir. Always have done, always will.'

At this point Humphries concluded that first interview, and rose to leave.

'Mr Greene, I thank you for your time. We do have a further opportunity to meet later this week. I will prepare a reasonable case in your defence which we will discuss at our next meeting.'

Humphries drew the guard's attention and he came to the cell and applied, unnecessarily Humphries thought, handcuffs to escort Greene along the dark and dank corridor to his shared cell. Humphries accompanied them on that short trip and bade farewell before leaving Newgate and walking the quarter of a mile to his chambers in the Middle Temple to consider the presentation of any line of defence.

The notes he had taken were minimal and he had had no reason to refer to any that he had been given by the clerk for the Detectives; except Humphries simply noted the suggestion that the injury could potentially cause insanity.

There seemed to be no reasonable defence. His client admitted the crime and was not able to give a reasonable defence. He had already concluded that the only direction he could take this case would be to suggest, and try to prove, that Greene had undertaken the murder whilst the balance of his mind was disturbed. But he struggled to see how he would be able to suggest that a madness, acquired through an incident during the killing, could be a defence for a decision to kill. He would need to imply that Greene was already an unstable character, and that the action was an aberration derived from an unbalanced mind.

Humphries wanted to explore those ideas at a second interview two days later. Greene, however, was not prepared to have his mental capacity questioned in court, and offered to provide witnesses to declare he was the sort of person who always knew what he was doing and why. Humphries had managed to contact the Brigadier's doctor – and he would certainly, he said, have sided with the Brigadier on the matter. The only other person he had spoken to was Clive Butler, Greene's night-time companion at Westminster Abbey, also ex-military, and, Humphries felt, he might be persuaded, if it might save his fellow-guard's life, to state in court the view he had expressed in their interview that "no sane man would do this". Butler, possibly Greene's closest confidant, had not heard, and could not believe, the ridiculous story of the Queen's letter. Humphries would have no problems identifying people who would vouch for the Brigadier's good character.

Chapter 40

The Old Bailey
Monday September 15th 1851

The journey from the Newgate cell to the cell beneath the New Court at the Old Bailey was a matter of a few yards along an unlit brick corridor. For the Brigadier it was a journey from hope to fear. He had believed whilst incarcerated in Newgate that someone would listen to him and accept his story. He would not compromise his position. His lawyer had failed to persuade him to enter a plea of guilty but insane, 'all this talk about the Queen isn't going to impress the jurors' was a constant refrain. Humphries, as a matter of precaution, had contacted officials at The Queen's House, only to meet with incredulity that such a question should be asked. The story of the letter had not featured in the many lurid accounts and speculations in the Penny press or in any of the more formal journalistic enterprises. Humphries still believed insanity would have to serve as the trump card in his defence, indeed the only card.

The layout inside the courtroom was confrontational. The Brigadier sat isolated. His diminutive height and his bent head exaggerated the sense of being in a pit, as did his distance from the sounding board above his head. He briefly tried to look up across the room towards the witness box where his accusers and supporters would stand – but which he would never have the opportunity to inhabit (no one was allowed to speak in their own defence). Behind the witness box, and with an even greater sense of looking down on the Brigadier, sat the judges. Seated at tables immediately below where the judges sat, were clerks, lawyers, and the writers who took the shorthand notes. To the Brigadier's right sat the twelve jury men – in two rows of six. Tightly packed – and looking grim. There were also seats for spectators, these proved a lucrative benefit to some Old Bailey staff – a prime seat in a murder case could secure an income of at least a pound. Through the window of the courthouse behind the judges the Brigadier, when, with a struggle, he lifted his head, could see the recently erected wall that had the positive effect of preventing the public gazing in on the proceedings, but the negative one of obscuring any sunlight from entering the building. The gas lights gave limited visibility and several people were in shadow.

Away from the courtroom there were luxurious facilities exclusively for the judges and their servants, and a separate room for witnesses, so that they would not be obliged to wait their turn in a nearby pub. A luxurious jury room was appointed with eighteen leather seated chairs and three tables – though this was rarely used in court cases other than as an assembly space: the jury made its decision in court. There were also separate parlours for the Sheriff and Lord Mayor, a Lord Mayor's Clerk's Room, an Indictment Office, and a drawing room for the sword bearer and judges' clerks. The lavish provision for the judges contrasted dramatically with the prisoners' quarters in the basement

Arnold Greene's was the first case of the day. Once the public had been admitted, and the clerk had achieved what he considered adequate silence, the Brigadier was asked to stand, awaiting the procession that admitted the judges and various other dignitaries. In reality he was briefly held in an upright position before being unceremoniously dropped back into his seat.

Mr Christopher Gifford would be leading for the prosecution.

The clerk read the indictment. 'The prisoner, Arnold Greene, is charged with the offence of Murder. That on or before Sunday August 24th 1851 he did, at or near Abbots Yard, Westminster, wilfully, and with malice aforethought, take the life of Mr Thomas Marshall of Victoria Street, London.'

Judge Ebenezer Bartlett asked, staring directly at the prisoner. 'How do you plead Mr Greene?'

'Guilty,' came the almost whispered, but uncompromising, response. It was such a novelty that some present visibly shook. It would be the only word that Greene was allowed to contribute to the trial. He had been clearly instructed that he could not qualify his plea with any explanation.

The judge declaring that the coroner's court had also determined that it was a case of murder, and he asked the prosecution lawyer to invite his first witness.

The prosecution had not felt it in order to summon senior members of the Abbey staff, especially because the prisoner, they understood, had decided to plead guilty. They did feel that Mrs Burrows, who had discovered the body, would be a valuable, and sufficient, witness as to the place and time of that discovery. They also did not wish to cause further stress to Mrs Marshall. She would not be required to declare that the body was that of her husband – no one had contested the identity.

Esme Burrows was the first witness called by the prosecution.

Mrs Burrows stepped up into the witness box, unwrapped a sheet of paper that she had written on and smoothed it out on the lectern in front of her. The oath was administered and the judge requested that she identify herself and give her account.

'My name,' she began confidently, 'is Mrs Esme Burrows, widow, I am 55 years old and reside at room 12 the Deanery, Westminster.'

She went on to give an account of the discovery of the body of a person she recognised and whose identity had been readily declared on the occasion by Canon Brooks.

Mr Gifford, acting on behalf of Regina, chose not to question his witness – he had, after all, compiled her testimony.

Mr Humphries, for the defence, possibly for no other reason than to make sure that his voice level was at the right pitch, chose to make a couple of points in the guise of questions, but nothing of substance was achieved. No one contested the time, place, or person.

The prosecution then chose to invite members of the Detective Branch. They each gave their accounts of their involvement in the events that led to the identity and arrest of the Brigadier.

The officers of the Metropolitan Police were only briefly called to the stand. They believed that the correct man had indeed been arrested, but were unable to claim that his identity had been ascertained through their labours, great though they had been.

Mr Humphries then called Clive Butler and gave an extensive pre-amble to his question, so much so that the Judge was close to bringing it to a halt, believing it to be an unrequested statement.

He continued, 'My client, Brigadier Arnold Greene, believes that he had undertaken this act on behalf of the Queen.' This unexpected declaration shocked the whole assembly, cries of 'what' and 'nonsense' could be heard and jurors turned to each to exchange both looks and words. The equally amazed Judge did call for silence for Mr Humphries' question.

He began again. 'My client, Brigadier Greene, believes that he was undertaking this act on behalf of Her Majesty the Queen. He maintains that he received a letter from her, dated June 29th 1851, requesting him, for no stated reason, to dispose of Mr Marshall at a certain place on a certain date. The letter included a request that it be destroyed to protect him. He thus no longer has the letter, but maintains that it is true. Her majesty's private secretary suggests that the claim is both false and libellous. Mr Butler, could you please introduce yourself and tell the court whether this claim is likely to be true.'

As Clive Butler stepped forward it could readily be seen that this was as much a surprise to the Brigadier as the claims about the letter were to the rest of the court. The Brigadier leaned forward in the dock but was restrained by the arm of an officer standing before him before he could speak.

'My name is Captain Clive Butler, I am fifty-nine and live at 48 Market Street, Bromley. I was an officer in the Kent Regiment. I have worked with the Brigadier for over two years. Every Sunday and Monday evening and night we keep guard together at Westminster Abbey. I have always found the Brigadier to be an honest and careful man. He has an exemplary service record, and Westminster Abbey would not employ anyone who did not. He is a loyal servant of the Dean, and has proved himself as a loyal servant of the Queen. I have never known him to tell a lie.' There was a short pause as Butler looked across the courtroom at Greene, who did not return his gaze. Slowly, and in evident sorrow for his friend, he concluded, 'I do not believe that he could have been in his right mind when he told the story which his lawyer has just mentioned.'

Mr Gifford rose to address the witness. 'Mr Butler this court is gathered to determine whether Mr Greene committed the heinous crime that we have been hearing about. Do you have any doubt as to whether he was the perpetrator of that crime?'

'None sir. I believe he did it. He doesn't lie.'

'Then do you not believe that someone who has done such a thing would readily construct a story to avoid a hanging?'

'I do not believe that Mr Greene in his right mind would do such a thing – but I believe he done it. I believe he also believes he had received a letter – but it is obviously ridiculous to believe that he had.'

Mr Gifford abdicated from his questioning, and Mr Humphries felt he could not add to Butler's account. It was time for the judge to invite summoning up statements from the lawyers.

Mr Gifford was complimentary about the work of the Detectives, but felt that their work was incomplete. There should have been other questions asked, he believed, before the case had come to court. He could not be sure that Greene acted alone, he could not be sure of Greene's motive – but what he could be sure of, he said, was that the man before them was indeed the person who had cold-bloodedly brought Mr Marshall's life to an end. He could give no credence to the fanciful story about the Queen's letter. He believed that the death sentence would be appropriate.

Mr Humphries rose slightly nervously, much rested on his next few words, to conclude his involvement in the hearing. 'I also believe that Mr Greene did indeed take the life of Thomas Marshall, but' and here he turned very deliberately to scan the two rows of the jury as he spoke, 'but I believe that the crime was so horrendous, and the excuse so ridiculous, that they cannot reasonable be accepted as the actions and beliefs of a sane man. I believe that the appropriate verdict would be manslaughter.'

Before inviting the jury to reach a verdict Judge Bartlett informed them that they might consider a second charge in their deliberations. He asked them to decide, 'Is Mr Greene guilty of wilfully, and with malice aforethought, murdering Mr Marshall?' But added, 'and you may also ask yourselves "Is Mr Greene guilty of taking Mr Marshall's life, but doing it whilst the balance of his mind was disturbed?" You must all agree and you may deliver verdicts of guilty or not guilty on each charge.'

The jury turned to one another, the foreman, the locus of opinions, sat at the centre of the upper tier. Throughout the courtroom the jurymen were studiously being observed, their head, lip and arm movements closely watch for any betrayal of the views being expressed. Silence from the observers was not a sign of respect, but a desire to overhear any conversation among the twelve men. After no more than five minutes all 12 men sat and turned to face the judge to indicate that a verdict had been arrived at.

'Will the chairman of the jury please stand.' A bearded man, probably in his sixties, dressed in a suit that had seen better days (and had probably seen a few years) arose and turned towards the judge, who addressed him directly.

'Is the prisoner, Brigadier Arnold Greene guilty or not guilty of the wilful and predetermined, murder of Mr Thomas Marshall?'

The chairman looking directly at the Judge and declared, 'not guilty.' There were audible gasps.

'Is that the verdict of you all?'

'Yes, it is.'

'Is Brigadier Arnold Greene guilty or not guilty of the crime of manslaughter, in that he took the life of Mr Thomas Marshall but did so whilst the balance of his mind was disturbed?'

'Guilty.'

The verdict was now less of a surprise and drew little response, except from the dock where the Brigadier was not sure whether to express his anger at not being believed, his fury at being declared insane, or his relief in discovering, as he had not anticipated, that his life would continue.

'I therefore find the prisoner, Arnold Greene, guilty of the manslaughter of Thomas Marshall and instruct that he be detained at her majesty's pleasure, with penal servitude, for a period of 10 years. Please take the prisoner to the cells.'

Steps from the back of dock led directly to the basement. Within a few seconds Greene was removed to the cells. He would be stripped of his military title and pension and, with an absence of family, would effectively disappear from the world. He would not survive long into that decade of imprisonment. Within days he had what appeared to be a stroke and lost much of his physical and mental capacity.

Part 5
Why was Thomas Marshall killed?

Chapter 41

The Detectives return
Friday September 19th 1851

Significant questions were being raised by the press.

Pathetic images of Greene in court, and reproductions of previous sketches of the murder, made the front pages. The words "guilty" and "insane" appeared in large print in most descriptions; but they all drew attention to the judge's view that there were unanswered questions. Particular attention was paid to the supposed letter from the Queen. Questions were raised about the Brigadier. Questions of motive – who would want to kill Thomas Marshall?

These were questions that the Detectives had not asked – maybe the chief of which was "who wanted Thomas Marshall dead"? The Detectives soon realised that although they had "got their man" there was no real sense in which it was felt that any justice had been achieved on behalf of Thomas Marshall.

The death at Abbots Yard brought with it another nagging question, "why there?" Jones and Roberts of the Detective Branch knew they had further questions to consider. They needed to talk to the people at the Woodworking yard, and to Mayhew – to find out more about Marshall's involvement in his work.

Jones applied to Pentonville prison for permission to speak to one of their prisoners. They learnt that Greene had not only had a stroke but seemed, as they described, "off his head". Maybe that meant that he was persisting with a story that it now seemed might merit further investigation. However the prison graciously said that one of the Detectives could come the following Monday, but that any conversation would be in the presence of a prison officer – and only a period of 15 minutes would be permitted.

Why had they persuaded themselves that the presentation of what seemed like a 'cock and bull' story about a letter from the Queen was simply to cover up a murder that Greene had committed in the Abbey? Once Greene had admitted the crime their desire to find out Why? and Where? had disappeared, they had the guilty party behind bars. The court's decision that he was insane had, they thought, addressed any outstanding questions. This new, inconvenient, approach of the press had opened everything up. They needed to move quickly.

That urgency was enhanced when the next edition of the Evening Standard landed on the front desk. The story, emblazoned across the front page and under the name of Gerald Bourne had moved on from the court case. "Police succeed where Detectives fail", which, although it contained an element of truth, or maybe because it did, angered Jones. A quick glance at the text suggested that it must have been written with the connivance of the Police; he immediately demanded a meeting with the Westminster B Division Chief Superintendent. Such a meeting could not be arranged for twenty-four hours, but in the meantime, there was much to get on with.

Detective Chief Superintendent Jones also wanted to speak to Brigadier Greene's lawyer. Had he been concealing information from them? They had dismissed the ludicrous story about the Royal Letter. Maybe it was more important than they had thought. Did the lawyer know more about it? And why would the Queen wish to get rid of a Bank Clerk who was also a Chorister? The request by Jones to the Middle Temple for an interview with Clement Humphries was rejected. The head of Chambers declared that client confidentiality meant that without a writ from the court there were no circumstances in which members of the Chambers would comply with a request for interviews after a verdict had been delivered. It would later emerge that Mr Humphries had not been made aware of the request but that a junior had issued the standard "response to requests after verdict" letter.

100 yards down Whitehall, with a copy of the Evening Standard at his elbow, the Home Secretary, the recently ennobled Whig George Grey, was removing the necessity for Albert Jones to take any initiative. A summons issued to the Detective Chief Superintendent to meet with him next day was already in the hands of George Grey's junior assistant travelling towards Scotland Yard. The message, delivered to the front desk, was in Jones' hands twenty minutes after its composition in the Home Office.

Jones needed to have something positive to say at his meeting with the Home Secretary next day. He saw the Evening Standard story was credited to Gerald Bourne, with whom he had spoken on several occasions in the past. Although he resented the tone of the newspaper article, he believed that the offer of an exclusive interview might secure some better publicity – and a breathing space to resolve other issues. He knew that Bourne regularly frequented the Red Lion and dispatched a runner to ask for his attendance at Scotland Yard immediately if he wanted to secure an exclusive for a morning edition.

At six o'clock that evening Gerald Bourne was seated opposite Albert Jones knowing that both had a lot to gain, and potentially a lot to lose, in the thirty minutes allocated for the interview. Detective Sergeant Francis Roberts would take notes.

'Gerald, you will not be surprised to hear that I am greatly offended by the article you produced today in the Standard. I didn't have you down as a spokesman for the Police department. The things that you mentioned reflect no better on them than on us. Confidentially, and this isn't for your article, I have been summoned to a meeting with the Home Secretary tomorrow. I need to have something to say to save my skin – and you need to have something to say to balance what came out earlier.'

30 minutes later their conversation concluded, half an hour after that – having spent the time in a holding cell –

Bourne had a draft copy of an article. The terms of the confidential arrangement meant that Jones had insisted on a right of veto. By eight o'clock, half an hour before the paper went to the compositor, a text had been prepared for the next day's edition of the *Morning Chronicle*.

Chapter 42

Meeting the home secretary
Saturday September 20th 1851

Neither Jones nor Roberts had the mental capacity to initiate any further contacts ahead of the meeting with Grey which had been set for ten o'clock the next morning at the Home Office on King Charles Street. The newspaper article could only go so far in assuaging the Home Secretary's clear frustration at the competence of the Detectives. What Jones was not aware of was that a similar despatch had gone from Grey to Richard Mayne, the recently appointed First Joint commissioner of Police (having spent 21 years as Second Joint Commissioner). Mayne's office door was literally ten feet away from the front door of the Detectives. His recently retired former colleague, who had helped to create both the Metropolitan Police and the Detective department, had fiercely argued for the independence of the two bodies. Although they were in adjacent buildings, communications between the two were perfunctory.

It was a significant moment of embarrassment as the men emerged from their offices in Whitehall Place together and greeted one another, neither knowing that they had a common destination. That information quickly emerged through the single question, 'where are you off to this fine morning?' Neither Jones nor Mayne were encouraged by the knowledge; both wanted to blame the other for the necessity of the meeting, but for the moment held their fire. Their walk was accompanied mainly by silence until the doorman at the palatial King Charles Street offices checked his list and directed them to a waiting room on the first floor.

The fifty-two-year-old stern-faced Home Secretary having bid them sit opposite his large mahogany desk, which had folders piled to his left and right, rose from his chair and stood silhouetted against a tall Georgian window that allowed in the bright morning light. He picked up recent copies of both the Standard and the *Morning Chronicle*, and declared, 'we cannot have this, I will not have this.' The documents were evidently the articles written within the previous twenty-four hours by Gerald Bourne at the behest of the two departments represented by the men present.

'It is intolerable that such a public spat should be taking place. Blaming each other for what I believe has been the incompetence of you both.' He had not yet concluded as both men indicated that they would like to contribute.

'Lord Russell, the Prime Minister, has instructed me to resolve this matter. I am not looking for your excuses.' Both men felt intimidated as the newspapers were thrown onto the table and a pointed finger from his extended right arm was directed at them by turn.

'The Prime Minister has instructed that you,' the hand explicitly identifying Jones, 'and your senior officer at B Division,' the finger had moved towards Mayne, 'shall both be suspended from duties without pay for a period of one month – to commence when this Marshall case is concluded, and that you shall both ensure that any further communication with the press shall only be sanctioned in your joint names, having been cleared by the Home Office. During that period of suspension, I am to initiate, with your help during that period of suspension, a review of the relationship between the Detective department and the Metropolitan Police.

'Your priority now is to work on the Marshall case. The only material I want to see in papers are reports that you, together, are making progress. Do you understand?' Grey looked from one to the other demanding an acknowledgment that that was their priority as well.

Grey rang a bell, which was evidently a sign that the meeting was at an end, for the office door opened and an assistant entered.

'I don't believe you'll have anything to say,' was Grey's way of forestalling any further contributions.

With an apologetic “thank you”, both Jones and Mayne stood.

Grey’s final instruction was ‘I want progress today. I will have a joint report on my desk within ten days. Goodbye gentlemen.’

At the foot of the steps up to the Home Office, the Chief Commissioner of Police declared that he was going to Millbank Headquarters of B division and would be instructing Captain Watson to go immediately to Jones’s office at Whitehall Place. He would also make him aware of both his impending suspension and the Prime Minister’s demand that the Marshall case be resolved quickly and with amicable co-operation with the Detective Department. He trusted that this would be satisfactory to Jones; who readily accepted the proposal. As Jones turned left at the end of King Charles Street to head up Whitehall, Mayne turned right towards Parliament on his way to Millbank.

Chapter 43

Co-operation
Monday September 22nd 1851

In order to be available for Sergeant Watson when he arrived Jones despatched Roberts to go to Pentonville for the arranged interview with Mr Greene, the previously attached 'Brigadier' had been removed with his manslaughter conviction.

It was not an unusual venue for Roberts. Detectives often had to interview people there who were on remand, or if they had extended periods of being held in custody and the cells at the Police Stations were inadequate. There was, however, a novelty in going to see someone who had already been convicted. He would be being detained under a very different regime, with significantly greater restrictions in terms of access.

Pentonville inmates were held under the 'silent' system, forbidden to speak to each other. When outside, on their permitted hour-a-day exercise, they would tramp in silent rows, wearing brown cloth masks and holding on to a rope with their right hand. Even in chapel, which they had to attend each day, they sat in separated spaces, or "coffins" as the prisoners referred to them, their heads visible to the chaplain but hidden from each other.

Mental disturbances were common – as yet there was no specific provision within the prison system for those categorised as insane. Sir Joshua Jebb, who had designed Pentonville, would soon be considering the construction of a separate Lunatic Asylum at Broadmoor in Berkshire, but for the moment Greene had to receive the sort of treatment that led to many reported cases of insanity or delusion, and several suicide attempts.

Once Roberts credentials had been accepted, he was escorted by a warder along one of the prison's four units radiating from the centre where the individual cells, of standard dimensions, were located.

Each prisoner worked from six in the morning until seven at night, mainly in picking oakum. But Greene had no such occupation as Roberts and the warder entered. Greene's respect for authority, and possibly a hope that the police officer had come to correct an egregious error, encouraged him to attempt to stand, but he failed. What to Roberts were the evident consequences of a stroke had been determined by the prison medical team to be signs of Greene's insanity. He had no capacity to stand or to speak. Roberts was pained to see the human wreck that Greene had become. His pain only increased as, with bowed head, seated on his fixed stone bench, Greene began to weep. It was such a pathetic presentation that Roberts found himself weeping too as he left the cell, after a visit that did not extend beyond ninety seconds.

Sergeant Watson was already in Jones' office when Roberts returned from his uncomfortable visit to Pentonville; and both were disappointed that he was unable to shed any light on the alleged letter or the circumstances of the death of Thomas Marshall.

Jones resumed his conversation with Watson.

'It seems evident that someone wanted to get rid of Marshall. But who and why? Who had he upset, did he have enemies? Between us we have some knowledge of his life and activities in recent times.'

The next hour was dedicated to reviewing the results of the investigations conducted by both the police and the Detectives.

Watson sought to give a summary.

'Incredible as it seems we now seem to accept that someone deliberately arranged for Thomas Marshall to go to Abbots Yard that Saturday evening. His wife tells us that he tended not to tell her where he was going, or why. She last saw him when he went out about half past six on the evening of Saturday August the twenty-third. We know that Mayhew didn't ask him to go there. We are confident Greene inflicted the fatal wound. There is a consistency between what the coroner observed and what Greene claimed about a wooden club of sorts. It could have been lying around the yard – though Greene says he brought it himself and then threw it in the river. The first person to see his body was Mr McDougal. That was on the shore of the Thames around 9.00 a.m. on the Sunday morning. We are confident it was Marshall; together with the Nelson brothers, McDougal brought the body into the yard.

' So where did the request come from? Who was he expecting to meet? We can assume it wasn't Greene, although they knew each other a bit. Did Greene make the arrangement, or did a single person summon them both to the fateful meeting?'

Watson continued, 'we know that he was dead before eight o'clock on the morning of Sunday August 24th. Greene said he committed the crime on the Saturday evening, and that is not inconsistent with the evidence. McDougal and the Nelson couple concealed the body for several hours before transporting it to the Abbey. There they deposited the body in the Jericho cupboard, and returned to Abbots with the cart – and that was witnessed by the Beadle nominally, though not actually, at the College Street entrance.

'The body was revealed and identified by Mrs Burrows and others later that Sunday afternoon, and I was in attendance at the location where it was found at four o'clock. Both you, the Detectives, and the coroner were informed that day – and Canon Brooks informed Mrs Marshall. The coroner's inquest took place the next morning and all parties were convinced that it was a deliberate and pre-meditated murder.'

Watson paused to look around to make sure that the others were being attentive; they were. He concluded his summary, 'within a few days, due to the fortuitous co-incidence of Greene and Nurse Wight having previously met, you', nodding in the direction of Jones, 'were enabled to identify and apprehend Mr Greene as the murderer. We,' referencing the police, 'through contacts with the Beadles, ascertained a connection with Abbots Yard. Greene's trial at the Old Bailey a few days ago initially gave us cause to celebrate that the case had been resolved. But the interests of the press, and, it must be said, the tensions between our two agencies, has brought demands from the Home Secretary and others for us to determine both a motive and the identification of the person or organisation who commissioned Greene to undertake the crime, we have no reason, at least at present, to believe that Greene had any personal grievance about Marshall, and he has stuck to his story about the Queen's letter from the moment of his arrest.'

'That sounds right,' said Jones, who turned his head to Roberts, who confirmed he was of the same opinion.

Jones picked up the summary. 'From our enquiries there seem to be three areas where Thomas Marshall was in dispute with others. His work with Mr Mayhew and Mayhew's newspaper led him into confrontations with those who felt that their observations about several occupations were erroneous and harmful, and Thomas was specifically involved in commenting on the woodworking and tailoring workers.

'We also know that there were a couple of issues where he had fallen out with the Dean of the Abbey. The longest standing one was over the reorganisation of both the worship and the interior of the Abbey. In this he was in close liaison with Canon Brooks.

'The other, and I think very interesting issue, which has only come to light through our conversations with his colleagues at the bank, and was not mentioned to us by the Dean, though Mrs Buckland made some reference, was Marshall's accusation that Mr Buckland had not only represented the work of Mary Anning, the sister of one of Marshall's work colleagues, as his own, but had also failed to fulfil an undertaking to pay Miss Anning for her contribution to his thesis. We know that Marshall confronted the Dean on this account not very long before his death.

'We are also aware that the leadership of various Trade Unions are very much opposed to the material that Marshall contributed to Mayhew's publications. It seems evident that he had been identified as the supplier of those articles. He foolishly made himself known at the Street Traders meeting recently.

'If Greene did get an instruction to undertake the murder, that must have been received from someone who knew both Greene and Marshall, and had also been aware of Marshall's connection with Abbots Yard. That might suggest someone associated with the Abbey was involved, though it doesn't rule out connections with the unions or Mayhew or the bank – we don't know that much about others that Greene knew – and it's too late to ask now.'

Watson, nodding at this conclusion, said, 'that does suggest that maybe we ought first of all to talk again to the Dean, and there is also Canon Brooks, right from the start he was said to be a close friend of Marshall's.'

The new policy of co-operation seemed to be bearing fruit already. It was decided, much to Roberts' annoyance, that for any further interviews there should be a common front and that they would be conducted by Jones and Watson together; Watson would make the arrangements and Jones would lead the questioning.

A runner was sent to the Abbey. Fortunately, the Dean was again in residence, he had attended the funeral of Robert Dundas, the second Viscount Melville, who, like Buckland, was a luminary of the Royal Society. He was anticipating returning to Islip within a few days, so an interview with him was set up for two days later, a Wednesday, and with Canon Brooks on the Thursday. Contacting Anning, Mayhew and the union leaders of the woodworkers and the street traders would be arranged by Jones over the next couple of days. There was an urgency because of the deadline set by the Home Secretary – required by the 30th, not much over a week away.

Chapter 44

Visit to the Dean

Wednesday September 24th 1851

Mrs Buckland was obviously irritated by the imposition of a further interview. She felt that another visit from the Police was a violation of the sanctuary that she was seeking to build around her ill husband – nevertheless she instructed Medley to give them admission.

In the presence of her maid Jenny, as the Police Sergeant and Detective Superintendent entered the drawing room at the Deanery, Mrs Buckland was gracious. Once Jenny left and the door was closed, the Dean's wife stood resolutely between the officers and the Dean.

'I don't know why you are here again. For heaven's sake a man is in prison for the murder of Thomas Marshall, that crime is solved. Haven't you got better things to do rather than bully my sick husband?'

It was Watson who sought to calm the situation.

'We are most sorry Mrs Buckland, we really are. It is true that Brigadier, sorry, Mr Greene has been found guilty of killing Mr Marshall, but we believe that he was acting on instructions from a third party and that to have a satisfactory conclusion to this investigation we need to discover who it was who instructed Greene to undertake the crime and, preferably, what reason they had for so instructing him.'

Sounding rather pompous Jones added, 'the prime minister has particularly asked us to do this.'

'It really is too much. We shall be returning home' (a very deliberately chosen word) 'to Islip tomorrow. I do not anticipate returning for some time. This will be the last interrogation I will permit.'

The officers were uncertain whether the Dean had heard this conversation, they thought not, as they looked at his slumped figure across the room.

Stepping past the belligerent Mrs Buckland with an 'excuse us', Watson and Jones sat in chairs adjacent to the Dean.

'Mr Dean,' the Detective assumed his questioning primacy, 'we are very sorry to disturb you so shortly before your return to Islip. I know that you will be very pleased that the killer of Mr Marshall is now in prison. However, to fully conclude our investigations, we want to find out who was behind Marshall's murder and why he was killed. We believe we are close to working that out; but would value a few more moments with you.'

'If I can help,' the Dean responded weakly.

'We understand that Mr Marshall came to see you not long before he was killed. Do you mind telling us what that meeting was about?'

Mrs Dean angrily contributed, 'I'm sure you already know, you've talked to Anning I understand.'

'We have indeed Mrs Buckland. But we heard from neither of the people who were involved in that conversation, and now only the Dean will be able to enlighten us. Sir?'

'Yes, he came here. He was aggressive, yes bullying. I'm not a well man, I needed my rest, I didn't need his insults and violent threats.'

'Did he actually threaten you sir?' asked Watson, lifted his head from the book on his knees on which he was making notes.

'Yes, he did. Not physically, but he said unless I did something he would publish a story around about me.'

Jones continued, 'what, specifically, was he suggesting that you had done?'

'I wrote a book, a big book, many, fifteen or sixteen, years ago about the evidence of God's design in all creatures, those alive today and those extinct. A lady called Mary Anning, Anning's sister, helped me a bit with it, and I said I might give her something for her help if I could afford it. I gave her fifty pounds. I couldn't afford any more and I didn't think about it again. That's it.'

'Mr Anning seems to think that there was something more than that. He understood that you had offered Miss Anning half your fee, which we understand was £1000, for what he called the exceptional amount of work she did. That is what Mr Anning tells us he told Marshall.'

'That may be what he told Marshall, it may be what Marshall said to me, but that is not my memory, and there was certainly no contract. Marshall was threatening to portray me as a cheat and a liar, as someone who had deprived a young lady of what she was due.'

The Dean added after a few seconds' pause. 'She said nothing about it in the many years between the book being published and her death.'

'Nothing in public; but she spoke to her brother not long before that death.'

'So he says.' Here Buckland, still not having raised his head, paused again.

'I am sorry that I couldn't help her more than I did. We had great fun together, we made discoveries together. I saw her often at her home in Lyme Regis. We walked beneath the cliffs together. They were very happy days. But things have moved on. I couldn't have Marshall ruining my reputation.'

'What were you planning to do Mr Dean? You haven't said.'

'I don't really know. I had been thinking of writing to her brother, maybe even meeting him. I don't know.'

Mrs Buckland now decided that this was the point at which the interrogation should conclude. 'I don't think you'll learn anything more. I think it's time you left.'

She rose and walked to the door. The maid wasn't summoned. Mrs Buckland opened the door and issued the single word, 'Gentlemen.' Obediently, but reluctantly, Messrs Jones and Watson departed.

Leaving the Abbey by the cloister door Watson suggested, ‘Maybe we need to see Anning again. The Dean obviously sees the situation differently.’

Jones reflected, ‘I think we’ve had our last meeting with Dean Buckland. We’re seeing Canon Brooks in the morning tomorrow. I don’t think Anning would be keen to see us at work again, he did come over to our offices to see Roberts and I – maybe we can ask him to come tomorrow after work.’

Chapter 45
Meeting with Canon Brooks
Thursday September 25th 1851

'Familiar faces,' said the Dean's Yard Beadle as, once more, Watson and Jones passed below the archway adjacent to his security box.

'Thank you, sir. Maybe our final visit.' This was expressed by John Watson more out of hope than expectation. 'We have an appointment.'

Without enquiring further, the Beadle replied, 'I'm sure you have. You're welcome.'

Both men had met with Canon Brooks previously. They decided to adopt the same approach as on the previous day, Albert Jones would speak first.

'Welcome gentlemen. Please come in,' was the affable greeting. Today his maid was available and the officers accepted the Canon's invitation to have a cup of tea and some biscuits, which the maid would bring up to the drawing room on the first floor.

The Canon opening with the familiar refrain, 'I thought this crime had been solved,' and Jones and Watson rehearsed their explanation once more.

The Detective Superintendent wished to identify one of the issues that they felt was worth following up in their pursuit of a motive, and their desire to identify the person who enlisted Greene.

Jones began by stating. 'We still have not finally identified the reason for this killing. We are exploring several options. One of these is the debate over recent years about the worship and some structural changes to the Abbey. We understand that you and Marshall were not supportive of some of those changes. We are aware that Mr Marshall did occasionally express views contrary to those of the Dean, and that there were those amongst your colleagues who took offence.'

Canon Brooks paused for a moment before responding. 'I would not have thought such matters would be grounds for such a barbaric attack. Marshall essentially held the same views as I did, as I do. Changes to the liturgy have the effect of detaching the church from its traditions and history. Language which has been familiar and used for hundreds of years, has been replaced by words that are brash and sometimes vulgar; and the removal of the transept screens was a sacrilege. The final vestiges of the rich Benedictine monastic tradition that was the foundation of the Abbey, and had survived for a thousand years, torn down to admit what can only be described as the vulgar plebeian hordes. The mystery of the sound emanating from the Quire now open to public gaze and scrutiny.'

Brooks paused in the rehearsal of his grievances. 'Sorry, I got carried away. Yes, those were views that Thomas and I held. I know he was on the choir committee, as a representative traditionalist, and he may have made enemies there.'

There was a brief pause, but not one of such a length as to indicate to the Police Officers that Brooks had concluded his diatribe.

'In fact, curiously, one of the most powerful advocates for change was Arnold Greene. He would occasionally come here, and he was quite intemperate in his opposition to my views. It would sometimes be embarrassing as he shouted out his opinions, as if addressing me as a junior member of his regiment. I would occasionally have to go and re-assure my late wife that everything was in order.'

'We had not heard that,' said Watson.

'I hadn't made the connection until you mentioned it. Thinking about it, there were occasions when he let fly his views while Marshall was here with me. Marshall and I would occasionally meet to console each other over the changes being made.'

'Can anyone confirm those events? 'asked Jones.

'I suppose no one can. We would sometimes meet after choir practice, on a Thursday evening, before, it now seems, that became the evening when Marshall met up with Mayhew. That meant he came on a Friday occasionally in recent times. The maid would have finished work. Very sadly, both my late wife and Thomas are no longer with us. No surviving witnesses. You could ask Greene - but I suspect he'll still come up with his preposterous idea about the Queen.'

'Sadly,' commented Jones, 'Greene has suffered a stroke and seems to be deeply infected with blood-poisoning, my colleague tried to speak to him recently, without success.'

'I am sorry to hear that. Not only for poor Greene, but because it means that you can't eliminate the possibility that his motive was to silence opposition to the Dean.'

After some reflection Watson concluded, 'indeed we cannot. I don't think we need to take any more of your time. Thank you for the tea and biscuits Canon Brooks.'

'If I can be of any further help, please let me know,' were the Canon's parting words before closing the door on his Canonry; Watson's first words to Jones after that door closure were, 'that's an interesting thought.'

Watson and Jones returned to Whitehall Place to write up an agreed version of their notes, and to prepare for a further meeting with Joseph Anning.

Chapter 46

Meeting with Anning
Thursday September 25th 1851

Joseph Anning had still not told his closest colleagues about his previous meeting with the police. It had caused a momentary hiatus in his friendship with John Durdin, but that was quickly overshadowed by their common grief over the death of Thomas Marshall. It was that event that coloured their lives day by day. Clients who had been on Marshall's books had been transferred to other members of the Bank's team until a reliable new member of staff could be appointed and so, most days, there were meetings with people either sharing anecdotes of their time, business, and personal dealings with Thomas, or asking awkward questions about his demise. There had been no significant mention of Thomas's work at the bank at Greene's trial, and the issue concerning Mary Anning was not in the public domain.

Joseph Anning's arrival that evening after work was less flustered and more punctual than his previous visit to Whitehall Place. He was welcomed by Albert Jones, his previous interviewer, and introduced to Police Sergeant John Watson.

'Thank you for coming back to see us Mr Anning. Although Arnold Greene is now in prison for killing Thomas Marshall, we are still seeking to establish both a motive for the killing, and to identify whether other people were involved in a conspiracy to kill him. You'll have followed the Old Bailey proceedings no doubt, and we now believe that Greene may well have received a message instructing him to kill Mr Marshall, we wish to find out more about that.' Watson felt it appropriate to explain the state of play, this meeting was not going to be simply a repeat their previous encounter.

He added, 'we are pursuing a few lines of enquiry – and one of them concerns the matter that Thomas raised with the Dean on your behalf.'

There was an immediate protest. 'I never asked him to. I never meant him to.'

'That may be so, but we do know that after his conversation with you that followed your visit together to the Great Exhibition, Mr Marshall visited the Dean and issued what the Dean perceived to be a threat. A threat to expose him as mistreating your sister. What we are wondering is whether there would be any grounds for believing that that threat was of such a serious nature that the Dean, or others, may have wished to find a way to get rid of him.'

'I can't believe that. You don't believe that do you?' asked Anning, looking directly at the faces of the two Officers for either confirmation or denial.

'Our personal beliefs are not relevant. We are looking to see if there is a way to eliminate the possibility, or whether we should make further investigations,' was Watson's contribution.

Jones continued, 'we met with the Dean yesterday.'

'What did he say?' was shot out by Anning like a bullet.

'He said that he had anticipated getting in touch with you; can you confirm whether he has ever done so?'

'No, I've never met him or heard from him.'

'Did you speak to anyone else, anyone apart from Mr Marshall, about your concerns?'

'I never mentioned it to anyone, but,' there was a brief pause, not for any deliberate dramatic effect but because of Anning's uncertainty about how to express himself, 'yesterday I took on one of Thomas's small accounts, a butcher from Westminster.'

'And?' expressed a renewed interest from the policemen.

'And I introduced myself, and he said "the brother of Mary Anning? Mrs Buckland mentioned you". I was taken aback. "Indeed, I am". I wasn't going to pursue it, but he came back, "she said that Mr Marshall mentioned you when he came to see them. I'm afraid she didn't think you were a nice man", and then he asked if someone else at the bank might take on his account.'

'Do you have the name of this Butcher?'

'I don't, I did not take a note of it. I pointed him back to the door clerk to be allocated to someone else. I don't think the bank would be at liberty to disclose his name to you . You could ask the Dean who his butcher is. I was just very upset that someone was talking about me in such terms. It made me regret, once more, that I had ever said anything to Thomas.'

'I don't think we are going to be able to get in touch with Mr and Mrs Buckland, they are leaving, I believe today, for Islip and will be away for some time. But what you tell us does mean that someone has spoken about Thomas's visit, and about your sister.'

'I really don't want to talk about it anymore. You know everything I know. I wish I had never said anything to Thomas, especially if you think that that may in some ways have led to his death.'

Watson quickly came back, 'we haven't said that Mr Anning, and please don't suggest that we have. We are following up a line of enquiry.'

'But it is possible. Of course the Deanery wanted rid of him; he could have ruined the Dean's reputation, And it's all my fault.'

Rising from his seat Jones said, 'we ask you, Mr Anning, to say nothing more of this. We appreciate your time.'

It was evident the interview was at an end. It was obvious also that Joseph Anning was leaving the meeting in a very distressed state.

Watson and Jones wrote up the interview. They were not sure how much further they should go. A casual and brief conversation with a tradesman probably meant very little; and neither were minded to find a way to get in touch with Mrs Buckland.

It was with sadness a couple of days later that in the daily route-paper there was a report that Mr Joseph Anning had been found dead in his flat, and it was evident that he had taken his own life. There was some relief among the Metropolitan police and Detectives that that information was not picked up by the press.

Chapter 47

Meeting with Chipper
Friday September 26th 1851

When Jones and Watson met next morning, on this occasion at the Millbank Divisional police station, they were very aware that their joint submission to the Home Secretary would be required just three days later. A brief review of their activities over the previous three days, against their earlier assessment of potential leads, meant that the meetings arranged that day, with Mayhew and Chipper Clarence, should mean that they would be able to prepare such a draft report next day, and a full report for Lord Grey by the following Monday.

Their first appointment was at Abbots Yard at ten; a convenient stroll from Millbank. It was an embarrassment to the Detective Chief Superintendent that this would be his first visit to the site where Marshall's body was found – and it was decided that the local Police Sergeant, who knew the site, would lead the conversation.

The yard supervisor, Chipper Clarence, welcomed his visitors at the site entrance. He was accompanied by Scotty McDougal.

Watson's opening greeting was slightly barbed. 'I need to remind you Mr McDougal that you are still facing a charge of concealing evidence from the police. I hope that today we can be fully confident in the things you tell us.'

Although not phrased as a question it received the response, 'Yes you can.'

After a more formal introduction, and an explanation of the meeting's purpose, the group walked down towards where Marshall's body had been found. The value of that morning's meeting was mainly to give a sense to Jones of the physical context of Marshall's death. Scotty was not able to add any detail to what he had reported previously.

Watson's concluding remarks contrasted with his introductory ones. 'We do appreciate the way that you have supported our enquiries Mr McDougal. I would like to say, though I can't guarantee it, that I would anticipate that when we review your case, and that of the Nelson brothers, we are likely to recommend to the court a small fine and a suspended sentence. Although your actions were, obviously, both illegal and ill-conceived, we do understand that you were not motivated by a desire for any personal gain or any desire to conceal a death. Thank you for your time today.'

'I accept that what we did was wrong. We wanted Mr Marshall to be back home, and the only home we were aware of was the Abbey.'

With these words, and an added "thank you", Scotty doffed his cap and walked away across the yard.

The real benefit, however, of their time together came when Mr McDougal had returned to his work and Chipper was able to speak about Society matters.

Sitting in his office, Miss Temple once more excluded to sit outside updating time-sheets, Chipper was able to bring the police officers up-to-date with the wider concerns of Woodworkers across London.

'What Thomas Marshall wrote, and what Mayhew published continues to incense a lot of people. You'll know that the Tailors have had public meetings, as have the slop-workers. Although I'm sure Mayhew thought he was exposing wrongdoing what he has in fact done has revealed that many people are prepared to work for less. The owners of this yard are looking to reduce our pay. The Society is gaining members, but we are being told we need to make higher regular contributions to the Society because people are being laid off and others brought in for lower wages. There is a lot of anger.'

'We are sorry to hear that. We thought Marshall was acting and writing for the best of motives.'

‘I’m sure he believed that. But I need to tell you about a Society meeting I attended last week. People there were getting at me. They had learnt that Marshall had written the pieces for Mayhew on Woodworkers. They realised that his murder here meant that we had something to do with his reports. I was denounced as promoting Mayhew’s views and, contradictorily, if that’s a word, supporting Free Trade. The people here aren’t happy.’

‘Again, we are sorry to hear that. We thought, from reading Mr Marshall’s reports, that he was presenting you as an example to be followed.’

‘If only,’ was the sober response from Chipper before he continued.

‘What I did discover is that some people knew about Marshall’s work before it was published. One of the local Society leaders, Morris Chapman, is sometimes a server at worship in the Abbey. He somehow learnt about Thomas Marshall’s involvement here, and had mentioned it to the Society chairman, who, Chapman says, thought nothing more about it until he learnt of Marshall’s death.’

‘That is interesting,’ said Jones, ‘we know that the leadership of some of the organisations behind the mass meetings was co-ordinated. It was a as a consequence of the work that had gone in to organising the Chartist campaigns of forty-eight. It was informal, but we now know that both the leadership of the Woodworkers and, because he attended, and made himself known at their meeting, the leadership of the Street Traders knew him as well.’ Turning his head to talk to Watson he added: ‘We must address this when we meet Mayhew this afternoon.’

Chapter 48

Meeting with Mayhew
Friday September 26th 1851

Since the discovery of Marshall's body Mayhew had adopted a very low profile. His publications had ceased, though this was maybe more to do with his inability to pay the printers. Poisonous attacks on him, mainly from the pen of Mr Martin of the Street Traders, questioned his integrity, his honesty and even his faith. He had also moved house. Fortunately, Jones had been able to establish contact with him through his publishers who were reminded that it was an offence not to co-operate with the police Detectives in the execution of their duties. Mayhew was nevertheless reluctant to meet either in his own home or at Whitehall Place, so both parties made their way discreetly to a small police office in the City of London for their afternoon meeting.

Jones began. 'We are grateful to you, Mr Mayhew, for meeting us today. Although the killer of Thomas Marshall is safely behind bars, we are still actively involved in looking for both the motive for his killing and any parties involved in arranging that crime.'

'I understand, and obviously want to help you.'

'One of the possibilities is that agents of one of the organisations that you, and he, have been critical of, might have wanted rid of him.'

'I have to say that that is indeed my belief. It seems that many people learnt that Thomas was a major contributor to my work. Naturally I feel very responsible for that, though it was never my intention to expose him to such danger as might threaten his life. He knew it was risky – and he rather foolishly got himself identified, particularly it seems through the Street Traders meeting but also, he told me, somehow people at Abbots Yard and in Spitalfields knew of his connection with the Abbey.'

'Do you feel your life is in danger Mr Mayhew?'

'Yes, I do. I read of threats in some newspapers, and accusations in some of the Penny Dreadfuls. One or two of your colleagues know where I live and I occasionally see them and they report that there have been anonymous death threats, and there is a belief that a price has been offered to get rid of me. I tell you, confidentially, I intend to leave this country within days. Arrangements are being made.'

'Can you identify any specific organisations or individuals that you believe might have been involved in Marshall's death?'

'The location of his death might suggest the Woodworkers, his presence at the Street Traders rally and the vitriolic campaign of Mr Martin could point in their direction. But it seems we have annoyed a lot of people. But he certainly never mentioned to me any specific group or people that caused him undue anxiety.'

With Jones' concluding word, 'Mr Mayhew, we are grateful for your time. I hope that you can safely travel abroad soon,' the interview came to an end.

Chapter 49

Writing up the report
Monday September 29th 1851

Conscious that the ten-day period set by the Home Secretary for their report was rapidly becoming exhausted focussed the minds of Jones and Watson. They were seeking to provide both a summary of their work across the previous weeks, and a view about what remained to be done to draw their investigations to a conclusion.

They were not feeling confident that their efforts would be seen as conclusive. Several options remained – but many of those who might make further valuable contributions were either dead or no longer available. They were aware that their report needed to be on the Home Secretary's desk by ten the next morning. They felt fortunate that no one in the press seemed to have been made aware of Grey's requirement. The "Murder at the Abbey" story had lost something of its appeal with Greene's conviction; the reporters were not establishing any new leads, and editors and proprietors needed new information to justify continuing their involvement. The uneasy relationship between the Metropolitan Police and the Detective Agency still carried some weight; and the front page writers were trying to discover new and exclusive examples from elsewhere to elaborate the tension. As Jones and Watson sat down together at seven that Monday morning, they were not anticipating leaving the office until their document was completed. At eleven, relatively satisfied by their morning's progress, they decided that they needed some external air and left their Scotland Yard for a brief walk, they would only be allowing themselves fifteen minutes.

At the end of Whitehall Place, going on to Whitehall, a glance at a billboard changed all their plans. "Government Falls". They intercepted a lad bearing copies of the special edition of the *Morning Chronicle* and read that Lord Russell had lost a vote of confidence the previous evening following failures to implement an agreed system of support for Ireland, with the nation in the desperate throes of the potato famine. Talks over-night had brought no resolution and Russell, and his Home Secretary Grey, had resigned earlier that morning with immediate effect. An election within a month was anticipated.

'Do we go on?' asked Watson, 'the urgency seems to have gone out of the situation.'

'We'll consult Mayne. But I can't imagine that there will be much we can do. Grey's not going to be hanging around waiting for us. He's got a reputation and a career to save.' There was a noticeably more relaxed atmosphere in the office as they concluded the editing of their submission. They filed a copy with other material in the folder marked "Murder of Thomas Marshall – August 1851". They decided to give a copy to Commissioner Mayne, delivered to his office in the adjacent building, but would wait for any further advice to deliver it to the Home Office.

Chapter 50

Later
October 1851 and after

The general election of October 1851 led to a change of government. Lord Derby, the incoming Tory Prime Minister, appointed Walpole as Home Secretary. The short-lived administration was mainly focussed on survival and the police review was first suspended and then quietly dropped when Aberdeen's Whigs regained power the following year. Sir Richard 'King' Mayne reined in the independence of the Detectives across the next seventeen years of his commissionership. He had studied the joint-report and would cite it as evidence of the need for, and benefits of, co-operation. It was he who felt that the investigation could be laid to rest – there were other more immediate needs.

By the end of 1851 Dean Buckland was physically much worse, Lord Jack Thynne, the sub-dean, had taken on many of his roles, and Queen Victoria had signed an authorisation for him, Lord Jack, to formally perform in practice, though not in name, the role of Dean. For a few months Buckland stayed in bed at Islip, mentally deteriorating and becoming, at times, hostile. Mary Buckland consulted some London Physicians and it was suggested that he be sent to an Asylum, the one recommended being in Clapham under the leadership of John Bush. It was there that he died in his seventy-third year on August 14th 1856, still technically Dean but having taken no part in Abbey life for most of the previous four years.

Mary Buckland, who had been brought up by an Oxford professor and his wife after the death of her own mother, had first encountered William Buckland, thirteen years her junior, when they were travelling on the same coach, he was on an errand to track her down and noted that they were both carrying a copy of the same geological text. They had married in December 1825. After the Dean's death she moved to be near their son Frank. Mrs Buckland suffered from bouts of unconsciousness, said to have been brought on because of the same carriage accident that damaged her husband. She died in 1857 during one of those periods of unconsciousness. Frank would later present his father's vertebrae to the Hunterian Museum of the Royal College of Surgeons. The family long blamed the diligence driver for the injuries that lead to pain and dementia in the Dean and his wife.

Albert Greene was moved to the hospital wing at Pentonville Prison. He was detained there for three months before being moved to an asylum, but one without any of the advanced approaches displayed in Clapham for the Dean. The former Brigadier, died before the middle of 1852.

John Durdin continued working in the bank and would go on to make a name for himself, but not in a good way. A stroke led to his temporary absence from the bank, and the discovery that he had been embezzling funds. That discovery led to the overnight sale of the Commercial Bank of London, for fear of a run on the banks, in 1861. Durdin, like Greene, would experience the separate and silent system in prison.

Henry Mayhew, from a discreet base in France, published a compendium of his pieces shortly after Marshall's death; it was significantly revised for republication in 1861. He remained in hiding for some years. Mayhew influenced the Christian socialist movement and several writers, including Charles Dickens, together with future researchers, among them Charles Booth who published a multi-volume book Life and Labour of the people of London in 1902. Mayhew continued to live a precarious financial life until his death in July 1887.

Early in 1856 Mrs Marshall – by then engaged to Canon Brooks – went to the Clapham asylum with Mrs Buckland, and a third party, a priest from the abbey, who had longed to see and meet Buckland. The Dean appeared to be delirious – he told some crude jokes, to the embarrassment of all, and then declared that he had a need to confess – the priest, certain of his vocation but uncertain about what to do now, stepped forward. The Dean could not stir from his bed, but he closed his eyes and attempted to cross himself.

'I freely confess that I badly cheated and mistreated one of the greatest women of England, and am responsible for the death of Thomas Marshall.'

The priest looked, and was, shocked. Mary Buckland drew the priest aside to confide in him, 'I'm afraid he is always saying things like this – you can't take him seriously, but to give him rest and peace could you give an absolution – we'll stand back here.'

Not quite sure what to do the priest moved forward. He spoke quietly, out of the hearing of the Marys, to cover his embarrassment. The priest raised his arm in an absolution and blessing, making the sign of the cross over the Dean. He bade them farewell. Buckland died during the following night, absolved and at peace.

Upon his death the role of Dean became vacant. Lord Jack Thynne, who had effectively undertaken the role for four years, declined to be considered – he would eventually serve 45 years as sub-dean.

Those advising the Queen were looking for a man who had experience of the Abbey, but who was not going to further change the 'feeling' of the place. Buckland's time had not been without controversy, the monarch's advisors were looking for a safe pair of hands. Their eye fell upon Canon Brooks. Within a month of Buckland's death Brooks was installed, on September 13th 1856 into the Deanery; within six months he had married Mary Marshall in a colourful but also solemn marriage service. Many people in the Abbey had known Brook's late wife, and had lived through the trauma associated with Thomas Marshall's death.

The new Dean and Mrs Brooks held their small reception in the Jerusalem Chamber; a few feet from where her late husband had been found, and close to where Canon Brooks had once picked up a discarded envelope with its pencil-written letter on regal headed notepaper. The envelope no longer existed; nor the repurposed letter that had gone to Greene. The letter that Thomas Marshall had received instructing his final movements, which he had carefully filed in his office, had been removed by his disillusioned wife, and destroyed, when Thomas left home that fateful Saturday evening.

The newly married couple's secret was safe.

Printed in Great Britain
by Amazon

41440528R00158